3 4143 00

CN00375673

G[illegible]

was b[illegible] in 1967. On leaving school he [illegible] Berlin with a punk band. His 'year out' before university stretched into six, during which he travelled and did various jobs. He began writing in 1994 while supporting himself as a bookseller. *The Octopus Hunter* is his second novel. He lives in London.

WITHDRAWN FOR SALE

From the reviews for *The Octopus Hunter*:

'The literary thriller is far from dead, as Stewart aptly proves in this top-notch characterisation, with crisp, cutting style. Echoes of the great literary thriller writers may be found here, but Stewart is very much his own man, and this gritty adventure is totally individual in style. Apart from brilliant atmosphere and detail, it is the overriding threat of violence that gives the novel its pungent flavour, with the author's language perfectly judged in conveying tension.' *Amazon.co.uk*

'Building towards a gripping conclusion . . . *The Octopus Hunter* goes some way to capturing the time-tangled nature of Balkan politics and blood feuds.' *Glasgow Sunday Herald*

'Book of the week. A well above average novel' *Irish News*

'A stubble-faced account of nationalism, whose terse, gritty prose suggests that Stewart's much-praised first book, *Kenny Rogers Sings the Gambler*, wasn't simply a one-off.' *Jockey Slut*

Also by Grant Stewart

Kenny Rogers Sings the Gambler

The Octopus Hunter

GRANT STEWART

WARRINGTON BOROUGH COUNCIL	
H J	10/08/2001
F	£5.99

Flamingo
An Imprint of HarperCollins*Publishers*

Flamingo
An Imprint of HarperCollins*Publishers*
77–85 Fulham Palace Road,
Hammersmith, London W6 8JB

Flamingo is a registered trade mark of
HarperCollinsPublishers Limited

www.**fire**and**water**.com

Published by Flamingo 2001

1 3 5 7 9 8 6 4 2

First published in Great Britain by
Flamingo 2000

Copyright © Grant Stewart 2000

Grant Stewart asserts the moral right to
be identified as the author of this work

This novel is entirely a work of fiction.
The names, characters and incidents portrayed in it are
the work of the author's imagination. Any resemblance to
actual persons, living or dead, events or localities, is
entirely coincidental.

Photograph of Grant Stewart © Tony Davis

ISBN 0 00 655188 2

Set in Bembo by Rowland Phototypesetting Ltd,
Bury St Edmunds, Suffolk

Printed and bound in Great Britain by
Clays Ltd, St Ives plc

All rights reserved. No part of this publication may be
reproduced, stored in a retrieval system, or transmitted,
in any form or by any means, electronic, mechanical,
photocopying, recording or otherwise, without the prior
permission of the publishers.

This book is sold subject to the condition that it shall not,
by way of trade or otherwise, be lent, re-sold, hired out or
otherwise circulated without the publisher's prior consent
in any form of binding or cover other than that in which it
is published and without a similar condition including this
condition being imposed on the subsequent purchaser.

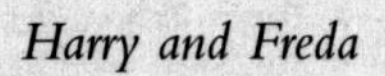
Harry and Freda

AUTHOR'S NOTE

This is a work of fiction. I began writing it in late 1996, and finished it in the summer of 1998, many months before the escalation of terrible events which made Kosovo a place we have all heard of now. I have resisted rewriting the story to make it tally with real events, because this is, and was always meant to be, just a story.

In two to three years a man should be able to write a pretty good war book.

Ernest Hemingway, letter to F. Scott Fitzgerald

When I'm with you
I want to be the kind of hero
I wanted to be
when I was seven years old
a perfect man
who kills

Leonard Cohen, *The Reason I Write*

This is the Balkans: anything could be true.

Robert Carver, *The Accursed Mountains*

Part One

1

ROBERT READS:

'Paracin Barracks, central Serbia, September 1987

A bad day at the barracks begins roughly thus:

It's midnight.

Aziz Kelmendi sits up in bed. He peels away his wool blankets, and sits absolutely still. It's chilly, and he shivers. Then he blinks and begins weeping. After about ten seconds he stops as abruptly as he started.

Aziz steps out of bed onto the cold floor, and opens the top half of his locker. He buttons up a clean shirt and tunic over his damp vest, and pulls on pressed combat trousers over his grey underpants. Next, clean socks and his nearly new boots. The poor quality leather creaks up a din in the near silence. The springs of the rusty cot make a racket, too. But nobody stirs.

Dressed, Aziz sits on the edge of the grey mattress, staring into space. Aziz Kelmendi is nineteen.

A moan drifts over from an adjacent cot, and Aziz appears to look around him in the dark. But you can't read him. He could easily be thinking: well, as barracks go this is not a bad building, and we're pretty lucky recruits. It's a nice night, if a little chilly. Yeah, a tad cold. Or he could just be breathing the sugary odour of twenty sleeping men, and thinking nothing at all.

Aziz slides an arm in far behind the locker, and the arm comes back holding a rifle. He tosses the weapon into his other hand with a casual gesture that doesn't suit him. Aziz, always so afraid of weapons.

He fishes two magazines out of the foot locker and empties the thirty-two rounds from each onto the mattress. Next out of the locker is a steel helmet. From its lining he pulls a rag, which he uses to wipe each bullet clean in turn.

He strips and cleans and reassembles the weapon, and refills the magazines with the polished rounds. He checks the loading and firing mechanisms three times. Aziz picks up the magazines and drops one in his right tunic pocket, and clicks the other into place in the gun.

He walks the length of the barracks. At the far wall he swivels on the balls of his feet, like a footballer, and patrols back again. The other men sleep on. He tracks back to his locker and squats, fumbling inside, before something appears to distract him. Still crouching, he turns on his heels and raises his rifle to semi-readiness, then turns his head both ways in the dark, and pisses in situ.

He stands up, and sweat drips from his forehead into the pool of water.

His stare pans to the south-eastern corner of the room, where the cots stand in diamonds of dim moonlight from the curtainless windows. He patrols toward the south-eastern door, focusing on four illuminated beds nearest the exit.

He closes one eye, sights along the barrel, and fires.

There are four ear-splitting half-second bursts, one at each cot, before the room comes alive with figures leaping up like jack-in-the-boxes into the flashes of the gun. For a moment in the dark it looks beautiful, like a stroboscopic ballet. The men leap from the beds, and the empty shells leap around Aziz's boots.

Aziz then sprays blanket fire against the south-west wall, and there's some clicking as a cordite smell fills the room. As eyes focus in the dark, shapes dive beneath cots.

Aziz takes a step closer to the four bloodied heaps, and hits three of them with one precise shot each. The heap nearest the door heaves itself up and around, and Aziz pins it in the back, one shot.

The whole thing has taken seconds.'

Robert reads on. It's a heck of a story.

'Moments pass until the paralysed silence is broken by a racket outside. There are shouts, and the sounds of men keeping pace with frantic dogs. Aziz drops the empty magazine and snaps in number two. Shadows duck once more all over the room, and someone squeals, but Aziz Kelmendi is gone now, out of the door.

In the barracks the recruits begin a chorus of exhalations, and moans of disbelief. Several of the boys have messed their underwear and the room fills with the stink. Some are weeping while others, still and mute with shock, sit there and smell the shit all around them, and listen to the sounds of men weeping.

Aziz gets about half a mile.

His body is dragged back to the guardroom and covered and put under close guard while it is still dark. There will be questions and the beginnings of an investigation, before events take a strange turn. Before frantic phone calls are made, and certain people in government, people who will be elated to get this call, are consulted.

The barracks is photographed, then briefly searched and cleaned, before five boys from an overcrowded hut are assigned the vacant beds. The evidence of the shooting is hastily painted over, and the recruits told to speak to no one.'

Aziz Kelmendi's story, the story of a lonely and disturbed young man, is skilfully manipulated. According to Belgrade television, he was an Albanian separatist terrorist: certain newspapers rage about a mission to murder the youth of Serbia as it sleeps.

'This is only the start of something! He was one of many agents of genocide in our midst!'

Robert reads:

'Aziz Kelmendi shot dead two Bosnian muslims, a Croat, one Serb. But a minor figure in the government, a man named Slobodan Milosevic, rants and rails, fuelling the fire.

The Serb boy's father pleads with thousands of inflamed mourners at his son's funeral not to use the murder as an excuse for reprisals against Albanians living in Yugoslavia, and even for war.

But no one hears him. They hear Slobodan Milosevic.

They are listening to *Slobo* now.'

2

London, May 1996

ROBERT WAS BEING pushed toward the edge by reasonable questions.

It's my own fault, he decided. I thought I'd explained myself. Obviously not – as usual. This always happens with me. Why does no one understand what I say? Why don't I have that gift?

'I'm still not with you.'

Exasperated: 'I've explained it plenty of times.'

'Yeah, I heard all that, I understand all that. But I still don't understand why – why you came up with it in the first place, and why it has any appeal *for you*. I can see the logic, I just can't see the sense. The will. The *fun!* Get me?'

A typical exchange.

And he'd go through it again, counting off the reasons. 'The money, the weather, the potential for –'

'That's still not answering my question.'

Which was: 'Why Albania?'

Followed by: 'You can up sticks and zoom off anywhere in the world, and you have to choose the last place on earth – the ring end of beyond. No one's even *heard* of Albania.'

'Which,' Robert would reply, through gritted teeth, 'is precisely the fucking point.'

Etcetera, all the way back to square one.

People and their reasonable questions. He couldn't really complain. They were right, he wasn't doing a great job of explaining. But he was ready to start a small war over the next reasonable question.

Shit.

Robert's radar flicked on as he saw Declan, at the far end of the table, peeling off his T-shirt and showing a traumatised Alice his Maori tattoos. Several people were staring. Robert could see Declan's lips moving now, and knew, to the syllable, what he'd be saying.

'These took three days. Imagine it. No food, no water, three days. Just the pain and the needle. But it means I'm purified now, Alice. *Purified.*' And then that madman smile.

Jesus wept. And I thought I was going to miss these freaks.

Robert sighed and raised his red eyes ceilingward. He took a swig of Chianti with one of black coffee, sloshed them together in his mouth, and swallowed. He repeated the process, and winced.

Maybe it was the name of the place. Just the sound of it. If he'd said: I'm going off to live in Madrid, there'd be no problem. Madrid has chic; it rolls off the tongue. You can see Madrid. You can reason Madrid.

Whatever it was though, enough was enough, Robert told himself. It was time to take control.

First time for everything.

So, after fortifying himself with another black coffee and Chianti cocktail, he smacked his palms on the edge of the long table in front of him, and pushed his chair back. He cleared his throat loudly and waited, still sitting, until the dozen people at the long table were all listening.

'People!' he began. 'Dearly beloved, arseholed people.' His voice sounded pretty good echoing around the marble interior. Like a Roman senator's. 'People I know, people I love, people I'd *like* to love.'

Tina giggled into her drink, and someone crooned: 'Hey, *smoochin'*.'

'People I invited out of a sense of pity, such as that fat bastard opposite me.'

The fat bastard, who was really only stocky, stood and executed an exaggerated low bow.

'People who have come tonight just to make sure I really am actually leaving.'

'Hear, hear!'

There was a squeal and some sexy giggling from another table, and Robert raised his voice still further. First though, he caught a glimpse of the giggler – who looked good – fell in love with, married, and finally lost her to a tropical storm or a plane crash which he miraculously survived, all this in between sentences.

'It seems, good people, that a collective and FINAL explanation for my, ah, somewhat, ah –'

'Eccentric?' the merely stocky bastard prompted.

'Thank you, Sir Raymond, thank you. A final sodding explanation for my somewhat eccentric career move is in order.'

Knives tapped glasses.

'Well,' Robert went on, less theatrically. 'It's a lot more simple, and a lot less daft, than it sounds.'

'Yeah, right,' Iain heckled. More chuckles.

Somebody signalled a waiter and held up two index fingers.

'I picked Albania mainly because it's so cheap. And I mean *stupidly* cheap. If you ask me why it's so stupidly cheap, I can tell you chapter and verse why it's so stupidly cheap: Albania's the poorest country in Europe, for starters.'

There were some cheers. Robert wondered why should they cheer someone's poverty. The waiter who had been signalled returned with a bottle each of house red and white.

'But the main point is that it's so *damn* cheap. Because it comes down to money, and I only have enough money for somewhere as cheap as Albania. Get it now? Sinking in? Yes? Comprende?'

Some moans. A few nods. Of course they comprende. But they weren't going to make it easy for him – these were his best friends, after all; they felt they owed it to him to give him a hard time.

'If you knew the sums involved you'd see what I mean. Fuck. You knew the sums involved you'd be packing your bags and coming with me.' Robert was getting into it. He could show off when required.

'My initial investment is next to naff all. The *weather* is the absolute plums, the beaches kick bottom, and in a couple of years I'll be coining it in – albeit it in a currency I've forgotten the name of.'

'Lek!'

'I am taking my money –'

'LEK!'

Big laughs.

'I am taking my LEK! to a place where it'll instantly multiply in value simply because of where it is. And within a couple of years I'll be making shedloads more.' Nobody looked like heckling now, and Robert started to milk the vibe.

'Much more. Because when the disillusioned backpackers of the world cotton on to how cheap and sunshiny it is and how spoiled it's *not*, they'll be over on the boat from Corfu in droves, and hammering at my door looking for a cheap room. And I will be waiting at the threshold to my modest establishment, attired in my most hospitable smile and my most attractive trousers, ready to pocket their LEKS and dollars and drachmas, and shag their single birds to within an inch of their self-respect.'

Bangs and whistles of approval.

'The Sarande Hilton, ladies and gentlemen! Ladies, gentlemen, and fat bastards, I rest my watertight case. And you're all invited to visit, you godless infidels. Every effing one of you, because I love you all –' and in a deliberately audible aside '– although fuck knows *pourquoi*.'

He concluded with a flourish of his cloth napkin, signalling vigorous applause and whistles and even *Bravos!* from all parts of the room.

Robert flinched when it clicked how many people had actually heard his speech, and then he leaned back and laughed.

The place seemed to go crazy over the next few minutes. Music started up somewhere in the kitchen, and someone at the next table began singing along. Behind him, a drunk thirty-something in a too-new Arsenal shirt was waving at our boy and shouting: 'Count me in! Count me fucking in! I'm fucking comin' with you, mate!'

Robert rose to his feet, sweeping up his glass. Raising the wine high he bellowed: 'Albania!' Then he laughed at himself and sat down.

But the fat bastard was on his feet, only a split second ahead of the rest of the table and a good half of the restaurant. Several waiters and a minicab driver stood looking bemused by the door as, for a good ten seconds, the Porchetta Pizzeria resounded to the bellowed toast. Passers-by gawped through the glass before hurrying away from the putsch gathering steam in the famous pasta joint.

Albania! Albania!

Robert sat and watched the continuing reaction to his little speech. A roomful of suggestible drunks and a word they had no conception of. *Albania!* Just bawling, just following the lead of some other drunk who talked up better than they could. It could have been Nuremberg. Robert laughed again and drained his glass.

Robert wasn't one for formal goodbyes, or these self-conscious soirées, but his friends had insisted. And he'd at least got to choose the venue. His only worry was that this was a potentially fractious bunch to be breaking bread together – his old crowd of never-grown-ups, alongside a fairly straight, easily shockable set from the drawing office. But on the night even the least predictable of the old crew made a fair stab at decorum. Ray must have had a word.

Robert had known Raymond since college, more than ten years. The rest, apart from his present workmates – whom Robert did genuinely like, even admired – were driftwood from his travelling days, the ones who hadn't disappeared without trace to start new lives somewhere in south-east Asia, or the States.

That had been a good time, having the travel bug. But Robert had been cured of it a few years now. That, or it had dumped him. More likely the latter. These days he couldn't imagine pulling the kind of stunts they'd once been into. But then he had never been alone back then; there was always some lunatic like Iain or Declan from whom he could suck courage. And then there was the little matter of the world back home being far more frightening, in its way, than backpacker land. Which was probably why the likes of Iain and Declan were still dedicated wasters and career nutters.

No, Robert didn't have the bug or the buzz any more. This trip wasn't about that.

It got late. Robert saw off most of a bottle alone while he tried to blot out parts of the talk.

Okay, so they were all good people, shirt off their back blah blah, but he wished they'd change the record. Oh, there were endless hilarious things to say about him emigrating to the poorest country in the world. The general consensus was still that, sound economic sense though his plan appeared to make, Robert had skipped well and truly round the twist. If he'd reckoned on his little speech being an end to the matter he'd reckoned wrong.

Right now the questions were coming from Tina, sitting at his left. It hadn't escaped our boy's notice that Tina had made a disproportionate effort tonight – you didn't scrub up like that just to eat. By leaning four or so inches to his left and clandestinely inhaling, Robert was treated to a high on a par with anything available at the bar. He had harboured dreams of Tina for a wee while now, but working in the same office, the same design team, well. But he didn't work anywhere now. So far tonight he'd done the inhaling trick, oh, sixty or seventy times.

She'll smell better on my bedroom floor in about an hour, he thought. For the seventy-first time, Robert inhaled deeply, imagining it. She'll smell of wine and of sweat setting off that maddeningly horny perfume and body heat and . . .

The feeling faded.

It was no good. Could she sense it?

Sod's fucking law. Tina.

It was sod's law because right now she wouldn't change the subject. He tried to concentrate, but it was no good if she talked about that. Get *off* the questions, please? Unless he was way off the mark Tina was a definite possibility – if she'd only let him talk about something else. She was getting under the surface now, away from the Albania thing and just onto the general Why.

Why was he going at all? she wanted to know. Why was he going anywhere, for good? What was driving him away – or beckoning him? Robert cringed inside. She expected big things of the answer.

He closed his eyes, and something clicked off in his head. Now he just wanted to get away from here and be with his thoughts – thoughts that had nothing to do with this evening, and these people and their questions. You could keep Tina, he just wanted to escape. There was too much thinking: sometimes a man just needed to *do*. 'Not the ones you do,' he recalled from somewhere, 'but the ones you don't.' Fuck. The ones you don't.

From across the table Ray caught his eye and then glanced at Tina, then adopted an angelic expression. Robert laughed and shook his head. When he looked up again Tina was blushing, but looking pleased. Other people were looking pleased. Tina was up for anything and people were happy for them.

Sod's law.

The goodbyes lasted a good five minutes. Robert was kissed and hugged half to death by friends of either sex.

Tina tried not to look pissed off when he went home with Ray. He tried to explain how he needed tonight pretty much by himself, to centre his thoughts and all that life decision stuff, blah blah. With some little-boy-lost eye contact thrown in it didn't actually sound too hollow, and maybe even scored some sensitivity points. If she does ever come out to Albania, he thought. If I've sorted things out. If I'm happy.

'I'll keep in touch,' he told her.

'Yeah.'

'I will.'

'You do that.'

'Count on it. It's just –'

She nodded, understandingly. 'I understand.'

She understands.

'Take care.'

'Ditto.'

There was a longish kiss, and then somebody said the name of the damn place again and it made Robert start. Robert still couldn't picture Albania.

He forced Tina to take money for a cab, then splashed out on one for him and Ray, but got it to put them out at Archway. He liked a walk after a drink, and Highgate Hill was a walk, all right.

Ray said: 'You're a moron. You turn down a perfectly good shag – no, a better than perfectly good shag – after which you make yourself walk up a hill. And you make me walk up the fucking hill with you. If I'm not careful I'll sober up, and then woe betide you, young man. Then woe effing betide you!' He began to pant as he tried to talk and keep up at the same time. 'What are you doing, torturing yourself? You a fucking martyr? No, you're a fucking moron.' He laughed. 'Call *me* Sir Raymond? You're a knight of the fucking round morons.' The phrase obviously tickled him, because he used it a few more times. Ray was a good way gone.

Once Ray had calmed down, they walked most of the way in silence. It was a nice spring night. Clear sky. Stars. Highgate Cemetery was just over the wall, with all its dead heroes among the trees. Half way up the hill you could hear John Prine's *Sam Stone* from the flat above the Rose and Crown, and Ray recognised it. 'That's three of us in the world, then,' he said, and hummed along.

Robert Maidens was somewhere else, though. Although he was thinking about Ray. Pondering how, with each year that passed, nights like this were more apt to take their toll. It was a sign of age: extended hangovers, panicked bowels, nasty coloured phlegm, non-optional afternoon naps the next day.

Naps? Naps were for old people. He was getting the start of a double chin as well, and lines around his eyes. It didn't show this much on some people. Some people were like Peter Pan. Sickening. But then lines were the product of worry. Maybe some people just didn't worry. Hard to believe.

The night bus was catching them up as they approached the stop, and Ray looked across hopefully at Robert, who ignored it.

Ray began humming *Sam Stone* again.

'. . . came home to his wife and family,
After serving in the conflict overseas . . .'

There were two kinds of lives, Robert decided. One where you had Things, and the other where you had Memories. And the one with Things implied responsibilities and all sorts of procedures which were a mystery to him. He shook his head – he didn't want to get into that now. It could all be a meaningless wine-thought. Just his Thought for the Day.

He reflected on tonight, and on other nights of drink and talk with Ray. This was the best part, going back home to talk, although you had to go through the social bit first. You had to gather some of the raw material of human contact. That's something you'd never get with a woman – those times, those memories – Robert Maidens and Ray had said often to each other. Something a lot of men say and don't know if they mean.

Robert shared a one-bedroom flat with Patricia. Patricia had a futon in the living room, which was cheaper than paying for a two-bedroom place.

Patricia worked as a cocktail waitress, but insisted that that was only what she did, not what she was. Her real ambition was to direct plays. She'd directed a few smaller ones, but there was no money in it. Still, Robert admired that she was doing what she wanted, when she could.

She'd found another man to replace Robert. A man, mind, not a girlfriend. Patricia said she was sad to see Robert go. She was always saying how cool he was to live with, not like some men who were just wankers, and certainly not like girls, who just fluttered around in pants and vest having crises and running up phone and heating bills. Girls? She got enough drama directing, thanks all the same. She often talked about Robert's natural, considerate charm.

Robert would always nod and try to look comfortable, and wonder what he was doing that was natural and considerate. How could he isolate that and replicate it? What have I missed?

What Patricia said surprised him. He considered his grasp of women, and what they wanted, to be lousy. But if Patricia said different, maybe he was doing something right after all.

In the clean flat they smelled like men back from the pub. Patricia was working. They dropped their jackets over the stringless guitar by the hall door.

Robert Maidens cracked the seal on a new bottle bought especially, and Ray put ice in the good glasses. They carried the glasses and the bottle through to the bedroom and took off their shoes. Ray sat back on the bed, Robert Maidens on the small sofa. A trendy Ikea lamp, the one homely item in the room – a present from Patricia – was on in the corner near the window.

Ray dug out a Kristofferson and pressed random. *The Pilgrim* came on and he adjusted the volume so they could talk but still join in on the good parts. Robert poured downright silly measures of Jack Daniel's, and they raised their glasses.

Ray spoke first. 'Albania,' he said quietly.

'Yep,' Robert Maidens answered, and they drained their drinks, then coughed and giggled. Ray poured refills and this time when they sipped the bitterness was gone and the whisky felt soft and tasted smoky.

'Shall I roll one?'

'I'm okay with this.'

''keydokey.'

'It wasn't too horrendous tonight,' Ray said.

'Nobody died.'

'No. No strippers.'

'Iain didn't set light to anyone.'

'Nope.'

They sipped.

'Tina was after your parts.'

Robert Maidens shook his head. 'Sod's fucking law.' He laughed quietly. 'The ones you don't.'

'What?'

'Nothing.'

'How come you weren't up for it? This isn't the Bobby Maidens I know. She's the absolute plums. And she was after your parts, no wind-up. Jesus wept, Robert, she'd have screamed the fucking Hail Mary.'

'Sod's law,' was all Robert said.

Ray looked into his drink and shook his head. 'What lips. What a *mouth.*' He made sucky noises, and sighed.

Robert Maidens sipped his whisky and sighed back. 'Albania,' he said.

'Yep. Albania.'

They raised their glasses in salute.

'I'm outa here, Raymond, ole pardner.'

'You are that, pilgrim. "*He's a poet and he's a picker.*"'

'I'm well out of it all.'

'That you is.'

'That I is.'

'Unless.'

'Unless?'

'Well, it's volatile, still. You must have thought about that.'

'That's right, you bastard, reassure me.'

Ray shrugged. 'Could happen. I'm just saying.'

'Nah.'

'Not worried?'

Robert shook his head. 'It flares up. I think it's one of those things that's blown out of proportion. There's the Basques but people still go to Spain. And there's the Troubles but people still go to Ireland. It's not even like Ireland. It's not going on all the time.'

'You never know. You read the Update. What if Kosovo's next?'

'Is it Kosovo or Kosova?'

'Does it matter when they start lobbing bombs?'

'Perhaps Iain should go.'

Robert frowned hard and jammed his eyes shut. He smacked his glass down on the dresser, stared ahead dramatically, and began warbling: '*Maria Helena, I'm going away to war!*' Ray joined in on the next line and they were both singing: '*I'm going to fight, I may not be back again!*'

The song playing on the CD couldn't compete with the boys' crooning, and poor jilted Kristofferson sounded more sorry for himself than ever. Richard leaped up and began miming castanets. Robert stood on the bed and adopted a bronze memorial pose. They hummed the bits they didn't know until they got back to the chorus: *Maria Helenaaa, I'm going away to war! I'm going to fight, I may not be back agaaaain AH*!

Robert jumped down off the bed and retrieved his drink, and they both sat down as if the musical interlude hadn't happened.

'You could always come? Be a lark. "What larks, Mister Pip!"'

'You could always forget the whole fucking thing.'

'Not now.'

Ray squinted over at the silhouette of his friend in the corner of the dark room. 'Is that it? Please don't tell me that's the reason you've gone through with this – because you think you've come too far to back out. You're not worried about what people will think?'

Robert made a face. 'Give me some credit.' A night bus, or a lorry rumbled by, sending vibrations through the floor, rattling the ice in their drinks. 'Well, there is an element of that.'

'Oh, man,' Ray murmured. 'Jesus just kept weeping.'

Robert drained his drink and did the refills. 'Not how you think, though,' he said. 'No, I really want to go. What I mean is that I started the whole thing, set it rolling, and it's hard for me to see around it now, or beyond it.' He pondered. 'It's like nothing else can happen until I do this. God, your face. I know what you're going to say: that it sounds like a test.'

Ray didn't argue. 'Like I said. You're a martyr all of a sudden. It doesn't sound like an adventure. It sounds like a suicide mission, or going into a monastery, or the wilderness.'

Robert laughed and shook his head. 'No, I didn't mean it like that, either. But this plan has become so big and so all-encompassing, it's taken so much of my time and thought, that the alternative just seems too small to bother with. Like, the alternative is not doing it. And apart from feeling like I would have chickened out, well, it just doesn't seem like any alternative at all. You're making it sound like something terrible, but it's not.

'It's a new life. A fresh start. Everything bad behind you, you know? I know how, with all the preparation, you can lose sight of that. But that's what's behind it – that's what we talked about, both of us, if memory serves.' Robert caught his friend's eye. 'And you could still change your mind and re-join the programme?'

Ray looked down at his shrinking ice cubes. 'I enjoyed talking about it. A new life. But I must have changed in the time it's taken to organise it all. I just don't feel sufficiently pissed off with the old life as you seem to be. And I certainly don't need to go just because I once said I might.' Ray paused before saying quietly: 'There's nothing to prove. It's not a test. No one'll think less of you.'

Robert looked at him, and let it go. After a moment he said:

'You know, I can't give you perfect answers. I feel a push to do this, for right or wrong. I recall you thought it was a pretty good plan yourself once.'

'I still think it's a good plan. I just wonder if you do, and why.'

'I don't know. That's what I'm trying to say. It's pulling me both ways. I don't do things like this any more. But I want to do this one. Jesus. Maybe I can give you the why of it in hindsight.'

Ray nodded and raised his glass and smiled. 'That sounds okay. Come back in tatters you know where to find me.'

Robert nodded. But what he thought was: things change, people move on. That's part of what I'm trying to say. So, maybe I won't know where to find you, and it won't be anybody's fault or even anybody's idea. It will just happen that way.

Minutes later and their eyes were drifting, and the words – even the important words – weren't necessarily anything other than the whisky talking. And it wouldn't be fair to remember any of that.

Ray yawned and shook his head and said: 'We'll worry about you.'

'Royal We?'

'Yeah. Me and the Queen.'

'Cheers.'

Robert woke a few hours later in the middle of a cruelly realistic Tina dream – lots of sweating and lycra gymwear. Damn. The whisky buzz was still on him, but he couldn't get back to sleep. He worked a windscreen wiper across his mind. Stop kidding yourself. She's cute but she won't seem so cute tomorrow. Most days she looks three beers and you know it, and you're way over three beers. You're just clinging to the idea of her, because you're really going and you're afraid. She's an anchor to a world you know.

His thoughts wandered back to the Porchetta, to feeling her warm thigh pressing against his under the table. Thin stockings and a short lycra skirt. When he pressed back with equal pressure, her leg stayed. Although he couldn't look at her yet.

She spoke, but quietly, just for him.

'I don't know how you can do it.'

Her voice was breathy and deliberate.

He risked a glance and she was definitely flushed.

'I think it's incredibly brave,' she was saying. 'It would terrify me to death. I mean, *to death*.'

He could feel himself losing control of his breathing. Yes, oh, yes.

Then Tina said: 'I suppose I just wanted to let you know I really admire you for what you're doing. Something so certain, so permanent. I wish I had the guts to do something I really loved. I mean it. I really, really admire you.'

And she moved her leg so he could feel it moving against his, and slipped her right hand under the table to move along the length of his thigh, and closer. But the spell was broken.

She admired him.

Robert lay in the dark thinking about what he might have been doing now if only she hadn't said that, that she admired him, and he groaned and turned over and tried to sleep. Ray was snoring in his chair.

Fucking Albania.

3

ROBERT VISUALISED IT as like Greece in the very old days; say, twenty or thirty years ago, only with a lot less money to go around. Albanians apparently had a lot less money than just about anyone.

Robert had once imagined himself in love with Greece, back when something about that landscape, and about an authentic quality in its sounds and its silence, had called out to the mellowing side of a stern and serious young man tired of trotting the globe in a stimulant haze.

He'd been plenty of places by then – often in that state of oblivion, usually with his inner eye slid firmly shut. But it took a place as simple and functional as the harbour at Piraeus, and as small and holdable as the cluster of tiny islands off Naxos, to soothe his breast, and convince him of the benefits of a good night's dreamless sleep.

Maybe it was just timing. But to Ray he declared that it was the *pain* of the place: the pain of a place like this was so ancient, its scars so old and smoothed off, that you felt under the patronage of a heroic calm, protected by a talisman of legends from the fresh agonies of modern history.

Ray told him: Stick to Marlboros for a couple of days, mate.

But by around 1990 Greece had changed so much that it was hard to imagine there had ever been any old days, or any silence. Robert watched the vandalism in disbelief: the lego hotels springing up, the discos bullying out the kafeneions: the place dying. Who could do this? he raged. It's the Greeks, it's not us! They've misread what we came here for. We don't want what you're doing! Leave it as it was!

Don't change.

Anyway, he watched the last of the secret, whispered about islands build new harbours so bigger ships could arrive with bigger crowds to see less and less of the little that remained of the old and the small. And Robert, being Robert, took the insult to antiquity personally.

And, although the Greek tourism industry survived Robert Maidens' sense of loss pretty well, he was far from alone in the way he felt. Yes, many like-minded wanderers shouldered their Karrimors and Lowes, and followed the cheap and authentic trail to new havens such as Turkey.

But by 1990 they could see that even Turkey only had ten good years left at the outside. And even south-east Asia – too convenient a stop on the tour from Oz – would head the same way before long.

It seemed the world was shrinking, or maybe not so much shrinking as homogenising. The parts you were allowed into were not so much global village as global theme park. Global mall.

Travellers, Robert Maidens observed, finding himself every bit as culpable, have a special kind of snobbery: *everyone is bogus but me*, went the lament. *Once you let in the rabble, the mysteries are not mysteries. Everywhere is ruined, ruined, ruined.*

Whatever.

But where was left? Which magic land rated lowest on the spoiled scale? Well, there were the urban museums of the old Eastern Bloc. Prague and Budapest, for starters. They were special and beautiful cities. But they were cities, not an island paradise. Not the same. Everyone wants an island, or near as dammit.

And then Albania fell.

And hardly anyone noticed.

Okay, strictly speaking – or even not strictly speaking – Albania was not an island paradise either. Not yet.

But it had potential. It had promise. And Ray, who, to Declan and Iain's horror, had just begun working at the Foreign Office in Whitehall ('Job for life, man: spiritual death! Don't do it!'), had the information. And it was Ray who suggested something seemingly insane.

Which, when they looked into it, didn't seem quite so crazy. Could this be the perfect place?

The hook was in Robert. It tugged, it whispered to him, louder, until it spoke up and eventually begged. And Robert Maidens, so long disillusioned, so long in limbo in so many ways besides where to spend his summers, got his place in the sun.

After protracted investigations and deliberations, and a good deal of soul-searching, he initialled each one of a sheaf of papers on the strength of a video. Okay, so he hadn't seen what he was buying apart from on the tape. But he didn't consider he was taking much of a risk. Even a total swindle would only cost him £1500. A grand and a half, and that included lawyers and back-handers as well as the house and the sixty acres it stood in. Risk? At worst it was a costly adventure; at best an unbelievable investment.

Not that the notion of investments was one Robert understood.

What he was beginning to want to understand, though, was the idea of owning something. Time had caught him up: he wasn't a traveller any more, and he wanted somewhere that was his. Somewhere he could put Things. But you couldn't have that in Britain because it required the kind of money he couldn't imagine, and the kind of security he didn't believe in. The possibility seemed a world away.

So he decided to go a world away.

Sixty acres. He tried imagining the size of it. As a kid his parents' quarter acre had seemed huge to him. More than enough for one-man World Cups, medieval sieges and heroic last stands.

What was four of those gardens times sixty? He tried fitting trees and water and fields and rocks into the space. Sixty acres on the western shore of a lake.

And a grand and a half. How could you buy a farmhouse with outbuildings and all that land, for a grand and a half? He had taken some convincing.

Part of the truth was that he was buying land Albanians just didn't want: land rendered useless by mismanagement and migration, and requiring a level of investment that just wasn't going to happen.

Robert made himself read and understand. He read everything he could get his hands on – the travel guides and *The Albania Update* and *Yugoslavia Dismembered* and *The Death of Yugoslavia*, as well as a recently published sociological study called, appropriately enough, *Albania*.

Albania, he'd read, was littered with these potential prime sites:

land once covered in collective farms, now tossed aside with the rest of the old regime's broken toys. The collective farms had all been burned down once the communists finally lost control. There was no longer the manpower to work the land, when people could and did migrate to the northern cities of Tirane or Durres, or even the unimaginable prosperity of Athens. In places, whole villages had left.

Many of the old collective farms had been virtual prison camps. No one wanted to stay in prison. No one wanted the land, even the people who owned it – it had been tried.

The EC had sent hundreds of tractors to the farmers. And the farmers had driven the tractors in convoys to Macedonia, sold them, and used the money to emigrate to Greece. The land was there to take if you wanted it.

But Robert needed to be sure.

He had obtained written assurances that the land he was buying was not technically anyone else's – that it hadn't officially been given back by the Berisha government to its pre-communist owners, who would one day appear brandishing a valid prior claim, and worse. Not that all his bits of paper would necessarily protect him in a country whose primary political process appeared to be the due course of blind anarchy. But no, it looked as though it really was his. And if one day it turned out it wasn't, so what? He'd lost a grand and a half. He could come home with his pride intact and a hell of a story to tell. That would be enough. No one could say he had failed.

He watched the video again.

The opening shot was of a town square.

You got a brief impression, maybe a few seconds, of quaintness, before the cameraman scooted off for a long look at a place selling ice cream, then a prefab pizza joint. Then a too-short shot of a lovely church which, you could see on freeze-frame, had been converted into a volleyball court, and then a fuzzy cut to the harbour. Next, some seagulls and another cut, this time to an old man driving a horse-drawn cart on a country track in bright sunshine. Flagons and demijohns were on the back of the cart, and a bale of something yellow.

Robert opened a beer.

The old man had to shade his eyes to look into the camera and smile. Robert paused the picture. It was the same geezer he had just seen eating ice cream and pizza.

The film moved on to the property. You couldn't tell much about the house except that the exterior looked white enough to suggest a fairly recent paint job, which was something, at least. Inside, the quality wasn't terrific, and you had to play with the contrast. If you did that and turned the lights out you just about got piles of furniture and a younger man demonstrating how to change a gas cylinder. And a lot of dark.

The land was something else, though. The camera began with a slow pan around from a quite breathtaking lake scene, Lake Butrint – the brochure hadn't exaggerated that part – toward a small forest. Behind the lake was more forest and behind that the humped backs of low, distant hills. Hemingway's *Hills Like White Elephants*, Robert thought. The camera slipped over the lake and rested on a foreground of sand, rocks, and scrub, fading into ferns where the trees – his trees – began. Like Greece, Robert thought. A grand and a half. Too good to be true.

And there was another worry.

Where were the big Western entrepreneurs, investors who could manage a risk of more than a grand and a half? Why weren't they buying up places like Robert's farm? Surely they'd seen the same videos and recognised the potential in what they were seeing. Okay, there was the odd retail and fast food outlet in the cities, but where were the big tourism and industry players? Didn't they want this lake? What's wrong with my lake? Some evidence of a few people intent on ruining the country for vast profit, *à la* Greece, would, paradoxically, have made Robert feel quite a lot better. This way he felt totally alone. Why is no one else doing this?

The answer, he found, was pretty simple.

The big players wouldn't be dealing with one farmhouse and a grand and a half: they'd need paper yards of coastline, whole ring-binders of lakes. And the bottom line in their case was that, notwithstanding the climate and the scenery, everything else about the place was simply too unstable.

Recent social unrest – in plain English, rioting and looting and a whole bunch of shooting – just as the country seemed to be getting off its knees, had scared away most big investors. Although Robert's lawyer assured him that this had been exaggerated. Still, labour for any scheme had to be imported, as few of the locals wanted to work – work was what the communists had made you do, and nobody wanted the communists back. The country was surviving largely on food aid and foreign loans. And soon, Robert hoped, a bit of backpacker business.

Simple truth: the image of Albania as a virtual anarchy, the next domino in the genocidal Balkan wars, was still backed up by enough solid possibility to make it too much of a risk for anyone but people like Robert Maidens and his grand and a half. Prices had collapsed and died, then been dropped in a hole and buried.

Robert couldn't believe his luck.

But then he had his ace, his priceless informant – not that Ray was passing on documents in the James Bond category, just damn useful stuff you don't find in the *Blue Guide*.

In the end it came down, he decided, to one thing: when you had that kind of information it was a *sign*. And if you could raise the money and summon up the will, you didn't pass on this kind of chance.

So Robert Maidens had made enquiries. He wrote – in English – to some of the contacts listed in *The Albania Update*, a foolscap-sized leatherette monograph from the Foreign Office library which he photocopied whole and virtually memorised. He contacted the lawyers, property agents, town mayors and deputy mayors listed in the back of the *Update*. He didn't know if these titles meant anything at all. Albania, the document warned, was in many respects not even a third world country.

Some of the details disturbed him. During bad winters people went hungry, but only after a damn good riot. Besides which they displayed a penchant for complex and ancient blood feuds: whole clans wiped out in vendetta killings stretching over decades, and longer. Although, the *Update* promised, things were rapidly changing for the better.

How rapid was rapidly?

Faced with facts like these, Robert wondered if some of the people with these titles of lawyer and mayor would be able to read, even in their own language. But he was to be surprised and a little ashamed as, one by one, his preconceptions were proved unjust. And he began to worry less about starvation, rioting and offending someone's brother's mother's second cousin's dog.

Yes, the lawyers and mayors could read, and their English, although somewhat Edwardian in flavour, was often as good as his. With his guesswork and prejudices he had been prepared to hear a big *nada* back to his enquiries. But he heard back with bells.

The new capitalists informed him unstintingly and professionally. They sent him videos – he couldn't believe they had videos – and beautiful hand-drawn maps (because there weren't any printed maps in Albania), and in one case even a professionally-printed brochure. And the prices were ridiculous.

Because they didn't need to cheat him, not yet: first world money was still worth fortunes. What the names in the *Update* needed initially was a foot in the door of trust, a chance to prove that you could count on stability and profitability when doing business with Albanians. They needed to inspire the good reports he would send back to the second wave of investors. So right now fifteen hundred quid would buy you whatever you wanted.

It would buy you a whole world all to yourself.

4

Corfu, May 1996

A SHORT FERRY ride takes you from Corfu to the southern Albanian port of Sarande.

From there it was a few miles by road, if you could call it a road, to Lake Butrint and Robert's property.

In the books Sarande crops up as an important port throughout Albania's history. But Robert noticed that the guides didn't give it much of a mention any more, other than for its proximity to the archaeological sites at Butrint. On the trusty Bartholomew map, the port merited a mere two-ring dot. But then, unspoiled was the whole idea, after all.

Robert's Albanian lawyer, Mister Bejteri, was to meet him at a pre-arranged time on a pre-arranged day. He would drive Robert out to the lake, and Robert would see his new home for the first time. With this in mind, transport was one of the questions Robert needed to bring up with the lawyer right away. The farm was isolated, and he'd need to get about. It would be like living in the countryside.

Wake up, Bobby, it's not *like* living in the countryside.

As well as transport, there was also light, food, firewood, sanitation, and building materials to ask about. It was plenty to think on. You can be as prepared as you like, but some things only occur to you once you're *in situ*. It was exciting. It was many things.

In the meantime, Corfu was not exciting, and was definitely not like Greece in the very old days. The contrast between the resort island, and what waited for him across the water, gave Robert cause to reflect.

Would swathes of Albania wind up like this neon sticklebrick jungle? Barring riots and blood feuds, what could stave off that kind of progress? Ten years from now, what would they be building around his lake? You had to hope. That was all you could do.

He strolled and scuffed along the wide grey flagstones at the waterfront, killing time. On other islands you could see shoals of small fish through the translucent water at the quaysides. Other islands actually felt like islands.

He watched the distance for boats.

This was the lousiest place in the world.

That sounded like a film: *You're in the asshole of the world, captain.*

No, that wasn't altogether fair. Corfu had its share of photographable things, and scenes that you could put in a guide book to please most of the people. And probably some translucent water and shoals of tiny fishes as well.

But to Robert the sounds and the motives behind Corfu were ugly. It made him think of those fake western street scenes and interiors the KGB supposedly used to construct to train its agents. Maybe that was pushing it. No, it wasn't pushing it. You had to want to lie to yourself here: you had to want to be convinced, like in a theme park.

Have a drink, Robert.

The two-ring dot on the Bartholomew was looking better by the minute.

Except that Robert was dead scared.

Why is that? Why wasn't I fretting like this ten years ago in Thailand?

Because I was barely twenty then: I didn't know enough to be scared. It's the wisdom of age. I'm wise. I'm an old fucker. God, have I really changed so much since then?

Being alone, really alone, was a new and strange feeling. The night before it had hit him so hard he'd left half of the best meal he was likely to find in this damn town, to run half a mile to the discount telephone exchange. He suddenly wanted a long talk with Tina. He was going to tell her how he was too old for this shit; he knew what he wanted! He knew what mattered now and he was leaving here and coming home!

He'd stood hunched in the booth with the old-fashioned black receiver jammed to his ear, hearing the buzz of the never-to-be-spoken in one ear, the patient crunch of the sea in the other. The panic had passed, and he'd felt stronger, and reflected that what he had nearly done was probably one of those moments you keep to yourself.

After that, he'd wandered out of the telephone exchange and along the street into an Irish bar, for Pete's sake, and got spinning on frozen margaritas, picking out English voices over the omnipresent techno beat, and not starting conversations with anyone.

The next morning Robert couldn't imagine how he'd ever considered staying a week on Corfu – which had been the original plan: a bit of a holiday before knuckling down to patching up the house. But, as well as hating it here, he found he couldn't chill into holiday mode with his destination just a few miles away. At first he couldn't relax for worrying over the work to be done in his new place. And finally, he just worried. When it reached that stage, just focusing on the work was a relief.

Jesus wept, what a mess is my mind.

Mess, no mess. Work of the sort he would have to do, although daunting, struck him as ultimately a good thing now: a way to work off extraneous concerns, sweat out some rat-race toxins. A way to be proud of yourself, to do something with grace.

D-day for fixing up the house was August. That gave him three months. Between August and the end of September he had thirteen friends lined up to visit. Or fourteen with Tina. Even allowing for the inevitable four or five blowing him out that was still a steady flow of people to look after. It would be good practice. He promised himself he'd have the place fit to knock them all sideways.

And the year after that he would be open for business. And with Sarande only a hop across the water from Corfu, or a drive through northern Greece, he could do okay. More than okay.

Butrint was mentioned in all the books as a mecca for archaeologists and historians. It also struck Robert as perfect dopehead material: a Garden of Eden for neo-hippy backpackers with a good attitude. He could get on with those people. Hell, as lord of his own place, he could get on with Germans.

Maybe within a few years he'd be the proud owner of one of those special guesthouses he'd been lucky enough to find from time to time in Greece. Places which you just knew were put there for you to find. Places of relaxation and friendship and the best kind of memories, and of time spent with good people giving the best of themselves. Places, sadly, that it was always hard to go back to for fear they wouldn't be the same again.

Unless, of course, you owned one.

Robert could see himself on a veranda. He could taste a rough chilled wine and hear Ry Cooder's *Paris, Texas*.

What he couldn't envisage, ever, was six more days of Corfu.

He turned on his heel and dog-trotted back along the waterfront to his hotel and used the desk phone to call Bejteri in Sarande. He packed quickly. Bugging out like this, he felt a mixture of total relief and sheer terror. Old Mrs Prasinos nodded as he paid the bill, her face expressionless. Mrs Prasinos had likely seen many people come and go, in a hurry or otherwise.

It was hot sitting in the sun and the ferry was due any time in the next few hours, possibly depending on whether the Greek police had commandeered it to repatriate another load of Albanians desperate enough to try swimming to civilisation. Even though Albania was supposed to be free and democratic now. Big words, Robert reflected.

And Robert was going the other way voluntarily.

He backtracked to a harbourside bar where he had a good view of the boats and settled down to wait. Three gin and tonics later he switched to ice-cold bottled water and black coffee, to try and get his head straight.

By the time he was sober again the fear was back, and now a week in Corfu wasn't looking like such a miserable prospect.

Is Ray right? What is this need I have to put something behind me, and why this drastically? What do I think I have failed at?

And as the tub appeared, bobbing pretty damn quickly towards him over the horizon, and it sunk in that he was going to get on that rustbucket and sail away to fuck knows where, the town behind him looked suddenly like a perfect picture postcard.

5

May 10 1996

Ahoy Ray!

First week and no major fuck-ups. How's Blighty? Don't tell me, I don't care any more.

This place is something else. Not always in a good way, but something else, all the same.

Anyway, everything's been jam and kippers with Bejteri so far. He made a big deal of telling me I'm under his protection. They call it besa. *That means if anyone messes with me they have to deal with him and his whole* fis *– that's his extended family, or clan. I think he's serious, and that protection comes with a capital VV for Vindictive Violence.*

He's a specimen, all right. I think he thinks I'm his passport to international tycoonery. Although I don't know how he expects that to happen. He can't have made much more than a hundred quid from this whole deal, but he thinks he's the Albanian Rupert Murdoch. Still, he's bending over backwards to help me settle in, so I shouldn't judge.

The one time he really freaked me out was the day after I arrived, and he turned up out of the blue and gave me a rifle!

I jest ye not. A .22 rifle. That's all I can tell you about it, what with my extensive knowledge of firearms. But it looks to me like most things out here: cobbled together from spare parts. I know it's not very '90s man', but I tell you what, I'm fascinated by the thing. I don't think I've ever seen a real gun before. I haven't had the nads to go out and fire it yet. I'm still learning how to take it apart and clean it and put it back together.

I know what you're thinking and, yes, I was a teensy-weensy bit put out when the man who sold me my house turns up on my doorstep appearing to suggest I need artillery to defend the place. But the Update *says that giving weapons as gifts is some kind of ritual here, all very kosher and traditional. A cake would have done, frankly, but I might as well enjoy it now I've got it. And cakes are probably harder to come by.*

Owning guns is supposed to be illegal, but I imagine that it's about as enforceable as the rest of their laws that no one pays any attention to. The main job of the police seems to be to look cool while extorting bribes from anything that isn't dead.

I mean it. Bejteri warned me that, me being a foreigner, they'd really take the piss, and he gave me some excellent advice: DON'T PAY! *Once they get the message they'll leave me alone, he reckons. And it seems to be working.*

I did spend twenty minutes at a roadblock the other day while two Gestapo types tried to make out my passport was fake because I wouldn't play ball – that is, give them $20 just to get through the roadblock into town, fuck that – but they eventually let me go. I tell you what, if that's an example of what people can be like here, I'm glad I'm armed.

It gets you thinking, though. Those army stores that were looted a while back would have had a lot more than .22 rifles in them.

Anyroadup, my second acquisition was transport, which I realised straight away was an absolute must. Good old Bejteri came through yet again. Just so happens he has a cousin or a brother-in-law in the secondhand (third? fourth?) vehicle business. None of them stolen, honest, guv.

Bejteri's one of the few people around whose car doors aren't held on by rope.

I'm not kidding.

But then again there's a couple of okay-looking Mercedes taxis. I'm not kidding about that, either. How the fuck can these taxi drivers afford Mercs? Best not to ask, one reckons.

Anyway, so we motor down to Bikes-R-Us and I pick out the one machine that doesn't scream OBITUARY *at me.*

Hop on, motorcycle vendor says, give it a try. Isn't she a beauty? he says.

All I can think of is the last verse of 'Bat Out of Hell'.

But he was right, she purrs like an asthmatic kitten.

It looks like a 125 or a 250 (says the expert). The fuel tank has a stain on it that might once have said Honda. But the rest of it is probably the same story as the rifle: spare parts. Picture something out of Mad Max 3, *you're there. God help me if she packs up. Although, mind you, everyone and his dog here seems to be a mechanic. Necessity, I suppose.*

I probably paid through the nose, but not as much as I'd have done without Bejteri, and it's still pennies when you've got foreign currency. I've actually seen bikes pulling trailers here, but I don't think mine would stand for that. I thought about getting a car, but the bike's nippier when you get stuck behind a horse and cart. That's not a joke either.

On a more serious note, the food situation's not as bad as I'd been led to believe. There isn't much variety, but they seem to have plenty of the basics. I can see myself nipping back to Corfu for little luxuries, though. But I'm going to have to become mega-organised once you lot tip up.

Right. Hand knackered from writing. More later.

Evening.

I tell you what, I don't think I'll ever get it into my head that I own all this land. It's an unreal feeling. An absolute other world from where I was a few weeks ago. You'll see what I mean.

Ray, I think I might really have found something. Owning. I've never really owned anything before. It's a comforting feeling. And no mortgage, not in this world. A whole new world.

I'm starting to recall those reasons I'd forgotten . . .

On the other hand: okay, I own all this, but I've virtually got to make the chair I sit on. Nope, I ain't drowning in home comforts. But that's cool.

But the land, wow.

I'm sitting here on my veranda feeling all aboriginal, connecting with the land and all that. They're right in what they say about land, them and the native Americans. Land means something. Land talks to you. And, no, I'm not drunk. Sixty acres is quite a lot of land. Well, a lot of rocks, mainly, but you get my drift. It beats me how this place was ever described as a farm – I thought you needed fields for a farm. I wonder what they grew here. Rocks?

The country is surprisingly green. I'd expected it to have that blasted heath look about it, a mixture between Greece and the Scottish Highlands. But it's not like that at all. It's kind of a Mediterranean version of Hampstead Heath, only with more rocks and fewer faggots. Ha ha. There is heather (I think it's heather) and ferns and stuff and daisies and buttercups (ah, bless) but also palm trees and prickly pears and figs and orange trees.

I'd also expected Sarande to feel a lot poorer. So much for preconceptions. The port is predictably grotty in places but the town has its share of okay spots in among the really ropey Stalinist flats. I tell you, some of them sag so much it's like they're made of cheese. One imagines one wouldn't sleep terribly soundly in them.

I've yet to see all these wild animals I've been reading about. Perhaps they've all been hunted to fuck. Shame. Although I'm in no hurry to encounter wild boars and bears and wolves. I sound like Dorothy. Lions, tigers and bears!

One big weirdness here, though, is the spooky remnants from the Hoxha days. You keep coming across all manner of little concrete constructions, like electricity sub-stations, in the most stupid places. It takes you a while to realise they're the bunkers and gun nests we read about. They intrigued me so much, I did a tour on the bike, and the beach is covered with them. Every few hundred yards. They're all around my lake as well. A piece of the past you can't stop seeing. Talking of the beach, if I drive south a wee way, there's a strip of road from where I can actually see Corfu, and little dots of people on the sand, sunbathing. That's a weird feeling, I tell you.

Hoxha's a dirty word now, Bejteri tells me. They even dug him up and moved him to a pauper's grave. And in the post-Hoxha withdrawal they've got a major phobia about rules – a reaction against decades of repression. Now they just do what the fuck they want and sort out their disagreements in their own sweet way.

I hope that's not where the rifle comes in. Or the blood feuds. Call me Mr Scaredy Cat, but I'm not doing flick-flacks over these blood feuds.

We were right about the farm having no electricity, and there's no chance of getting any since no one seems interested in repairing anything unless you're prepared to pay $200 and wait six months. Then pay another $200. So, stuff breaks and just sits. Although it's no great shakes when you have electricity, with – so Bejteri tells me – an average of two power cuts a day.

All my lighting comes from these dinky little Davy lamps, I kid you not. I cook on a gas stove with cylinders. I get water from the lake or preferably from my well and I can boil the fucker or not, but I haven't got ill from it yet. It seems pretty damn clean. In Sarande a lot of people seem to have to rely on standpipes. At least there's no queue at my well.

You don't want to know about the latrine situation.

I know it goes against everything I've ever said about guns, but I feel good about having that little .22. It gives you a sense of security, almost like you're not out here in the wilderness alone. Like there's two of you.

Now, there's a point. Surprise surprise, it does get lonely here. I've got my little Roberts radio to carry around, and my wogbox – and six months' worth of batteries, last minute paranoia shopping in Corfu – but I'll be a happier ex-pat when you and the other losers get over here. Bring me some different tapes and CDs, especially acoustic stuff (suits the atmos) and something fat to read, and I'll have your babies. It's in the evenings when I have time to think – there's too much work to do during the day – that I get lonely. Talking of work, I've lost a few pounds, which is nay bad thing. Nay bad thing at all.

Hand knackered again, more tomorrow.

Tomorrow. Another day, another lek.

Anyway, the house looked every bit as lousy as it did on the video when I got here. And Bejteri kindly left a load of absolute crap inside. Oh cheers, a load of firewood.

Anyway, I've got two useable rooms now: the big living room with the fireplace, and a bedroom. I'll have to get my chimney sweep head on at some stage, which I'm not looking forward to. I'm sure there's something dead up there. I hope it's dead.

Everything else is as you saw it. The veranda is a recent add-on, as we thought. It really makes the place. Structurally, everything's surprisingly sound, apart from a few dodgy floorboards in the bedrooms, and the odd rattly shutter. The roof is okay, thank God. The roof could have given me nightmares.

It's going to be a little palace. I'll be happy once I'm used to the isolation – I tell myself that while veering between fits of loneliness and boredom on one hand, and excitement and euphoria on the other. It's not a healthy state, I know. I'm looking forward to having some visitors, which I keep telling myself is not too far off.

That's about all I've got to tell you up to now, except that I haven't checked out the night life yet. Ha ha. God, there's got to be somewhere in Sarande to hang out and get mellow. In the meantime may life in the corridors of power always leave you deeply fulfilled. SUCKER!

See you soon, mate.

Yours with big kisses, Dr Tarzan Hemingway Livingstone.

PS Give my best to Tina – preferably by e-mail from a long way away, you silver-tongued devil.

6

AFTER ONLY ONE supply run to Corfu, Robert realised he needed a new plan. Corfu was expensive. And finding his feet in the shops of Sarande wasn't working fantastically well, either. For one thing, he noticed that the prices tripled when it was his turn to pay. It wasn't meanness, just that there was a different price for everything if you were a foreigner. And with armed guards on the doors of any shop selling anything worth buying, you could only barter so much. But it couldn't go on. He'd have to bite the bullet and talk to Bejteri.

He was getting a wee bit tired of Bejteri. It was clear the lawyer meant well; but just asking him a simple question was an ordeal that could last half a day. He managed to turn every inquiry around so it became a demand for foreign investment and aid and a lecture on the benefits of democracy and the corresponding evils of socialism.

'What is the West doing?' he would ask, waving his arms through clouds of smoke from his Marlboros which were the status symbol of the successful Sarande citizen. 'The West should give us the money to help our business. How can we build democracy from nothing? And industry. How can we build industry with no money? The West must give us money and materials or this country will never change. We are Europeans, like you. The West has a duty to help us. Why are we given nothing?'

Something for nothing, it seemed to Robert, was the Albanian way in all things. Red Cross handouts, food aid, theft, backhanders – whatever you could get. In almost any other country this lawyer would be in jail. But here, the magnitude of the bribes Bejteri's profession entitled him to was, if anything, the source of his respect among the community. Robert would sit in the stuffy office with its ancient telephone and – amazingly – functioning fax machine, and suffer the whining tirades and lists of imperatives ('the West should; the West must; the West has a duty') and nod his head and wish he knew someone else to whom he could go for advice. Someone living on the same planet.

It crossed Robert's mind to suggest that a little Western-style hard work and enterprise might prove more effective than waiting around for handouts which, he suspected, were bound for the bottomless void of the backhander economy. But it wasn't worth the energy or the risk of causing offence. So, he would sit and smile and nod until the lawyer had burned himself out in the glow of his ever more ridiculous – and revealing – demands. 'The West must give us American cigarettes, and beer. Albanian produce is *skata* – shit. We must have American clothes and TV if we are to become Westerners . . .'

As if Albania's transformation into a modern economy was something white-picket America and middle England lost sleep about; on and on Bejteri would rant until any pretence of championing the cause of democracy was crushed under a catalogue of greed.

All this after Robert might only have asked where he could get thick string.

The bike was in the side street outside Bejteri's office where he always left it when he was in town. But he didn't go straight there. The weather was cool today and walking was pleasant, even carrying the Alp rucksack full of supplies. Robert liked to stroll a different route back to the bike every time. It helped you find your bearings, and you discovered things.

It was while exploring in this way that he found the old man.

He looked at least seventy, but his eyes were sharp and his features alert. He had that expression of knowing more than you do, like a cat, but without the cold torpor.

He looked different from the other men of his age in town who were, to a man, grey-suited, baggy-kneed, flat-capped. Robert's old man was dressed in a beige linen summer suit, not a million miles from the two-piece suits you saw in Hampstead or Notting Hill a few summers back. Only, this one had seen at least a decade's service.

His long hair was strangely, almost comically, Hampstead and Notting Hill as well: salt and pepper, wild, pushed back off his face.

Anyway, for some reason the sight of this splendid geezer sitting cross-legged at the table in the street made Robert stop.

He noticed the man, and then the small cafe, and then he was suddenly aware of feeling very calm.

He set down the Alp. He hadn't felt such calm since he'd left London, and possibly long before.

What was it?

Well, for a start, there was none of that ropey Greek *rembetika* music rasping out at an anti-social volume from someone's broken radio. That helped.

The street was almost deserted and very quiet. Robert stood for a few moments while the residual nerves associated with the day's chore fell away. He let the silence of his surroundings permeate him.

This was a new street to him. Nothing special, just the white fronts of houses and the grey backs of others. He smelled soap, engine oil, frugal kitchens. He saw clothes drying on lines, and sunlight on tiles, and basking cats.

It was an odd street for a cafe, though.

He leaned in for a look.

A few male faces glanced around from under flat caps in the near dark. The interior reminded him of those hostile-looking Cypriot places on Green Lanes and the Seven Sisters Road, only without the hostility.

The old man was the only customer braving the slightly chill air in the street. Robert had been standing there a good couple of minutes now. They caught each other's eye, finally, and Robert obeyed a second, stronger surge of wellbeing.

Sliding the Alp under the next table to the old man's, he lowered himself into one of the white moulded plastic chairs. The old boy raised his drink – a tiny glass of something brown – and touched it to his lips in a formal, but friendly, gesture. Robert felt like a late but welcome guest. It was a good feeling.

After a minute the old man said, 'Good afternoon.' He had an accent.

Robert smiled and shaded his eyes.

'You see no one now, but there will be someone soon. My

friend Safet will not make you wait thirsty for long.' The voice was croaky, but smooth and warm.

'You speak English,' Robert said.

'Of course.' The old man paused. He took a proper sip of his drink and licked his top lip, and cleared his throat. 'You are not here long. Many people speak English. I speak several languages. Greek, Italiano, and some German. I have travelled a little.' He pronounced Greek as 'grikk', and German as 'dzerman'.

'Your English is very good.'

'But my voice is not strong, and my hearing is not good any more. Please join me at this table, and we will not have to shout so loud.'

No one was shouting, but Robert did as he was asked. He glanced back at the Alp once, and left it where it was.

'Thanks.'

From the door of the cafe a man appeared, all belly and apron and moustache, like a cartoon. His face betrayed nothing at all except that he was clearly the proprietor of the cafe. Robert thought of the shopkeeper in *Mr Benn*.

Robert turned to him, but the old man raised a hand. 'I think,' he said, eyes closed, like a mindreader, 'that my new friend will drink cold *beer!*'

The word popped out of his mouth like a cork, and Robert was instantly thirsty. He laughed, and nodded at the proprietor, who turned and walked away, still poker-faced.

'Yes,' the old man went on. 'You look like a man who enjoys cold beer, I think. I am right?'

'Dead right.'

The old man's eyes didn't register the expression, so Robert added: 'Yes, I like cold beer.'

'And here is your beer, and it looks good.'

It was Amstel, the same as in Corfu. Not great beer, but beer. The proprietor placed the bottle, and a glass not much bigger than the one the old man was drinking from, on the table. Robert poured a glassful which was half froth and drained it in one swallow.

'Good?'

'Magnificent. Cheers.'

'For your health. *Gezuar!*'

'*Gezuar!*'

Robert poured and drank again. 'How did you know I was English?'

'I have heard of you. I have been looking out for you – Bejteri has been speaking. You are lucky. He is better than some.'

'I like Bejteri,' Robert said. It seemed like the diplomatic thing to say.

'Yes. You can trust him. And I know your business can do well, if you work hard, but remember to enjoy yourself.'

'That sounds like good advice. I'd like to enjoy myself.'

'It is easy when you remember one thing: don't work yourself to death. Give yourself a little –' He searched for a word. '– break?'

'I know what you mean.'

'I hope so. I hope you know what I mean. It is not good to work too hard. Here, and the other cafe in the street behind? These are good places to come to give yourself a break. In the evenings the other cafe is very busy, with more people, younger people, but I am always here. I like this place. I like to be outside.'

'It's a beautiful day.'

'Yes. Beautiful.' ('Byotifol' was how he pronounced it.) 'There will be many more beautiful days until the late summer, and then the land will look brown for a few months. And very old, like me.' He chuckled. 'But now it is beautiful.'

Robert sipped at his froth. 'Have you always lived here?'

'I have travelled a little.'

Robert pondered his answer. 'Wasn't it difficult to travel? Under Hoxha?' He gripped his glass, suddenly wondering if he'd said the wrong thing.

The old man nodded slowly. 'It was very hard, almost impossible for most people to travel.' Then after a measured pause: 'But I travelled.' The smile was still there. The smile never seemed to leave him. 'You have been travelling yourself, yes? You have been going to Corfu?'

'Yeah.' Robert reddened and shifted in his seat. He looked down at his legs and cleared his throat.

The old man lowered his voice. 'It is nice to go to Corfu. They have many better things than in Sarande. You will enjoy going there.'

Robert straightened up.

'There are good places to buy things here – but hard to find when you are a foreigner. And expensive. I think the people cheat you? But I will show you – one day when we are not enjoying our drinks.'

'Yes,' Robert said – almost whispered. He looked down at the table to see his bottle and glass both empty. He hadn't realised he'd drunk so quickly. He turned his head to the door to look for the cartoon proprietor, Safet, but he was already there.

The boss looked at the old man for a nod. But the old man looked back at Robert. The proprietor now looked to Robert for the nod for more drinks, which he duly gave.

Robert had to swallow a lump in his throat. The old man's tiny act of deference had made him feel better than anything else since he'd left London. He felt a gentle rush of relief, and another of trust in his own senses – of affirmation of something you know is true. Like waking after the worst kind of dream.

He was sitting outside a cafe close to the sea, in the cool breeze and the bright sun, and drinking beer and talking.

7

DAMN!

Robert heard the shadow scurry into the bushes, and the debris and twigs kicked up in its wake patter to the ground.

For a moment after that he stood looking at, and listening to, nothing in particular. Blowing out through his mouth he lowered the rifle to his hips and held it there. He could feel his hands shaking. He looked down and he could see them shaking. He chuckled quietly, and exhaled once more.

What was it? Rabbit?

He didn't even know if they had rabbits here. Oh, shit, they have rabbits everywhere.

But it was something like that. Something smaller, and faster on its feet than a barn door and therefore, it would seem, not in any danger from Robert Maidens. He ran down the list he remembered from the *Blue Guide*. Ferrets, wild cats, weasels, pine martens – what the fuck was a pine marten anyway? – was all the small stuff he could remember.

Perhaps the list should have included indistinct shadows and figments of the imagination.

The hunter wasn't having much luck. In over an hour spent stalking, creeping and straining his ears and eyes, he hadn't managed to keep bird or beast in his sights long enough to get off a single shot, let alone hit anything. He was doing things backwards, he knew. He should be practising with targets before even thinking about hunting. But he couldn't wait; he was in a hurry for something to aim at. Not that he'd seen much. A few small birds, something that might have been a pine marten, and the latest escapee: a thing. No, not much success.

But one hell of an exhilarating sense of failure.

It was like absolutely nothing he had ever done. He was a kid in the world's biggest walled garden. He felt ten years old again. Any responsibility seemed a world away.

The previous afternoon he had watched a pair of eagles circle the house for over an hour, amazed and delighted by their startlingly precise shapes against the sky. Like paper silhouettes scissored by street artists.

He'd wanted to write it down, get it in a letter to Ray. But he knew he'd never do justice to what he felt they had given him. When he watched them, he floated. Even the weight of his hand shading his eyes was lifted. He got drunk on weightlessness: they were telling him something. They were saying: this is beyond flight.

Remembering, Robert hooked the weapon with his fingers and closed his eyes. The eagles were hunters, he thought, like me.

In theory. Twit.

He chuckled out loud at himself and stamped his feet, setting off bird calls in the trees and scratching sounds in the scrub and bushes all around him. He looked through the trees toward the other side where, a long way off, lay the mountains. It didn't seem like any distance at all.

It was good to think as you walked, but no faster than your patient steps, and only simple thoughts: easy questions with easy answers, or none at all – it didn't matter. For once he wasn't torturing himself.

Yes, only simple thoughts like: this had been a real farm once. And so for a moment he mused about farms. Then his mind wandered to what might have happened here to change that – what meddling digit of the long arm of small-state bureaucracy had caused the farm to be reduced to this wilderness. That set off a tiny alarm: QUESTION NOT SIMPLE ENOUGH. And so the answer was SEP: Someone Else's Problem.

What mattered was that the process had worked out well for him, had made this place his for next to nothing, his to wander around with his real toy gun, with his new dreams and no old worries. Here he was: a man with land and a house made of strong whole stones, and a deed – and a gun – to say it was his. Robert liked all these things, and no more.

Days like this will change Ray's mind, he thought.

Another noise behind him and Robert's reflexes registered the rhythm and weight of a small mammal in the long grass. With the gun at his waist he pivoted to face the sound and, without thinking, squeezed the trigger.

Without thinking.

The unexpected impact jarred him and he swore and stumbled. It was only a small rifle but a shock is a shock.

He hadn't thought at all.

It was his first shot. God, but it was loud! And from the hip! He felt like a – a what? Like a cowboy. Robert felt himself flooded with sweat as he realised what he'd done.

He'd fired a rifle.

He was a thirty-year-old Londoner.

Thirty-year-old Londoners waited too long for tube trains and got ripped off by landlords; they wondered how long they could behave like teenagers before they got a proper life; they paid through the nose in Camden for clothes which were too young for them. But everybody wants to keep getting laid – so you kept paying. You did all that stuff. You didn't fire guns.

But he had fired his gun, on his land – and missed what he'd aimed at, of course. But he had done it. Robert was still for a long time, collecting his thoughts.

There is another world and I am in it.

This is one of the ways people change.

Five minutes and a long swallow of water later, Robert had set up a firing range of about fifteen stones, a foot between each one, some on top of larger rocks and small mounds of earth to make different levels. This not being the movies there were no tin cans scattered conveniently around, but rocks would do for now.

He turned and walked back thirty yards, then turned again to face the targets, which were spread against a backdrop of trees. It all looked good. The trees were mostly oak which was about the extent of Robert's tree expertise. One of the guides – the *Bradt* or the *Blue* – listed all the flora he would see, but how would he know which was which? To him they were just part of a scene.

He had a good two dozen shells in his pockets, but by the time he'd fired off the four left in the clip and rested to let the sound flow back into his ears, Robert knew he wanted to stop and do something else.

He was sweating again, and his breathing was stuttering and uncontrolled. He passed the rifle to his left hand and dropped his right to his groin. He tore at the button fly of his combats, and released himself into his hand. He gripped the rifle at the stock tighter in his left hand, and began moving his right. The open air on it felt good.

There was a sudden noise and he stopped and looked around. Oh, come on, who the fuck was going to see him?

He started again, thinking about – he didn't know what. Things he'd never let himself think about before.

Suddenly there didn't seem a limit to the images he responded to. The images were not all purely sexual. It was like a door had been opened. A slide show was in front of his eyes. Lust; violence; pain; strength; a clenched fist; lust again. He grunted.

Then it was over and he was holding himself and breathing steadily, and the music was visiting his mind as it always did, and the pictures were gone.

Those pictures. It must just have been the gun, he decided. And his nerves, and all the changes.

Strings played a theme over and over again until the melody left him and he buttoned up and shook his hand and wiped it, and clipped in another five.

Robert's aim improved as he relaxed and became familiar with the weapon. He was enjoying shooting. He didn't think about the slide show.

The weapon lay on the porch dining table to his left. Next to it were the gun-cleaning brushes that looked like Christmas trees. Robert faced the setting sun while behind the house the lake was coming alive with the cries of diving birds and the grunts and howls of the animals he couldn't yet name. The evening was pulling up to that dangerous juncture when, for the briefest of moments, beings are caught dozing off guard and things happen: when it is exactly cool enough for some creatures, and exactly dark enough for others.

Robert was looking forward to later on, when he would lie down alone and think about Tina. His mind felt clean, as though a lot of small things had been swept out of sight.

It was then that he heard the engine.

It was closer than the road. So, on his driveway, maybe two hundred yards away. Not pushing many revs. It was a motorcycle, coughing as it dodged the potholes on the way to his house. Without thinking, Robert slid a clip of five into the .22. It was a gratifying motion. He could see the bike now, and a person on it. Who would be coming here?

A thin boy with long red hair and a small face.

No, a girl.

He strained to see into the rising spiral of dust in her wake, but she was alone.

The rider coaxed the machine to within twenty yards of the veranda – no chest to speak of, and broadish shoulders for a girl, hence his mistake – then cut the engine and dismounted. The eroticism of the gesture as her legs scissored open and then closed took him by surprise – or rather it surprised him that he found it erotic on this girl who from this distance was plain and, if anything, a little ungainly.

The stranger shook her hair and a few strands fell over her face. It was a stunning colour, closer to brown than red now. No, it was red again, and almost to her shoulders, curling under its own weight and the ends brushing against her neck.

Good hair. Makes up for the tits.

But when she began to walk – slowly, one eye on the rifle – toward the veranda, and he could see the real shape of her moving under the clothes, her natural curves asserted themselves.

Okay, there's some tits. And her hair changed colour once more. Brown again.

Robert forgot all about ungainly.

He was beginning to feel silly about holding the rifle. She was eyeing it. Well, you would. She came nearer – still watching the gun – until she was close enough to reach out and touch his leg. Her face reached about level with his waist. It suddenly occurred to Robert that he could blow her head off. But why?

He wished he was wearing his Ray-Bans. He looked good in his Ray-Bans, and they hid your eyes so you could lech. That was a better thought to think about than blowing her head off.

Height about five eight, a couple of inches shorter than himself. Age maybe twenty-six. One hair grip with a plastic yellow flower, come loose. Green tailored T-shirt – very flattering. Virtually redundant bra, grey camouflage trousers, pink DKNY trainers, pink socks.

Her eyes were bright green and her posture good, her hips narrow and her bum, from this angle, firm and high, with no spare on her thighs. She did look great in those trousers. Face plain, though.

Before he had time to make any more snap judgements she spoke.

'Evening. Want to put the gun down?' The smile which followed made the face unplain, once and for all.

Robert cleared his throat, and said: 'Australian.'

'Is that a question?' The girl's voice was confident, but with a musical quality she couldn't hide with volume, and probably a higher natural pitch than she would have liked.

'What? Yes. I mean, you are, aren't you?' *Shit fuck shit you moron. Bad start. Start again.*

'Yeah. Look, you want to put the gun down? I'm not dangerous. Promise.'

He slid it onto the table and wiped his damp palms on his backside. They were damp again straight away.

She waited.

'You going to invite me up?'

'What? Yeah. Course.' He stepped to his right and offered her his hand. She took it and hopped up in two nimble steps.

'Thanks. Very chivalrous, I must say. Pity I'm no lady.' She smiled again.

Here's hoping.

'English?'

Robert nodded. 'Near as dammit.'

'Where from?'

'London among other places. You?'

'Sydney. My name's Charlotte. My mates call me Charlie when

they want to rattle me, but I prefer Charlotte.' She smiled and reset the hair grip.

Robert shuffled his feet, or they shuffled him.

'Charlotte it is, then. I'm Robert. My friends call me shithead when they want to rattle me. Only from now on I'm just going to shoot them.'

He held out his hand in the shape of a pistol, and she giggled and shook his index finger.

'Quite right, too. Pleased to meet you, Robert. And I understand about the gun, by the way. Place like this. Crazy, scary people. I've got one of my own.'

Charlotte from Sydney's right hand disappeared behind her back for an instant before reappearing wrapped around a nasty-looking little black number. Robert flinched and took a step back from the revolver.

The girl laughed out loud and shook her head. 'Bought it in Sarande. Adam made us get matching ones.'

Who?

'I've never fired it, though. I don't really know what to do with it, to tell you the truth. But just having it back there makes a girl feel a bit safer. You know?' She put the gun away and folded her arms over her chest, and toed patterns in the dust on the wooden deck. 'Adam's mate was here on his own last year, and got robbed blind. Then he bought a gun and kept it visible, and no more trouble. I'm hoping it keeps working for me like that.'

Robert sighed and smiled. 'I think you're right. It's a signal.'

'So.'

'So.'

'This is a lovely place.'

'Thanks. It will be.'

The girl pushed some hair behind an ear. There was a brief silence.

'Are you hungry, Charlotte from Sydney?'

They ate tinned tuna, and sliced cucumber and radishes, and bread, and condensed milk poured into a tin of pears, and Robert dug out a bottle of red wine he'd been saving.

They didn't talk much during the meal, just a little about the places they'd been: sounding each other out. They were easy in each other's company and the wine disappeared pretty quickly. Robert tried to find something atmospheric on the radio but could only get *rembetika.* Charlotte thought it was funny being called a Roberts radio – she'd never heard of the make. They toasted the meal as an unqualified success.

After dinner he lent her his fleece for the cold, and picked up a bottle of Cutty Sark, and they went out the back door and scuffed toward the lake. No torch – the moon was enough.

'What do you mean, you live here?' she asked him.

'I mean I live here. I bought this place. I'm going to do it up and rent out rooms to backpackers in the summers.'

'Cool!'

'You don't think it's a daft idea?'

'I think it's a great idea.' She looked at her feet for a few steps, then flipped her face up toward his. 'Hey, do you need a chambermaid?'

Robert laughed.

The girl looked at her feet again. A few moments later she said: 'So what are you going to do in the winter?'

Robert sighed loudly. 'That's a good question. Get lonely? Go home for a while? Depends how I feel. I'm trying not to think about it. How about you? What are you doing out in the arse-end of nowhere? – excuse me.'

She feigned shock, then smiled. 'Don't worry about it. What am I doing?' Charlotte shook her head and groaned. 'Same as every other Australian you've ever met.' She put on a Crocodile Dundee accent: 'Jobbin' me way round the world, working in bars, no worries, mate, blah-di-blah.'

Robert laughed.

'It's true. Have cliché, will travel. It's not a bad life for a couple of years, though.'

She was sturdy, and not fantastically feminine, not in a girlie way. But there was an undertone of elegance to everything she did. Robert couldn't work out which trait, if either – the sturdiness or the elegance – she was trying to hide and which she wanted to accentuate. For now, he doubted if she knew.

'How long have you been doing it?'

'Year and a half. I should be thinking about going home and doing something serious with my life. But I just can't seem to face it. I mean, Sydney's cool, but that's it. That's Australia. Don't believe what you hear about Perth. It sucks big ones – excuse me.'

Robert chuckled. 'Don't worry about it.'

She sighed. 'The rest of civilisation just seems so far away sometimes. It's not like you, with the world a hop away on the Eurostar. You start to feel trapped. Australia's not an easy place to escape from, you know? So I'm making the most of it.'

They reached the lake and sat down very close together on the sandy shore.

Robert said: 'But there's civilisation and there's this place. This place is pretty extreme.'

'It's different here, I'll give you that. I mean different to anything.'

'That's true.'

'I mean it. I like it. It's beautiful – especially here, you've got an amazing view. Thank God I've got the bike, though.'

'Where are you staying?'

'Oh, another place a bit like this? Down the road south a mile or so?' She scuffed sand, and looked at her shoes.

Robert gathered that she wasn't sure whether she wanted to explain. He was curious, but he didn't push. Eventually she said: 'I suppose we're neighbours.' He took it as a signal to go on with that line.

'Are you renting?'

'Nah. Look, I suppose you would say I'm squatting.'

There was that tomboyishness again – especially in her speech – but again under it that smoothness of movement like someone moving assuredly through zero gravity. And then a gesture with the wrists, or of the neck, more naturally beautiful than any catwalk pose. Robert decided that both elements of her were natural. It was lovely, or possibly a lovely form of torture, to watch.

Robert cleared his throat. 'Are you, ah, are you on your own?'

She looked at him for a long moment. 'I wasn't. I was supposedly very much with someone. But Adam upped and ran off back to

Greece. He said he couldn't stand my moods, or something? I was sick of him anyway – well, more like disappointed in him – to tell you the truth.'

'Wait a minute. He just left you here? *Here*?'

She dropped her face into her hands. 'Please don't say it.'

'I'm saying it! People don't abandon people in Albania. People disappear here. I mean disappear in a bad way. I've got *besa*, but Jesus, you have to watch yourself!'

'I know. But I'm careful.' She shook her head. 'Adam. There's people and there's people. Anyway, he's gone and good riddance. And anyway, if this place is so dangerous how do you propose to make a living renting out rooms?'

'It'll change. It has to. They have nothing else here.' Robert stared across the lake at the shadow of the hills beyond, as if he could see the future approaching from that direction. 'Tourism's always one of the first things off the landing craft with the invasion. When they realise they can make more money selling us booze and bottled water and sun cream than they can from robbing us, it should calm down.' Robert paused, then said: 'Look, these moods your mate couldn't stand. Are they something I should know about?'

She giggled. 'Oh, no. That was his problem, not mine. He just meant that I like to think about things and, heaven forbid, have the odd meaningful chat.'

Robert smiled and sipped some whisky. 'So, you were doing Greece? I used to like Greece.'

'Yeah. On motorbikes. Secondhand. Motorbikes are dirt cheap in Greece. I've always wanted to ride a motorbike. I never thought I'd be strong enough to handle it, and I was a bit scared. But it's okay. Tough on the bum.'

'They're cheaper here.'

'Looking at that thing parked in front of your house I can guess why.'

Robert snorted. 'Fair comment. So, go on. You did Greece.'

'We came across the border on the bikes. Then we found the empty place a couple of weeks ago and moved in, and I made it as comfortable as I could.

'I thought it was great. A real little paradise? Thought I could use the time and the space to get my head together. Reckoned maybe a little serious thought would be good for Adam's head, too. Needn't have bothered myself with thinking about him, though. He's not interested in nature, or having a bit of peace; just in how fast the bikes can go. Three days with me and his own caveman thoughts and he was out of here. Went back to join up with the rest. I suppose they'll want to know what he's done with me. I hope that throws him.' She laughed.

'Anyway, I've been on my own about ten days now. And I know I should be lonely, but this great feeling of peace keeps saying: no, Charlotte, love, just stay another day or two. You're in no hurry to catch up with the rest of the world. And being alone with myself has been a real revelation. You know, I think I'm more interesting and that I've got more to offer than people have ever given me credit for.'

She blushed. It seemed to Robert that maybe she thought she'd gone too far, and shared too much for now. He said: 'No, I know what you mean.' She looked pleased. Robert unscrewed the cap on the whisky and offered it to her. 'Adam was your boyfriend?'

'You'll get me drunk. I'm not used to this stuff. Still, when in Rome.' She took a sip, and coughed. 'Not really boyfriend. Tell you the truth. You just hook up with people, you know? I probably made it sound a bigger deal than it was. I thought there was a connection, but when it came down to it, we never really got past small talk. I think it was just the location, the trip, all making me feel romantic. Yep. I'm more level-headed about it all now. About a lot of things. Being alone is helping. But I was getting toward the end of that as well. We need people.'

She combed her hair back with her fingers. Robert liked the way she did it. She did it again and he liked it a bit more. Robert drank, and ground the bottle into the sand beside him. Just hooking up sounded good. The night sounded good. And now in the dark, and the blue reflected light off the lake, Charlotte looked good.

'Look, Charlotte, will you be all right driving back tonight? In the dark, I mean?'

'Don't you worry about me, soldier. I know my way home.

But thanks for asking. Ouch!' Shifting her bum, Charlotte pulled the revolver out of the back of her jeans. She retrieved a handkerchief from down near her knickers, and wrapped it around the gun. Robert cleared his throat. Charlotte laid the gun in the handkerchief on the sand behind her. ''at's better.'

Robert cleared his throat again and wiped his hands on his thighs. Then he picked up a stone and threw it in the water. They watched the ripples.

He said: 'It seems a funny thing to do, leaving your friends and coming alone to the middle of nowhere and squatting out here.'

'I wasn't alone. And it's not as funny as buying half the country, like you. Anyway, I was just sick of it all, the people I was with. Getting blind drunk, and watching the girls row with their blokes, and then arguing with my own bloke. When all I really wanted to do was share how good I was feeling, or wanted to be feeling, at any rate. And he wasn't even my bloke, not really. And crummy discos and crummier restaurants.'

'Do you have a bloke back home then?'

'Shouldn't think so. Not by now. Funny. I never knew a lot of boys until the last year or so.' She laughed at herself. 'Boys. What am I saying?'

'Do you think you'll hang around here long?'

'Tell you the truth I wasn't quite sure what I was going to do next. But now I've found myself someone to scrounge dinner off, I might just stretch it out a little.' She knuckled his shoulder. 'Long as you don't shoot me.'

'Cool! I mean, whatever.' For some reason Robert added: 'Although I go to Sarande a lot. And I work a lot. On the house. I'm not always around.'

No one spoke for a moment, then Charlotte said: 'No problem. I could pitch in.'

Robert threw another stone. A diving bird shrieked.

The girl creased her brow and turned to him. 'Okay, no pressure. Just what are you doing here, Robert Maidens?'

Robert sighed and chuckled. 'I'll tell you when I'm sure myself.'

Charlotte said: 'Oh, I see. Fair enough. Do you know anyone else out here? Any other friends?'

'No,' Robert lied.

'Two of a kind, then,' she murmured. 'May I enquire, do you have plans for tomorrow evening?'

'We-ell now, lady, that's pretty short notice. And, as you can imagine, I've a pretty full diary.'

She snorted. 'But of course. Maybe I'll just drop over on the off chance of not being blown out. You can leave a message with the maître d'. We'll see, eh?'

'We'll see.'

They both smiled in the dark, and then laughed again spontaneously.

'Listen, answer me something.'

'Ask away, soldier.'

'How did you know I was here?'

'The shots.'

'Hm?'

'The gunshots. I could hear the shooting all afternoon. I didn't like the idea of the neighbours marauding around with guns. So I figured I'd summon up some of my new-found confidence and check you out. I decided I'd either have to beat a hasty retreat, or I'd make a little friend.' She leaned closer so they bumped shoulders. 'And here we are. Actually, I was going to ask you about that.'

'About what?'

'About this afternoon. About what you were shooting at.'

'Oh, anything that moved at first – don't worry, it all survived. Later on I just set up some targets and took potshots at stones. It's good fun.' He glanced sideways. Charlotte looked interested.

She said: 'Not hit *anything*?'

'If I did it was by accident. Turns out I'm not much of a marksman.' Robert hesitated, then said: 'Listen, would that bother you? If I'd been shooting things?'

She shrugged. 'Who's to judge? Like I said, this place is different. Does it bother you? Shooting at living things?'

'I thought it would. But then it just happened. I found myself just leaving the house this afternoon and going out and doing it and not even worrying about whether it was right to shoot at fluffy creatures. In fact I didn't think about it until you asked me now. And now I think about it it seems back to front: like worrying about it is the weird bit, not the shooting. The shooting seems to fit in with this place perfectly.'

'I suppose it does.'

'Yup. And I suppose I should show you how to shoot that – from the little I know – and clean it.'

'I suppose. I might not be so scared of it then.'

They drank from the bottle again, then Charlotte leaned against him and yawned and shivered. He told her about seeing the eagles, and she dropped her head back and whistled in appreciation. ('That's what I mean.' 'About what?' 'Adam. He'd never notice anything like that.') And it occurred to him that he'd done what he hadn't believed himself capable of, and put the eagles into words. He relaxed, and smelled whisky and the warm, tired girl.

She stood up and stretched her arms and swept her hair back from her face. He still liked the way she did it. She stretched up on her toes and his face was about level with the top of her narrow thighs.

She said: 'Time to face that drive home.' Then: 'Tonight's been lovely, by the way.'

The diving birds went mad in circles over the lake.

8

'YES. YOUR HOUSE was once a farm. But not a collective farm. They were much bigger, with ugly buildings which boiled you in the summer and froze you in the winter, and cracked at the corners when you wept too hard.' The old man chuckled mirthlessly.

Robert noticed that he spoke slowly when choosing unfamiliar words. But always the right words.

'After the communists, the people burned and destroyed all the collective farms – these are the burned buildings you see from the road.' He shook his head – which in Albania is the gesture for Yes, a nod meaning No – and went on. 'So many people have left the land now. There is no new machinery to work on the farms and the life is poor.' He lowered his voice. 'But there are other reasons why they leave. The collective farms were prisons. People were crowded into the fields. Old men and women and children. Anyone. Forced to work. The fields had wire, and dogs, and men with guns. A field was a cage, nothing but a big cage.

'And the people never saw the food. It went to Tirane, maybe, to the army?' He shrugged. 'People starved. Many people can still remember, and they want to get far away from what they cannot forget. Whole villages have no young men. Maybe one day maybe they come back.' He didn't sound convinced.

Robert was fascinated to hear a first-hand account of the history he'd so recently read. He wanted to ask all sorts of things, but he wasn't sure of the limits yet.

The old man seemed just as curious about him. 'And how goes the work, my friend?' was a daily enquiry.

Robert took a swig of beer and wiped his mouth. 'Better. I'm still not ready to tackle those stairs. But generally better. I'm improvising a lot. Improvising? Oh, that means making things myself, and making tools. If I improvise a bit more I'll have somewhere to sit soon that doesn't give me splinters.'

'Splinters?'

Robert wondered how much of what he said was beyond the old man's English vocabulary – like 'improvising' and 'splinters'. But he wasn't going to insult him by talking down.

He got round this one by miming getting a splinter in his backside, and they both chuckled.

The two men were alone at the cafe. Robert had abandoned work early after an unproductive morning trying to level the legs of an oak dining table. The table was a beautiful thing, but it seemed determined to warp and render itself unstable. It mutated like a virus. Robert was close to conceding that it was a badly conceived misfit, and executing the bastard. But for some reason the idea of giving up on it disappointed him out of all proportion. Besides which Charlotte would probably have tried to have him arrested. She had all kinds of opinions about the work he was doing on the house.

Whatever, with the work and Robert's good mood stalled for the day he sought out the old geezer in the cafe to share some cold beers and complaints with. Yes, there were days like this when something vexed him out of proportion and life wouldn't boil down to simplicity, land, and guns. Yes, there were catalysts which made you doubt yourself and your choices. And sometimes it seemed there was just a huge void where you should have been able to see the sense in what you were doing. Where did you get that? Where was the well of simplicity you could visit for wisdom and blankness?

He had written to Tina.

He felt bad about that but he told himself that Charlotte was liable to up and ride off into the sunset any day now, and more than likely would.

The two men talked most afternoons, now. In the mornings Robert worked on the house – helped by Charlotte, who never failed to show up and who, in her words, 'worked like an Asian'. And, wouldn't you know it, our boy found her less plain and ungainly by the day.

He sought her input on the house, out of politeness at first, but pretty soon because it was clear she had an eye. She saw things he missed. She teased him, saying it was a gender thing, and he played along. But Robert remembered that, yes, Patricia had the same eye.

Remarks like 'Is this going to be a guesthouse, or a barracks?' usually swung a stalemate her way. 'Make your mind up. If it's a guesthouse, I think you'll find I'm right about this.' And she always was. Game Over.

In some ways, though, her behaviour threw him.

There was her disappearing act, for example. Okay, she tipped up in the mornings and got stuck in to the work. But come siesta time she'd casually announce she was through being someone's slave for the day and that she had places to be. And, zoom, off she went to them.

Robert knew why she went: she was waiting to be asked, in something approaching a proper manner, to move into his farmhouse, and these disappearances were her way of saying she was too proud to impose on him without that invitation. There was no question that Robert wanted her there. But somehow he couldn't say the words. He admired her determination to take nothing for granted; he just wished she would, thereby putting the onus onto her, and saving him the trouble of starting something he might not have the nerve to see through. He liked Charlotte, he just didn't like pressure.

Anyway, four or five hours later she'd rematerialise on the veranda, sipping a bottle of something she'd brought, and struggling through a Greek magazine, or searching through the radio for something civilised, or playing Robert's tapes.

The few hours on his own or in Sarande settled Robert, and returned him to himself. Their evenings together were pleasant and relaxed. It seemed an almost perfect arrangement.

The cumulative effect on Robert's emotional equilibrium of, say, a week of this perfect arrangement, was predictable enough.

Right now the work to which the old man had referred mostly meant emptying the contents of a particular room onto the level patch of dusty ground below the veranda, then deciding what was to be salvaged and repaired, and what broken up for fuel.

Charlotte was a good influence. She never let him get away with interrupting a job half-finished. Not a chance. Charlotte finished everything she started, and made sure he did too.

Between them they worked steadily, and by the time they clocked off for lunch Robert felt he'd earned the drive into Sarande for a drink with the old man.

He never mentioned his existence to Charlotte.

The old man nodded No, to another drink but Robert nodded, then corrected himself and shook his head to mean Yes.

'You do not seem to me like a man who wants to boss a hotel,' the old man said, suddenly.

'It won't be a hotel,' Robert answered.

The old man laughed. 'Here it will be a hotel. Here it will be the Ritz!'

Robert smiled. 'You could be right.'

'But you did not come here to boss a hotel.'

The Amstel arrived and Robert let it stand. 'Yes, I did.'

'No, you did not.'

'Okay.' Robert gritted his teeth and drummed three fingertips. 'Okay. What do you think I came here for?'

'No,' he said. 'The question is: what do *you* think you came here for?' He grinned.

Robert sighed. 'It would take a long time to explain.'

The old man shook his head. 'Probably.'

There was a pause. Robert held up a finger. 'But, for one thing, I didn't like my job.'

'There are other jobs.'

'Are there?'

The old man raised his eyebrows. 'Your country is rich. There is only one job in your country you can do?'

'I don't think I know my own country any more.'

'My friend, those are the words of someone who knows his own country more than he thinks.'

To anyone else Robert might have said: bullshit. Or not bothered to answer at all. But he always listened to the old man.

If the old man had company Robert was careful not to outstay his welcome. The other men – there were never any women – were patient enough, and included him in their conversation as far as was possible. Yes, they occasionally managed to make him feel just the right side of a circus freak. But they appeared to mean well, and politeness was preferable to feeling anonymous.

But today they were very pleasantly alone.

'You could be right,' Robert said. 'Perhaps that's the problem.' Then: 'But I don't – I didn't – want to be there any more. I wanted to get far away. And anyway, I didn't know how safe my job was. No one does anymore.'

The old man shook his head slowly. 'So you were not really coming here – to boss a hotel, for example. You were – what is the word? – escaping something.'

'I saw my chance.'

'And what is this chance?'

Robert looked straight at the old man, and spoke quietly and slowly. 'This is a one-off. This is a new beginning where my money means so much more than it would have back home, and it's a place where hardly anyone like me has been before. It's not spoiled. This is somewhere I can have things I couldn't back there –' He motioned vaguely with one arm, then went on. '– and not just the freedom and the escape from the modern world –' Was he following him? '– but a home, and space, and not the fear, not the constant *fear* about all the things which are disappearing everywhere else.'

He stopped and studied the old man's face for signs of comprehension, then continued: 'I think maybe this is a place and a way to slow my life down. Stop me from grinding myself away, wearing myself out with constant, pointless work, work, work. It's like I've come from the new world back into the old. And so far I like it here. Like I said, it's hard to explain.'

'No. You have explained something very well – perhaps not what you wanted to, but something. But be careful. The old world is a difficult place to live, also.'

'Its problems seem simpler.'

The old man said nothing.

'I have money here,' Robert went on. 'Back home it was worth nothing.'

'Back home?'

'This will become home.'

'Your hotel.'

'Yeah. If you want to call it a hotel. For six months or so a year, it'll be a hotel. And the rest of the time I'll get used to it. I'll work on it. And when – if – I go home, it will be like a visit, a holiday. Nothing else. I can have a lot here. In just a few years.'

'That is good. But you can always go home.'

'I won't. I mean, I don't want to.'

'But you can.'

'I won't, though. It would be like –'

The old man waited. 'Yes? Like what?'

'Like running away,' Robert said, forgetting local etiquette and nodding his head.

'Like running away,' the old man repeated, slowly. 'I understand.'

Robert didn't respond.

The old man was quiet a moment, then said: 'Come, drink with me. Pour the beer while it is cold and have a drink with an old man.'

Robert cleared his throat. 'You asked,' he said. His voice was quiet and breathy. He drummed his knuckles, now.

'Yes, I asked.'

'You wanted to know why I was here.'

'Yes.'

'And you already knew.'

'No, I did not know.'

'You knew. You knew just as well as I did.'

'No, young man. I know a lot less than you think. I do not know. I only hear, and see.'

'I don't believe that. You just told me why I'm here.'

'I know because you chose to let me know. And I am honoured

that you did so. It took courage. You talked about change, about things disappearing. And I know about change and things disappearing. And I know that running away is not always a bad thing – because it is not always a simple thing. Come, drink with a rude old man. And do not think too much about it. That is not for now.'

Robert poured the beer into two glasses. It had lost most of its fizz and was no longer very chilled. The old man shouted up two more bottles and sighed loudly and patted his belly two-handed, signals to let the subject drop.

Robert suddenly felt good. Despite everything – because of everything? Yes, because of the chance to tell the truth to someone who he believed was not judging him.

The old man sighed again, and Robert raised his glass to his lips for a long, deep swallow.

'It is good?'

'It's beer. Beer's good even when it's lousy. And there's no philosophy in beer, so don't try and catch me out on that one. It's just beer.'

The old man laughed. 'I like your new word. Lousy. What does it mean? Lousy.'

Robert grinned wide. 'Take too long to explain.'

'I think so,' laughing. 'So tell me, what was your job in England that was so lousy?'

Now it was Robert's turn to sigh. This old geezer would get away with murder if Robert let him, and he would probably let him. 'I was a draughtsman.'

The drinks came and Robert tipped fresh cold beer into his warm one.

'Draughtsman? Explain.' He said it like 'thrafzmann'.

Robert rubbed his eyes. 'A draughtsman is someone who makes big drawings. Pictures of buildings and mechanical services, like water and heating and air conditioning?' He looked at the old man and could see he was losing him. 'I drew big pictures. I made plans. For engineers and builders. Do you understand?'

'Builders, engineers. Oh, yes.'

'You sure?'

'I am sure. You copy other people's plans. You know something?'

'What?'

'It sounds lousy.'

They laughed and Robert slapped the table.

The old man coughed, then said: 'You read Albanian?'

'A little – I bought a book to learn.'

'You read Albanian newspapers? Greek newspapers? You can buy Greek newspapers here, sometimes.'

'I know. I can get the World Service, too. Radio. I got the Voice of America the other night but it was too trippy, very twisted, so I switched it off.'

The old man shook his head, for Yes. 'The World Service is better – you should listen.'

'I try not to.'

'Then you must try to.'

'Why?'

'It is a nice day. We are having drinks. I do not want to talk about the news on a nice day, with drinks, and with my friend.' He raised his glass to Robert, and Robert raised his in return, feeling himself blush slightly. 'But listen. Listen to the news.'

'Why?'

'First, it is a good way to stop thinking about yourself. It will give you something bigger to worry about. You think things are simple here. And you talk about change. Well.'

The old man laughed briefly, then his face turned solemn.

'But do as I say. Listen to the news, and keep listening. And –' He leaned closer to Robert across the table. '– remember where you are.'

'What's up, petal?'

'Hm?'

'*Always with the negative waves.*'

'Nothing.'

'Is it the curtains?'

That morning Robert had discovered his living room windows covered with squares of fresh, bright fabric, the sunlight casting red seahorses on a blue background across the wooden floor, with an effect like stained glass.

'No, the curtains are great.'

'You don't like the curtains.'

'I love the curtains.'

'You didn't like them this morning.'

How could she tell? He smiled. 'I suppose this house just always said shutters to me. Where did you find that fabric anyway?'

'A woman finds things. A woman knows. We can use the shutters as well, sometimes.'

Yeah, he thought. A woman knows how to make me feel redundant and usurped. But if Robert was honest with himself – which was by no means a given – he wasn't really irritated at all.

Charlotte sighed. 'Oh, come on. They stop the place looking like such an outpost, for a start – no offence.'

'I know. None taken.'

'I should think not. Guesthouse or barracks, Robert? Guesthouse or barracks? Something else is bothering you, isn't it?'

They were sitting on the veranda steps. It would be dark in an hour. In the bushes and clumps of grass cicadas were beginning their match of signal and reply, signal and reply, which would end up with them all screaming at once until morning.

'That table,' Robert said, sighing. 'Fucker's determined to beat me.' He picked up a pebble and threw it at nothing in particular.

'Don't you dare smash up that table. You've ruined enough nice things already to furnish two homes. You want to smash that table, you'll have to get by me first.'

Robert grinned. 'You really flip when I break up something we can't salvage, don't you? You look at me as if I'm about to fillet the family pet.'

'You tease me. You take that axe to things in order to get a reaction.'

Robert opened his eyes wide. 'Who teases *who*?'

Charlotte blushed and grinned. No one spoke for a moment then Charlotte asked: 'Is it me?'

'What?'

'This other thing that's bothering you. I'm not stupid. I know it's not the stupid table.'

Was it her? Yes, of course it was her. She bothered him, but not in the way she meant. She bothered him because she moved like an unsteady kid in a new school uniform one minute, and a tall pine in a breeze the next, and he wanted to tell her, and it was playing havoc with his heart rate and his imagination and his sleep. Yes, it was her.

Robert turned his face to Charlotte and slipped his left hand under her hair and rubbed the back of her slim neck. 'Yes, it's you. I loathe you with all my being. But you're all I have to use as a sacrifice.'

She closed her eyes and purred, and leaned back against his hand. 'Mmm. That's nice. I hinted for six weeks for Adam to do that. Big lump. Look, you want me to fuck off?'

Robert looked surprised. 'Nope.'

'Then why the big frown? Stuff like that can make a girl feel unwelcome, you know? Come on. What's bugging you?'

Robert stopped the massage. 'Give me a minute.'

Charlotte sighed, and clucked her tongue. 'Right. I'm going down to the lake and fish out those beers, and you have a good *think*, and by the time I get back be ready to tell mum all about it or else I'm going home to sulk. Okay?'

She marched away in an elegant mock huff.

Robert looked at her clothes – she'd washed everything out in the lake today and it was all drying over the rail. He still hadn't recovered from watching her do it.

He recalled now how she'd unselfconsciously undressed on the shore, and waded in and out of the water, relaying clean and dirty things: a ball of T-shirts, two pairs of Levi's, dungarees, a green summer dress about so thin, Lowe lightweights, and then her three small bras, and finally ankle socks and several shades of knickers.

He'd sat, supposedly tanning, with the *Raymond Chandler Omnibus*, occasionally turning a page so as not to give himself away, and she hadn't looked fazed by his presence. She wasn't teasing him, he was sure. He didn't think that kind of trick was her. Anyway, he'd sat and watched, and watched, just wishing there were more clothes to wash. The way her small breasts succumbed to gravity when she leaned over the water. Father, forgive me. Father and Jesus, Mary and Joseph.

And it wasn't only arousal that he felt, watching her. It was peace as well. Peace and simplicity – there was that word again. The simplicity and peace of watching a lovely woman do this simple, timeless task, out here in this virtual wilderness. It was like a page out of the Bible. .

A very sexy Bible, granted. Father, forgive me again.

Robert waited for her footsteps to fade away, then crept over to the rail to check out the drying knickers. Lordy.

Right now Charlotte was wearing sandals and Robert's Scotland shorts and his I AM SPOCK T-shirt and his fleece which, it seemed, he just wasn't ever going to get back – and *no knickers*. He knew that, because they were all here, drying, *clean*. Think about that, Robert.

He tried imagining a more sexy outfit anywhere in the world, and wondered if he had time for a really close inspection of the knickers before she got back with the beers, then laughed at himself.

Get a grip. He was supposed to be thinking what to tell her. The question was nudged forward by a pulse of genuinely selfless affection, which took Robert a mite by surprise.

He concentrated his thoughts on Charlotte. For all her apparent confidence, she was clearly floating loose of something; for all her bravado she probably felt more lost and afraid out here than he did. At least he had come here with a purpose, and not merely been abandoned. Robert wanted to make her feel welcome and wanted, at the very least – and to perv at her pants, of course.

She worried him, though. Something had pushed her here. It wasn't normal to stay alone in a place like this.

He heard floppy sandal footsteps and the clinking of glass and took a deep breath and exhaled. Charlotte greeted him with an exaggerated smacker of a kiss on the forehead and a bottle in the hand. She took the other bottles out of the daysack and lined them up on the table, then plonked herself back on the step.

'I get splinters off this floor and it'll be the back of my hand.'

Robert sniggered.

'Oh, please!' But she giggled. She took his beer back off him and deftly opened both bottles with a cigarette lighter. 'Adam taught me that. It's my one and only boys' trick.'

Adam again. What else did Adam know? No, that wasn't fair: she didn't go on about him. 'It's impressive.'

'Yeah, except it really hurts? I don't think I'll do it any more. The new meditative Charlotte doesn't need to impress the boys.' She handed him his beer and they took long swallows. 'So,' she said. 'Wanna tell mum?'

'That *fecking* table.'

She gave him a long look. 'Nice try, Robert.'

Robert put his bottle down on the step. 'Charlotte, what *are* you doing out here?

She sighed. 'Don't for one minute think you can fool me by changing the subject in such a hopelessly transparent way. But, okay, I'll go along with it if it'll get you there in the end.'

'So, go on. Why are you sitting on my porch steps in the middle of Albania?'

'You want to know?'

'I'm curious.'

'Take some telling?'

Robert nodded.

Charlotte took another long drink, and wagged the bottle in front of Robert. He stretched his legs and padded over to the table and opened two more.

Charlotte said: 'Put some music on. It'll fill a hole when I'm talking rubbish.'

'Yessum.'

There was still some light in the sky and it was a good-coloured light with pinks and yellows. He chose the *Romeo and Juliet* soundtrack. Obvious, but occasionally effective.

'You must think I'm downright strange,' she said. 'Don't worry, I can understand why.'

'I think a pretty girl squatting alone in an abandoned Albanian farmhouse is a weeny bit psychologically sus, if that's what you mean.'

'Granted. That's a lovely sky. Have you noticed that there's never a grey sky here? Just black at night. It's black, or it's day.'

'Who's changing the subject?'

'Okay. I think I've needed to do something like this for a long time. I reached the stage where having some real space was about all I could think of that would do me good. I mean, I didn't plan on getting abandoned here, but subconsciously I must have wanted something like that to happen. I aimed for a place like this. Make sense so far?'

Robert nodded attentively. 'What brought on the need for space?'

'Oh, my confidence. People's expectations of me? That doesn't sound like much, does it? But it was enough for me. I'd really had enough. I'd lost myself. If it sounds corny it sounds corny, but there you are.

'My folks didn't want me to come, incidentally. Didn't think I had the brains or the gumption even to get on an aeroplane. I doubt my sisters have even noticed I'm gone. Although they're okay, really.

'Anyway, for years, probably all my conscious life, I've felt myself being slotted into place in a life, and I wasn't sure it was my life. And being slotted, mind you, not slotting – it wasn't my choice. And I'm not like my sisters. My sisters are talking frocks. Walking pre-nuptial agreements. I'm not saying I'm the big rebel artist or anything. I just want to think about what happens to me.

'No, I could see my future being fitted over me like a cage. I've got nothing against cages, but this wasn't the right one. People love you to conform, don't they? Especially when you're not quite up to conforming, because then they can always feel like they're better than you. See, I was a gawky kid when I was little, and an even more gawky teenager. Tomboy, really. It's amazing the difference it makes when your sisters fill up and out at just the right time, but your own body gets it just a little bit wrong? It shouldn't matter but it does. And when you're quite a serious, intense little girl it matters more. To you and everyone, even your parents. Especially your parents. My parents never took the time.' She paused and shook her head.

'And if they don't look beyond the surface then they judge you in a totally different way from the little princesses. Oh, I love my sisters, really. But I was never going to be the elegant lady to anyone's real satisfaction – certainly not my own.'

'You've thought about this a lot, haven't you?'

'Oh, yeah. Oh, boy, yeah. And thanks for saying it, but I know I'm not pretty.'

Yes, you are.

'Anyway. I'm not a rebel. But nature's nature. I'm no blonde beach babe, never gonna be. Might as well be myself.'

'Which is?'

She sighed, and finger-combed her hair. 'Well, I know who I'm not now. And that's a start. Process of elimination. When Adam shot through it just seemed like I'd been given a gift. I mean, at first I felt abandoned, but then I snapped out of it and knew that this was it, this was the place for me to be right now. Anywhere alone. I think in a way that's what this whole travelling thing was about for me, I just didn't realise it at the time. But when I ended up here it just slotted into place, and all those other influences were gone. You know?

'I could be alone for a while and meet myself? Then I could take her back, the real Charlotte, and introduce her to people and at least know who she was and who she wasn't, even if she was no great shakes. I'd still love her. And I wouldn't be confused.

'And I think I was right about something. Without mum or dad to click their tongues and put me down, and try and shape me into something I'm not, I'm doing fine. I make decisions. I say things that don't sound dumb.' She grinned. 'I choose curtains. I think I'm going to find it hard to leave this place. It's some kind of an experience, it really is. And then there's you.' She turned to face him. 'You listen. And you don't judge.'

'Except with the curtains.'

'Watch it.'

Robert whistled and nodded. He said: 'Hang as many curtains as you like. And drop that "not pretty" rubbish – I'm the judge of that, end of discussion.' He wanted to say more. Instead he smacked the wooden step with the palm of his free hand.

Charlotte cleared her throat and didn't move or speak for a minute. Eventually she said: 'Those chairs must be nearly dry. We could sit on them soon. Where'd you learn all that DIY stuff, anyway?'

'Learn? Here!'

'No way.'

'Way. I'm making it up as I go along, I promise.'

'My dad tried to show me tiling once – just me, not my sisters.' She shook her head and tried to laugh. 'I was really hurt. I was busy trying to be like them. I should have listened, and learned tiling and grouting. Isn't that a great word? *Grouting*. Very ladylike.'

'My dad was long gone before I can remember.'

'Brothers?'

'Two sisters.'

'Snap! Grandads?'

'One estranged, one dead before I was born.'

'Aha! Lacking in male role models. Potential delinquent.'

'Depraved.'

'Close family?'

'Nope, nope, nope.'

'You through avoiding the subject yet?'

Robert groaned. 'Jesus, you don't let go, do you? Look, it's probably nothing. Just something someone told me today.'

'Told you where?'

'Let me finish.'

It was almost dark now. You couldn't see much more than outlines, and the landscape of silhouettes and spaces looked like a place where the unknown and the unfriendly could come from anywhere, if you let yourself think like that. Two people would be glad to have each other here.

'I was passing the time of day with someone in a cafe in Sarande. And he mentioned something that's been nagging me ever since.'

'What?' Charlotte's voice was quiet.

'He advised me to read the papers.'

She waited. 'Is that it?'

'No. He told me to listen to the radio as well. To the news.'

'Wow!' She slapped her thighs. 'Is that why you were giving me the negative waves? Listen to the radio, of all things. Fuck me sideways.'

'Look, it was something about the way he said it. He meant something by it.'

'So, tune in. Find out.'

Robert didn't answer.

'Really put the hook in you, hasn't it?'

He took a drink and turned to Charlotte and smiled. 'It can wait till tomorrow. I'll get the World Service in the morning. It's probably all about nothing.'

'But you're still itchy?'

'Yep. I suppose I don't want to start something. Get sidetracked by complications. And I have the feeling he was talking about complications. Well, if it's a complication which doesn't involve me down here in my little house absolutely directly it can go and fecking jump.'

'You're a troubled boy, Robert. There's depths to you.'

'I don't want them any more. I'm rising above them. Hey, that's not bad.'

There was a space.

Charlotte said: 'Listen, I don't feel like driving home.'

There was a bigger space.

Eventually Charlotte said: 'Rent your porch?'

'You'll freeze. You should come inside.'

'Where inside? The place is a building site.'

Robert looked at her.

She smiled and leaned into him and said, quietly: 'I'd like to take the porch, for now? Please trust me.'

'What happened to your new-found confidence and assertiveness?'

'I'm asserting it now.'

Robert cleared his throat and swallowed. 'No probs, whatever you want. But if you freeze your jugs off you know where the door is. No strings.'

'Says you.'

'What do you mean, says you?'

'I mean, says you. There's two of us here. Robert?'

Robert swallowed again.

'You're a nice guy. I'm glad I met you.'

He rested his cheek on the top of her head and breathed in deeply, and said: 'Ditto.' She couldn't have helped but hear his heart thumping. It thumped for a good long while, while they sat and didn't move or speak. The song of the cicadas was steady and even, and still peaceful.

June 4 1996, midnight-ish

All right, mucker? Time to register a few wandering thoughts? Use someone to bounce them off. You'll do.

How's this: you can never know a lover – or anyone you would like to be a lover – in the way you know a friend. The guard's just never down. Everything's tactical. But besides that, they'll always surprise you, knock you down from behind – because you care, it bothers you what they do, whereas if your mate says: I'm fucking off, see you in a fortnight, you say, yeah, a fortnight. No questions. No paranoia. And a perfect, neutral understanding of the motivation behind it.

But if your lover or prospective lover fucks off for three hours of an afternoon: suspicion city. Like, why am I not worth three hours? Who the fuck is this person? Shields up! I'm bored of you today, but if you go then you'll be outside of my field of existence, you'll exist all on your own until you're back here again. I'll have no control.

And there's the deception of it. Because there's never any control. You never know anyone. They keep shocking you with that knowledge, that sickening realisation that there is another facet of them which you didn't know about, which is beyond your control, just when you think you've pinned them down.

Love is the fear of being alone.

It frightens a man to death to discover that he has not invented the woman he is with, that she isn't his creation.

And anyway, I'm jumping the gun.

Oh, someone told me today to listen to the news. I did. The news was about Kosovo.

Sod's law.

General Kitchener.

Robert read over the letter, and wrinkled his nose. He might send this one and he might not.

Part Two

9

THE NEWS TO which the old man had referred did indeed concern Kosovo.

Historians called Kosovo the powder keg of the Balkans. It was where Milosevic had begun his campaign to bring about what he called a Greater Serbia – or a Greater Milosevic, depending on how deeply you want to delve. So, in a sense, it was where the Balkan War had started.

Robert, who had come across the name several times when cramming up on Albania, had learned the habit of thinking of it as a Balkan version of Ulster, or of the Gaza Strip. Not that he completely understood the reasons behind the conflict in those other places. Just that the name Kosovo, like the names Ulster and Palestine, seemed to be synonymous with a lot of trouble.

What Robert had read about modern Kosovo was roughly what follows.

The southernmost region of the new Yugoslavia was ruled, officially, by the Serbs from Belgrade. Only officially, because the Kosovars – 90% of whom were ethnic Albanians – simply ignored the official government.

Instead they had set up a parallel administration and economy, running their own schools, and even hospitals. Under the leadership of Ibrahim Rugova and his Democratic League of Kosovo, or LDK, this type of passive resistance was designed to pressurise Belgrade into granting the province autonomy or, at the very least, improved civil rights. The LDK had close links with the Albanian government in Tirane. In Albania there was, of course, much support for the Albanian Kosovars.

But in Belgrade there was Milosevic.

Milosevic, mastermind of the Balkan War which had fractured families and communities, displaced populations, and created voids where there had been union. Milosevic, who had replaced a workable and largely harmonious way of life, for people whose differences were negligible compared with their common interests, with an extension of his own clammy paranoia. An interesting specimen, Milosevic, insofar as the histories of stunted Hitlers are interesting.

Milosevic was no more interested in the people of Kosovo than he had ever been in any people. You only had to read. During the Balkan War he had used his people as pawns time and again; abandoned them to defeat, left them without defence and direction, as he alternately wore the masks of wronged diplomat, and patriotic warlord, as and when it suited him.

So far he had refused to talk to Ibrahim Rugova or to anyone else, and did not appear inclined to change his mind.

That was the background.

The World Service took up the story as a group calling itself the Kosovo Liberation Army, or KLA, grew tired of passive resistance and, with increasingly dramatic stunts, began attracting the attention of the world's media.

The KLA's agenda was more extreme than Rugova's; it wanted independence from Yugoslavia at the very least. Its ultimate goal – although why the hell it wanted it, Robert couldn't fathom – was union with Albania itself. To the Serbs the KLA was a terrorist rabble, to the Albanians and Kosovars freedom fighters.

The KLA, said the World Service – which hadn't yet decided what the KLA was – was funded by wealthy Albanian ex-patriots in Switzerland and Germany, and armed with weapons sporadically looted from poorly-defended Albanian army bases and smuggled across the border. The group's early exploits had included ambushing police patrols and assassinating Serb government officials, often in broad daylight; and dishing out extreme violence to anyone it suspected of being a government informer.

Now, however, the KLA was getting bolder, and the western media more attentive.

The rebels emerged from the woods by stages, until roadblocks guarded by tanks flying the Albanian two-headed eagle now controlled areas that only a few months earlier had been Serb strongholds.

The Serb security forces reacted as they had always reacted. This time, with the full backing of Mr Milosevic.

On the day Robert began listening, an audibly shaken correspondent recounted how he had been taken to a village where a farmhouse had been surrounded, then simply riddled with bullets, apparently by the Serb police. The bodies in the house were mostly those of women and children – people whom Milosevic had described as terrorists. In reality, the report said, any KLA who may have been in the area would have been long gone, escaped into nearby woods at the first sign of trouble. These casualties had been the people who lived – and now died – here; these were simply revenge killings.

The view of the World Service was that the region was in for many months of violence, with the possibility that an escalated version of the conflict could spread to neighbouring Albania, Macedonia, Greece, and even Turkey.

'Robert,' Charlotte said, as the programme moved onto news of Euro '96, which, to Robert's disappointment, left him a little cold, and which Charlotte hadn't heard of. 'Robert, just a *little-ittle* question. When this stranger told you to listen to the news?'

'What about it?' Robert asked, gnawing a fingernail.

'Well, how exactly did he say it?'

'What you getting at?'

'I mean, was he calm about it, or was he screaming blue murder? Was he panicking and grabbing the scruff of your neck? Or did he just casually say: "Oh, by the way, I reckon you should maybe listen to the news a little, you might find it amusing"?'

'Very funny.' Robert turned off the radio, and they were silent for a spell.

'Robert?'

'Yes, my chicken?'

'What I'm getting at is, could this be serious?'

He didn't know.

Could it get serious?

Two days later the main report was of more Serb retaliation. A village had been shelled for twenty-four hours by the Yugoslav

National Army, the JNA. The situation was no longer an internal police matter.

Thousands were homeless, as many as a hundred dead. Precise details were sketchy, but the place seemed to have been chosen as a target simply because no Serbs lived there.

Robert fixed his table again, and this time it threatened to stay fixed. He smashed up the crap stuff for firewood and made a start on re-priming the veranda – that was a job and a half. And he waited for the news now like he waited for meals. He dug out the Bartholomew map, and wished he had two copies.

Another day, more news.

Peaceful street protests in Pristina, the Kosovo capital, were denounced on Yugoslavian television as armed uprisings. Footage of the marchers being provoked and beaten was expertly edited to portray them as aggressors. There were more KLA attacks on police patrols.

Twenty thousand took to the streets in Tirane, the Albanian capital, to demonstrate in support of their countrymen across the border.

Could it be serious?

'Robert, did you hear me?'

10

June 25 1996

Yo, fat boy. Just call me Mr Back-to-Nature. Because back to nature I have come with a vengeance.

Also call me Mr Land-Clearance and Mr Furniture-Restorer and Mr Make-Do and Mr Yeehah-Hot-Shot with a rifle. I have many names, old friend.

Anyway, how's the auld countree? As if I give a flying one. Got your letter – eventually. The 3rd is dandy. Bring your drinking pants. As to friends, no, none to speak of. But I'm on gossiping terms with a few locals.

I have seen a few stray backpackers in Sarande over from Corfu, mostly daytrippers, but I doubt there'll be any more this year after the strife in Kosovo. The couple I chatted to told me they know people who've changed their minds about coming to Albania because of it. I'm not worried, next year is my time. I'll be laughing all the way to the bank. There is huge untapped potential here. This will all blow over. Trust me, as the man said.

Trying the new toy out this afternoon, incidentally. Shotgun. Can't have too many vicious lethal weapons around the cosy old homestead, I always say. What would the darn kids have to play with? Quite a little armoury I'm building up. Costs a fortune in ammo. But what the hey? A guy needs to get in touch with his masculine side. And anyway, owning more than one gun doubles your sperm count and your IQ, as well as enhancing your natural charm and sensitivity, everyone knows that.

Seriously, though, I can just see the two of us enjoying a good day's blasting. It's addictive, I swear. So chill out, cissy. You might find several surprises out here, you'll see.

On the house front, it's pretty much gutted of crap now. I did the mother, father, babysitter, and social worker of all bonfires last night – stuff I couldn't break down enough to fit in the fireplace or even the woodshed. You should have seen it burn. Way cool. Butthead cool. Gave me a hard on.

*I'm down to wood and plaster in most of the rooms, so it's looking good. I finally did the chimney yesterday – you wouldn't believe the shit that came out of there, mate. I mean, dead things. I retched. At least I found out where that cheeky aroma was coming from. So I suppose I'll be on firewood detail a good few hours a week from now on. It's a good big fire, though. I've got the booze cabinet (Gorbaschev vodka packing crate) to one side, and the radio on the mantel (plank). I've repaired a few of the salvageable chairs as well as my nemesis, the f***ing b***ard dining room table which, after God knows how many days w**k, is now as good as very old. I felt like Batman, battling with that damn table ('You made me this way!' 'No, you created me!' 'No, you sanded my grain first! Take that, pretentious arriviste Islington backpacker!' 'Aaaargh!!').*

Yes, I'm beginning to feel at home. I still get lonely. But never bored. If I stop working for one day it piles up and comes back at me with a healthy dose of self-loathing. I can't afford to be bored. I feel good when I've worked and bad when I haven't. So I know what to do, and there's no excuse.

But even the loneliness is receding. I've got three rooms in the house that I wouldn't be ashamed to show visitors now, and they're rooms that I've made that way and I'm very proud. I feel happy in these rooms – even when I am lonely. And if I miss anything it's not people in general, it's mainly you, you lardy tosser, or just voices. Just hearing the people I know.

I can see us here together, chilling on the veranda in the evening, sipping the Jack, wearing out the Pat Garrett and Billy the Kid *soundtrack, makin' believe we're back down in Ole Mexico. (Ray's voice → 'But, Robert, we've never been to Ole Mexico.')*

I know this might not be your cup of tea permanently, and I hope you're happy where you are, but I'm beginning to feel pretty chipper here. I wish you'd mellow out a bit about all this and stop giving me the feeling you think I need mental help. Maybe you'll see what I mean when you visit. I'm finding resources in myself – and not as far beneath the surface as you'd think – that I'd just never have unearthed back home. It'll hit you, too, I know it will.

I never knew, for example, that I was a stone wall fixer, or a salvage man, or a fish cleaner, or a fence mender, or a barbecue constructor.

But not even anything that specific. I never knew I was someone who *could look at a problem and at the resources I have around me and then build something solid and good from what began as a problem. It's a great feeling. It feels so pure and (*WARNING! CLICHÉ IMMINENT*) the work really is its own reward. It just empties you. It's a simple thing. You get to the end of each day, and there it is. What you've done on that one day is standing before you. Undeniable. Verdict, judgement, reward. It doesn't argue back, or go over budget, or need architect's approval. Because you're the only one.*

Some evenings I look at the stuff I've done in a day and I don't believe I could have been the one who did it. I don't want to go on, but the pride, Ray. The pride gets you through the evenings. I could cry sometimes.

(Tell anyone I said that and it's your nads.)

And in a few months I'm going to have to be a laundry-doer, and firewood stacker, and bedmaker, and breakfast chef, and all round good egg and big-johnsoned man of mystery. Yes, the summer after this it begins in earnest.

I have my low times. But I don't have the fear any more. I feel I could just about face anything now, after this, even going home – although I never want to do it. No, I shouldn't say never. But I'm making my mark on this house. I'm where I want to be. And when the business starts I'll have the money to stay here in style.

Take care, city boy.

Yours, Robinson 'two-gun' Crusoe.

PS Football's coming home! Go on, paint your ugly face just for me and look even more of a twat. Big Kisses.

Robert read through the letter, smiling every couple of lines. He added a PS about saying hello to Tina and read that through, then folded the pages and slipped them into an airmail envelope. He put it with the ones to his mum and his sister from a few days back and wrote POST THESE, YOU TOSSER! on the top of a pad in big characters. Then, with the trained timing of a man who never wears a watch, he flicked on the radio just as the news was starting.

He heard the main story, which was Kosovo, then turned it off.

More turmoil on the streets of Pristina. Milosevic ignoring appeals from assorted EC foreign ministers to get real. Heavy fighting in the Drenica region. Robert glanced over at the Bartholomew map, although he knew where Drenica was: he could have drawn most of the map from memory now. Drenica. Sarande. Kosovo was at the top of the map disappearing off the page and Sarande was way down at the bottom. The top of the map looked a long way away.

He left the bedroom and tested his way down the staircase – the next big job – and stepped through the porch door onto the veranda. The veranda, he decided, had been added as a western touch to make the place more saleable. And it wasn't as good a job as he'd first thought – hence the re-priming. The door was still not creaking though, and Robert swung it back and forth a few times, enjoying the smooth motion. Glancing to his left, he saw the oily bundle of Charlotte's pistol wrapped in a once white T-shirt – his T-shirt – on the newly sturdy porch table. He shook his head.

He was wearing blue GAP shorts and grey Adidas tennis shoes, no shirt. He hadn't shaved in a couple of days. His hair needed a chop. He ran his hand over his downy stomach, which was flatter than he could ever remember it. Almost a six-pack. Maybe one day. Robert liked his new muscles.

He stopped on the veranda and looked down to the space in front where Charlotte was on her knees facing away from him, trying to stretch one end of a stray spring back into its hole at the end of a bed frame. The job was too hard for her and Robert could hear her panting with effort and the odd sound like a sob.

A sudden breeze picked up from nowhere and sent a mist of dust up to the level of the steps. He watched the wind play with Charlotte's hair until the gusting receded, then her rubbing her eyes, and then he descended the steps and slowly walked the few yards to where she was kneeling. He knelt down behind her, his knees outside hers, and gently placed his hands on her hips.

She jumped, and whipped her head half way round, then turned and faced in front of her again. Robert caressed her hips for a few moments then moved his hands around to her tummy, which was damp with sweat. She smelled rich and distilled. He was leaning over her back now, breathing craters in her hair. She pushed gently back onto him. He found her belt and tugged, harder than he intended, and she gasped. His breathing became audible, and he grunted as he yanked open all the buttons on her Levi's in one go. He pulled hard and when he had her jeans around her knees she bucked her hips forward and whispered: 'No, wait.'

She crawled away from the steel bed frame onto a clear patch of ground, throwing up more dust. Breathing hard she tugged off her running shoes and jeans and tossed them aside. She slitted her eyes and resumed her position on all fours. Robert stood up, kicked off his shoes and shorts, and dropped down into the same position.

For a long moment he just looked.

Then he slipped his hands inside her knickers from behind, and felt her body jolt, and heard a sound in her chest like a lot of air escaping from a small space. His breathing slipped a couple of gears and time slid sideways to where it appeared to slow down. She moved her feet together so her knickers could be rolled off, and hissed through her teeth as he dragged them roughly under her knees.

They knelt there in the dirt for a long moment, her skin glowing in the sun, before a growl in his throat boiled over into something louder, and he suddenly shoved Charlotte hard in the back with both hands so that she slammed flat to the stony ground.

She barked in pain as her face and torso hit dust and pebbles. But straight away she raised her hips again and he entered her, and she sucked in air and dust, and coughed. The angle was awkward and he was hardly inside, so he used short shoves so he wouldn't slip out. She pushed back, gritting her teeth and hissing, clawing at the ground. As he pushed harder she turned her face forward so it looked like she was chewing at the dirt in front of her, dribbling saliva and now laughing. When she laughed Robert grabbed a fistful of her hair and shoved harder with his hips. He pushed down with his hand and mashed Charlotte's face into the ground and heard her choke. Still there was a sound like laughter, or coughing.

A moment later she wrenched her head free. 'No, no! Stop. Stop! *Wait!*'

Robert ignored her at first, then slammed the ground with his flat palms and yelled: 'Fuck!' and something else angry and wordless. He saw she had a cut lip, and that dust was stuck to the small patch of blood. But all she did was momentarily get to her knees to throw off her T-shirt and motion to him to unclasp her bra from behind. Then she lay flat on her stomach once again, again with her hips raised just a few inches, and he pushed inside once more.

In the scrub around them cicadas and birds started panic calls which radioed around the land and soon everywhere was noise. Charlotte allowed herself to be jolted and shoved against the dry earth, so that her breasts and face and hands weren't spared on the pebbles and rough ground. Robert looked at his own knees and knuckles, which were raw. Below him Charlotte was yelping now with each impact.

At the end he threw his hands underneath her hips to feel the tremor of the last seconds, and he fell on her back so that she was winded, their heads clashing. Grimacing, he pushed for a few moments more until a sound emerged from the body beneath him that could have been any combination of pain, frustration, and completion.

Minutes passed. The two of them lay panting until Charlotte said, quietly: 'Ow.'

Then Robert tried to move and it made him wince and he said: 'Yowch.'

They both started to laugh and to crawl gingerly to a sitting position. Robert picked up Charlotte's discarded T-shirt and gently wiped grit and sand and blood from her knees and elbows, and then from his. He wiped her face and kissed her bleeding lip. Every couple of moments someone said 'Ow,' again, and the laughter became louder and wilder, and they raised their faces towards the sun, howling and squealing.

'What do you think will happen?'

'It is already happening.'

'But do you think it will spread?'

'Kosovo is not an island.'

'Could it involve Albania?'

The old man sighed. 'The Albanian people will not want to be involved. They will want to forget it. They will want it to go away. They have their own problems.' He motioned around him with a sweeping arm. 'But I think, in some way, after the demonstrations, they must become involved. There are times when it does not matter what one person wants.'

Robert looked puzzled for a moment, then said: 'You mean individual people?'

'Yes, it does not matter at these times what individual people want. Then crowds think. *Crowds* want.'

The old man seemed studiedly indifferent about the subject, which didn't surprise Robert anymore. It wasn't, Robert realised, that he didn't care: just that there were some things you could change by caring, and some things that would just be a waste of an old man's remaining strength.

'Jesus.'

The old man narrowed his eyes at Robert. 'You do not look worried.'

Neither do you, Robert almost replied. Instead he said: 'It's exciting.'

The old man coughed. 'You are forgiven those words because you are a young man, and I know what you mean. But for me it is not exciting.'

'I'd noticed,' Robert said, then regretted saying it. 'I meant it's exciting but it's terrible.'

'No. You mean it is terrible – but it is *exciting*. Not the other way round.' The old man's voice was quiet and solemn. Now he looked concerned – now that they were talking about Robert. Robert wondered what he'd done – or what had happened somewhere beyond his control – for him to deserve having been adopted in this way. Whatever it was, he felt good about it. Any distance from his past felt good. No, it was more than that. Robert nodded.

'You will follow the fighting on the World Service?' the old man asked.

'God, I hope there won't be fighting.'

The old man looked into the young man's eyes. 'If I were your age,' he said slowly, 'I would say the same. And only part of me would mean what I said. And I would follow the fighting on the World Service. And if I were a young Albanian man there would be thoughts of fighting in my head. And I would think: it is terrible, but it is exciting.'

'But you think there'll be fighting?'

'This time I think there will be some fighting.'

Robert looked surprised, then nodded, and then there was a pause.

'But I do not know how much. It could be very short – the Serbs have no reason to come here, there is nothing here. And in Sarande we are very far away.'

It was the first time it had occurred to Robert that the Serbs might come.

The old man's voice became a little more upbeat. He asked: 'Have you seen other wars, my friend?'

Robert thought for a moment.

'I remember the Falklands War. I was barely a teenager. I was always listening to the radio before school, and watching TV when I got home to see what had changed. I don't know what my mum thought. I'm sure I worried her. But I thought it was wonderful.' He took a drink.

'And then the Gulf. But I'd changed by then. And it just sickened me. I suppose I thought I was pretty radical. But the theory behind it, all those bogus reasons? No. It was nonsense. The overkill. The oil. The Americans. Yeah, it was all about the Americans keeping the price of oil high, and needing a new enemy so they could justify their massive arms budget. That war had no reason to happen.' He screwed up his face. Then added: 'But I still watched the news.'

'Yes,' the old man said, quietly. Then: 'I have drunk enough of this stuff today. Will you have coffee with me?'

'Of course. What do you think the fighting will mean for Albania?'

'It is too soon to say.'

'I read about it before I came. Whatever I read gave the impression that incidents like this were inevitable.'

'Please?'

'Inevitable. It means certain.'

A blank look.

'Certain. Like destiny, or fate.'

The old man's eyes sprung open and he shook his head in comprehension. 'Destiny, yes. *Inevitable.* And you believed what you read?'

'I suppose I did.'

'Inevitable.' The old man nodded a negative. 'I have heard such judgements before. But I do not think it is inevitable. If you leave people alone in peace no such thing is inevitable.'

He chuckled at his own words. Then: 'I have been in Italy where they talk about us here like we are savages. They think we live like enemies to everyone. They say – to my face! They say it to my face! – that our hatred in this small part of the world is so big, so old, and so deep that one day we must slaughter every last one of ourselves. It is not true. It cannot be true.

'They think about Bosnia and Croatia and they think we are all the same. I tell you –' Leaning forward. '– the only way we are all the same is that we have all been fooled.'

'What do you mean?'

The old man waved his hand and looked tired. 'We have been fooled into thinking that we hate each other, just like in Bosnia and Croatia. Someone has told the people this and they believe it because the people are simple people and it is easy to hate. When someone tells you lies about history and blood, and food, and land, it is easy to hate as a –' He made an encompassing gesture, and searched for a word. '– a people, a *fis*. But look, the differences of the people are nothing. In the end the people hate who they are taught to hate. That is what I mean when I say we are fooled – and we will be fooled again.

'But you should never think that it is inevitable. No, it is not destiny, not fate. What is different between a Serb and a Kosovar and an Albanian is much less than what is the same. But they are not allowed to see it. Look at our friend Safet who serves beer and coffee here. Two weeks ago he was a cafe owner. Now he is an Albanian. Those fishermen in the harbour will stop being fishermen, and become Greeks.'

'I see.'

'It's true. Do you know who the Kosovars are?'

'Albanians living in Kosovo?'

'Not anymore. A Kosovar is now someone who is not a Serb; a Serb is someone who is not a Kosovar. That is how it will be for a long time now. And anyone who gets close to the trouble will have to decide what he is, before someone decides for him.'

'Do you really believe the people have no differences?'

'Not enough, do you see? Not enough to kill for! If you tell them other things about food and land, good things about their brothers the Serbs, or their brothers the Kosovars, then there will be marriages, and markets to trade in, and dances. Not hate. It would be easy. Look at an Albanian and a Serb. Is one black and one white? No. You cannot even see they are different by looking. This hatred comes from the leaders, from people like Milosevic. It is not a real thing until they say it is. And if the people are not allowed to see anything else then this hatred grows. Wars are not started by waiters and fishermen.'

'But what about the religious differences?'

The old man laughed, and slapped his bony hands on the plastic table top.

'Do you see any Muslim armies? Do you see any Christian processions? Do you see any of this here in Sarande? Of course not. I promise it was the same in Bosnia and Croatia. Milosevic will be scaring Serb children with stories of the Albanian Muslims. Yes, there are Muslims here – if he means people called Ahmet. But most have never even been inside the mosque, and they give their children Greek names now so they can fool the Greek police when they escape across the border. So, soon there will not even be any people called Ahmet. It is a lie, my friend. The hatred we are supposed to feel for each other here is all a lie.'

Robert interrupted: 'But in Bosnia and Croatia the people began to believe the lie. They suddenly remembered they were Muslims and Christians.'

'Yes. Robert, you are very clever. You see things – I do not know the word. But it is a good thing to be.'

Perceptive, Robert thought. He was pleased.

'But you are right, and it can happen here just as easily. In the same way that a shopkeeper in Yugoslavia became a Serb first and a shopkeeper second, and he then became a Serb and a Christian and not a shopkeeper at all and, in the end, *not even a man.* The same can happen here. A farmer called Ahmet will become an Albanian Muslim, not a farmer, and not even a man. He will be only a thing.'

Robert opened his eyes wide and exhaled. 'It's frightening.'

'Yes.'

There was a silence which lasted several minutes. The old man looked tired. His eyes slid shut and Robert let him doze. A minute later the old man sat up, coughed, and wiped his mouth with a clean white cotton handkerchief, and pushed his *raki* glass an arm's length away. He motioned to the proprietor, who gestured minutely and went away.

'It is a nice day. I have enjoyed many things in my life. But there is nothing now I can think of which is better for the *soul* than to sit out in the quiet street and watch life and drink something.' But his voice was soft and solemn and his speech slow. 'That is something to remember now.'

'It's good.' Robert nodded, and raised his glass with the last of his Amstel. He intoned: 'To many more,' and drank it off.

The old man became very still for a moment, and Robert watched him, waiting for his eyes to move, to stop gazing at – through – him. At last he said: 'That, my friend, is like everything else: it is not inevitable.'

Charlotte said: 'I bet you think I'm really dirty.' He grinned, and Charlotte punched him lightly on his bare chest.

They were in the one usable double bed. He'd used nothing subtler than planks of wood to fix the frame, but it was a good job and you could get seven good hours and not wake up crippled.

The windows and shutters were open, and the sounds from off the lake, of the diving birds and the cicadas, were in the room. They took occasional sips from a bottle of Cutty Sark, him more than her. The night was chilly but they lay uncovered, holding each other.

Robert liked to look at Charlotte, and she tutted when he

fidgeted. Once or twice he bent down and kissed a shoulder or nibbled on a nipple until she batted his head and made him stop.

'Fidget.'

Suck.

'You can't get excited about them,' she said. 'They're too small.'

'Says you.'

Charlotte giggled. 'It was good, wasn't it? All of it.' A pause for thought. 'What made you finally take the initiative? Without any warning?'

Robert rubbed the back of his neck. 'I don't know. It was really on the spur of the moment. In that respect I surprised myself. I've wanted you since you tipped up. I thought you were gorgeous straight away. Boy, have I wanted you. But I just saw you down there fixing the bed and suddenly you didn't look like a visitor any more. You looked as though you belonged here.'

She leaned into him and squeezed his arm.

'And I felt sure you wouldn't stop me – just because you seemed so much a part of the place. It seemed perfectly right. I don't want to sound like a caveman or anything, but you looked like part of *my place*. You know what I mean?'

'You do sound like a caveman. But in a nice way. I get what you mean.'

Encouraged, Robert pondered further. 'Maybe I just thought it was the only way it was going to happen. I mean, it wouldn't really have worked the civilised way, would it?'

'How do you mean?'

'It would have seemed corny out here in the back of beyond with just the two of us. Courting and all that nonsense. There was just no social thing involved.'

'No witnesses. No audience to perform for.'

'Precisely, my poppet.'

'I wonder how many things we've done in our lives that, given any real choice, we'd have questioned? But we did them because we were just part of the whole fucking dance. You get told something is the civilised way to do a thing and you go along. You think with the group.'

'Jesus, what a thought.' He drank and passed her the bottle.

'Robert?'

'Yeah?'

'Did you really mean it about me belonging here?'

'Of course.'

'What else?'

'What else do you want?'

She cleared her throat. 'Nothing. I feel like it, too, though.' She left a space. 'With you.'

'Good.'

Charlotte sighed and waited. 'Feel free to add to your previous statement at your leisure.'

'What?'

'For God's sake. Caveman. Robert?'

'Kvestions, kvestions!'

'Stop it. I need to ask you something. Seriously.'

'Okay.'

She cleared her throat again. 'This stuff in Kosovo. If it gets really bad, what will you do?'

He said nothing. Charlotte tried again. 'Have you thought about it?'

'I have.'

'And?'

'I think it would have to get really out of hand – I'm talking virtual World War Three – before it could affect us. So I don't think there's anything to worry about.'

'But if there was? If there were air strikes and refugees and all that stuff, like in Bosnia?'

'Then we'd have no choice. The Royal Navy would ship out all its nationals – although Australian females would probably be left behind as far too much trouble, or offered as sacrifices to the natives. I might even get to sell you, get my investment back.'

'But we'd leave, right?'

'Right. Why do you even ask? Of course we'd leave.'

'That's fine. It would break your heart, though.'

'Is it worrying you that much?'

'I'm just tired now.'

'How tired?'

'*Tired* tired.' She yawned and slid down the pillow. 'What's the matter?'

'I'm not tired.'

'Jesus. You're disturbed. How much do you want in one day? I'll be here in the morning, for Pete's sake.'

'I've heard that somewhere before.'

'Cover me up. Now kiss me and say nice things.'

'You have wonderful skin.'

'More.'

'It's like the top layer of a cake, now it's dark. Tanned cake.'

'More.'

'It's like tiramisu, dark and dusty, but thick. I could slice into it and it would be thick. It would take a quarter inch of slicing before I got to the cake. Then I'd eat you, but especially your skin.'

'That's good. That's lovely. Stop that. Just say more nice things.'

'Spoilsport.'

'Say nice things or don't do anything.'

'I'll wait till you're asleep and do stuff anyway. You won't know.'

'That's not nice. I'm leaving you.'

'Ah, well, easy come. Good night.'

'Night.'

Charlotte stretched and flopped onto her back and her eyes fell closed. Robert waited until he was sure she was down for the count, then pulled back the sheets, and took a long look. She really was as he had described her. He scratched his shoulders and sighed, and tucked her back in.

Then he got up and stepped into his tennis shoes and walked downstairs, and turned on the radio very low.

11

KOSOVO DOMINATED THE news now.

It puzzled Robert that the attention of the world should be riveted to such a backwater. Although, as the World Service kept repeating, if the trouble spread, what then? And governments in Europe and America seemed to be taking that threat seriously.

Robert checked out the Bartholomew map; also the maps in the *Blue Guide*. He expanded the conflict with an index finger. Macedonia, Greece, Turkey, Italy.

Turkey. Jesus, you could end up with a holy war. Or the Greeks and the Turks – now there was a war waiting to happen.

No! Robert remembered what the old man had said, and corrected himself. Nothing was waiting to happen. Nothing was inevitable.

Although Robert had been tuning in for a couple of weeks he still felt distanced from what he was hearing; something vital about the scope of it all that hadn't yet hit home. Here he was, maybe only two hundred miles from where people were shooting at each other, and yet he couldn't feel its reach. And that made it feel like no trouble at all. He sensed the danger in that, like a false sense of security. But he preferred to ignore it. So that, in a way, with every day that passed, every news bulletin he devoured, Robert actually felt safer. Stronger. There are bullets flying just up the road, he told himself, but they don't touch me. Thus, although he knew danger was there, he gradually lost his sense of what that meant.

His day was increasingly planned around fixes of World Service news. He took the radio outside with him when he worked, and even into the forest when he went to shoot, or just to wander. Charlotte told him she was more concerned about his obsession with the damn news than about the news itself.

'I'm not joking,' she said.

Robert just laughed.

Some of the latest incidents:

- A second demonstration in Tirane.

So, the support of ordinary Albanians, at least in the capital, still appeared strong. And under this kind of pressure the Albanian government had put the army – such as it was – on alert. Not a good sign.

- In Kosovo, Ibrahim Rugova had openly accused Milosevic of a campaign of ethnic cleansing.

He alleged that the Serb authorities had plotted to uproot whole ethnic Albanian communities, and even to poison Kosovar schoolchildren en masse. There was evidence that this last claim was not so far-fetched as it sounded.

Robert whistled and shook his head. 'Did you hear that?' he shouted to Charlotte.

'I heard. Poison. God love 'em.'

- Escaped witnesses to Serb atrocities were telling their stories in the West. One teenage boy related his dramatic flight disguised as a woman.

The Serbs shelled his village and then moved in on foot, separating the sexes. They shot most of the men, then tied up the rest, and beat them bloody. The escaped boy survived by wearing one of his mother's dresses, and a headscarf, and stooping among the huddle of women. When the soldiers noticed his subterfuge he ran for the cover of nearby woods. He was hit by two bullets as he fled, but he kept running.

Before escaping he had seen the other male members of his family marched away and shot.

Tactics like this, said Rugova, were aimed at terrifying ethnic Albanians out of entire areas. The Serbs had done the same in Bosnia and Croatia, he said.

'Did you hear that?' Robert called out. 'Dressed as a woman. I wonder how he could carry it off.'

'What?'

'I said I couldn't be a woman.'

'I can't hear you. I don't understand.'

'Never mind.'

Next, the villages of known KLA members were singled out for sustained shelling. Here, the Serbs did not bother to discriminate between the sexes. They shot anyone who ran. Anyone who ran was KLA, they said. Otherwise why should they run from the police? In some hamlets they killed almost everyone.

Charlotte looped the denim straps over her shoulders, and finger-combed her hair. She closed her eyes and dropped her head back, and sat on her heels on the wool blanket.

Robert loved to look at Charlotte. But this particular expression bothered him. It was the one he read as meaning she was swallowing a good memory, washing it down to where memories are wrapped and preserved. Robert imagined a bottom drawer full of memories with labels marked: *Perfect.* Memories, like so much ammunition.

Thinking about it made him itch. But was it a bad itch or a good itch? He didn't know whether to kneel and pledge his love to Charlotte, or slap her in the face.

The blanket had rucked up around Charlotte's ankles and knees so that it was barely under her, but she didn't seem to notice. Robert was shuffling his feet a few yards away. He asked: 'Are you all right?'

'Lovely.' She started to giggle. 'Sticky but lovely.'

Robert blushed, and dug a hole with his toes. 'Charlotte the harlot.'

She sighed. 'If I had a dollar. But would you look at the state of us? Rutting on the forest floor. Which, incidentally, is not as romantic as you'd think, not when you're on the bottom, anyway.' She stretched her arms above her head. 'What do you reckon's making us so horny? It can't be healthy. It's too intense. Too much of one thing.'

'Is it?'

'I think so.'

'Well, please stop thinking about it.'

'Caveman.'

Robert pondered. 'It's guns and motorbikes.'

'No, really.'

Robert squatted down and stroked her hair. 'Really. I think it has to do with freedom. There are no wrong impulses out here: everything's allowed. Think about it. Back in civilisation we don't work with instincts or impulses – just pressures. And they come from everywhere. It's an effort just to hold a damn relationship together, even when you – when you feel happy with someone.'

'Robert, you don't like to admit it, but you're a gentle, caring guy. A thinker. And you'd be that anywhere. It's not really anything to do with where you are. Don't you agree?'

She took his hand, and shook her head. 'You spend time figuring out all sorts of complicated stuff. But I wonder if you really have to. I mean, maybe you should stop trying so hard? Sometimes it's like you're writing obituaries for everything you see. Just waiting for everything to end.'

'I sound like a barrel of laughs,' Robert said. 'You must be having the time of your life.'

'I'm enjoying being with a complex and caring person. With an adequately proportioned willy. But you think too much about the wrong things.'

'Guess what I'm thinking about now?'

'Behave. And something else that's been bothering me. You never talk about your family, do you? I've bored you to tears about mine.' She hesitated, then said: 'Any reason for that?'

'You have a boring family?' Robert kicked a branch. 'Nothing sinister, I'm afraid. We're close enough. I write to my mum and my sisters. But we're pretty scattered. I always seem to need a drink after one of them phones. My own troubles are enough. That's generally what keeping in touch with your family means, it seems to me – crisis management.'

Charlotte frowned and kissed his fingers. 'I reckon you put too much behind you, and some of the stuff you choose to carry around is poison, frankly. You've got things backwards. And I don't like the way you get worked up about Kosovo.'

'Jesus, any more faults you'd like to pick on?'

'No, you're okay. And we're just jawing. But Kosovo scares me.'

'It's topical, and it's nearby, so that makes it interesting. But it's no more relevant than that. It won't touch us here. There's nothing to be scared about.'

'Then stop obsessing.'

Robert put on a voice: 'I do declare, Miss Charlotte, you sure do look mighty purdy in them there workin' dung'rees. I'll be a possum if it ain't enough to drive a feller plum crazy!'

The girl on the ground gave the dope in the grin a look of sheer theatrical pity. 'Why don't I hate you?' she pleaded. 'Please tell me? Come on.' She stood up and began shaking out the blanket.

'You're in a hurry,' he said.

'Places to go later.'

'Name six.'

'Just one, flower. Back to my home? Where I still live?' She deftly folded the blanket and dropped it into the daysack. Robert wondered how she did that so easily.

'Back to your isolated, unprotected, precariously-located squat?'

She whistled. 'Whatever.'

'I worry when you go back there.'

'So you've said.' She waited. 'Have you anything else to add?'

'Then get out of that place.'

'It's still where I live, Robert. Isn't it? *Officially*? If you can't say what you mean, *officially*, I'm not going to help you. And I'm certainly not going to do all the giving way.'

Robert shrugged. He knew where she was trying to lead him. It wasn't unreasonable. 'Give me time. But I don't like you going back there.' That's a start, isn't it? he thought.

She sighed and stood up. 'I'll only be a couple of hours.'

'Then why bother?'

She gave him another tired look, and said quietly: 'I'll tell you what. Besides the obvious, you know precious little about what goes on inside a woman. Inside her head, that is.' She sat down on the ground and took her pistol out of her left Timberland and began yanking the boots on.

'Think hard, Robert, and then come up with the right way to ask the same question. Is it so difficult to say it? Would it be such an earth-shattering commitment?' She caught his eye as she tightened the second lace, and said: 'It might do you some good to say it as well.'

Robert watched Charlotte's bike disappear under its cloud of dust. Then he drove off in the other direction, into Sarande, and bought four hundred .22 rounds and two hundred and fifty grapeshot shells as well as a belt with pockets, and a leather and canvas shoulder bag. The two gun shops were crowded, and ammunition was shifting in bulk.

He bartered with two urchins to carry the boxes of ammunition to the bike and stand guard over it, and then slipped past the armed guard once more, into the back room of the gun shop.

There they were. Automatic weapons. Cost a year ago: $600. Cost now: a tenth of that. Market forces, in the form of wholesale looting and desertion, had encouraged a buyer's market.

Robert could afford $60. But then, when he touched the grey metal of the barrel, something was wrong. He felt like he was being physically dragged back, the floor sliding forward under his feet. Sweat beaded on his forehead, and he belched acid.

Robert left the shop without an AK47. On his way back to the bike he thought about all the Albanian men stocking up on ammo. And what he thought was that it was bullshit. They weren't going off to fight the Serbs, no way.

Then he asked himself, if these men don't need all the ammunition they're buying, why do I think I might?

He pushed the question away.

The bike didn't enjoy the ride back with all that weight pressing on the back wheel. As he pulled up to the house, Robert could see Charlotte on the porch, sitting on the rocker with her nose in a book, sipping an Amstel. It was late afternoon.

He climbed the steps and stripped off his damp vest and took one of the beers from the bucket of cold water. He drank it in two and then began unloading the heavy boxes while Charlotte watched. Neither of them spoke. Once, he looked up at her, and thought she looked awkward and bulky, sitting with her legs tucked under her that way.

There was something about the shape of her head he'd never noticed before, as well. He felt his shoulders stiffen with annoyance.

He carried on humping the boxes.

He stowed ammunition in all sorts of different places. Some loose in a bowl on the living room table, some in another box out on the veranda. A mixed box up in the bedroom. Most of it he hid in the flood gap underneath the house. There was plenty of room, and this wasn't the flood season.

He ended up putting some shells of both kinds in every one of the rooms they used.

They still hadn't spoken when Robert walked out to the thinking rock, carrying his two guns, and his new bag and belt.

The thinking rock was a chair-height boulder, about a hundred yards from the house at an angle to the lake. Charlotte had named it because she said it was a good place to sit and think and be not too far from home. It was closer to the house than Robert liked to be for shooting practice, but not so far that he felt in the wilderness. It would be a new forest around it soon, he thought. I'm not a farmer. Evidence of any fields is being overgrown.

Robert walked around the rock, seeing if he could carry both guns comfortably. He couldn't.

What I need is a pistol. But a pistol doesn't have much aim or power.

He pondered the Charlotte situation.

It would be okay. He'd explain about the ammunition, the need for prudence and peace of mind. Jesus, though. Do you have to explain everything that doesn't involve curtains and furniture? And was he really going to have to effectively get down on one sodding knee and ask her to leave her squat and live here? Did she have to put him through that? Couldn't it just be unspoken? Shit. He needed to release some anger. But he didn't want the atmosphere continuing.

So, the man backs down, every time, it's the fucking rules.

He snapped open the shotgun and fished out two shells.

Why – he slammed in a shell – *the* – second shell – *fuck*? – snap shut. Then: bang, bang, he blew two holes in the dirt five yards in front of his feet. *Fucking* – bang! – *women* – bang! *Don't* – shell – *fucking* – shell – *know!* He fired again and watched, his rage spent, as the dust settled over the four small craters. He breathed deeply in and out.

Okay, so I'll explain. And the hell with it after that. I know what I know.

He walked back. His house was the only one for half a mile on each side on this shore. A good view of anyone approaching for half a mile each way.

Charlotte was asleep. It wasn't dark yet. She must be tired out. He left the bedroom and made a snack and drank another Amstel and went back upstairs. He liked to watch her sleeping. She was wearing a sheet, and her mouth was frozen midway between a sulk and a pout. He smelled her hair and listened to her stomach make gurgling noises. Like things under the sea. You couldn't be annoyed when she was like this.

He lifted the sheet and looked, then put it back. He checked her pistol was by the bed, then took his Levi's jacket and a wad of *lek*, and tiptoed downstairs.

Back in Sarande he bought six bottles of Cutty Sark. He'd get another six tomorrow, before it ran out. And another thing – he was going to take a gun everywhere now. It was just a feeling.

When he got back Charlotte was on the porch again. It was dark. Jesus, what mood would she be in? She had the dungarees on again, and the fleece – she felt the cold.

He said: 'Hiya.'

' 'Lo.'

Charlotte patted her knee. Robert walked over and he sat at the foot of the rocker, facing the dark land. She wrapped her legs around his chest, and he felt her hands in his hair, as she picked the dust and grit of the road out of his scalp.

He started to say something, but only managed: 'I got whisky.'

'Shut up, Robert.'

'It's a precaution. For our peace of mind.' He realised he sounded silly – as if he was talking about the whisky and not the ammunition.

'Shut up.' She tugged the fine hairs at the back of his neck. 'Shut up. Shut up. Shut up.'

He did as he was told, and felt her hands slide over his eyes, and heard the night make old and new noises.

The radio.

Repeating again that Robert's place in the sun was not the only world. A big part of him didn't want to hear this. Another part wanted to stay in the forest with the guns and sometimes with the girl, and just to have time stop, here and now.

And yet another part was boiling with curiosity. He admitted his confusion and curiosity to Charlotte.

She seemed relieved that he was telling her anything.

The radio.

• Milosevic was still insisting that Kosovo was an internal police matter, and that his troops were there to restore order, and defend the persecuted Serb minority.

A mandate for JNA butchery, Robert thought.

• An estimated 80,000 refugees were now on the move into Albania or Macedonia.

The statistics given out by Belgrade were lies, said witnesses; multiply official refugee and casualty figures by five or ten and you start to get the picture.

• A new development was the use of helicopters, which rocketed any houses missed by the shelling. Whole villages were emptied and then razed in this way. Some were not emptied prior to helicopter attacks. The helicopters also patrolled the border lands, incensing Albanian shepherds and hill people.

The Berisha government in Tirane screamed that this was provocation, which was true. Milosevic countered that arms were being smuggled to the KLA across the mountains from Albania, which was also true.

Robert closed his eyes and put pictures to what he heard. It wasn't the same as daydreaming about wars. (*But this isn't a war. Don't tempt fate with that word.*) He saw green figures crouching behind pockmarked walls; a faceless man showing himself to draw fire; tracer rounds, pretty in the night sky. Mental footage of long bursts careening up and away. *Dawn light on razor wire. Silhouettes of uniforms from indeterminate eras and a dozen wars; pillars of white smoke; desperate last stands, stills and movies. Slow motion, a trench. A line of men.*

You absorbed one piece of information, thickened your skin against a new horror story, then with the next bulletin there was something worse.

More troop movements. Escalating fighting. More refugees on the move.

Robert spread the Bartholomew map out before the hearth, and closed the porch door against the breeze, and made new marks. The map was getting tatty. He learned the names of northern towns and the snakes of unfamiliar roads.

If this was an internal police action, what had to happen before you could call it a war?

But there wouldn't be a war. The experts on the radio said there would be some escalation but no war. It just sounded worse to him because he was so close. Yeah, that was all it was. There wouldn't be a war. There would be him and his guns and then the guesthouse and the tourists and the money, and some wicked stories to tell. That would be exactly what it would be like. And now there was talk of the UN sending troops.

Robert froze.

The UN.

He turned off the radio as the truth sank in: the KLA was so bold because it was waiting for NATO to intervene, save its people, and guarantee them a big slice of territory when it came time to divide up the pie. Jesus. The KLA actually believed it: that the West would not abandon Kosovo the way it had abandoned Bosnia and Croatia; that this time it would be different.

Robert felt ice form down his spine. God help them, he thought. They actually think someone is coming to help.

Milosevic intrigued Robert.

It's hard to plan against a creature like Milosevic, Robert thinks, because he doesn't worry to plan ahead himself. He is infinitely flexible; he changes with the landscape.

The Devil laughs when we make plans. In that sense, Robert has to admire him. Milosevic has accepted the *illusion* of complete control, and mastered adapting to change. Milosevic may not always even be your enemy, that is how flexible, or devious (or is it now called pragmatic?) he can be.

But he is called a madman. Is it necessary, then, to abandon reason in order to deal with change?

Robert jumps as Charlotte crawls up behind him and slaps the map and jolts him from his reverie.

She says: you're really, really enjoying all this, aren't you? Well?

Every day new facts. Every day more explosions and crowds running and patrols massacred. Every day he listens to the World Service and thinks about his life and his choices, and the ammunition under the house. He sits in the house or on the veranda or by the lake or on the thinking rock, and sights birds along the .22, and draws dark lines around his thoughts to hear them over the cicadas – he thinks it's the cicadas – and wonders what will become of happy, lonely, happily lonely Robert Maidens.

12

As he turned west off the Xarre-Cuke road, Robert instinctively slowed down.

Something wasn't right.

He'd done this trip a hundred heart-in-mouth times; dodging potholes and dead dogs and suicidally slow donkeys. But today the hazards were not in the drive. Today, at the instant he turned west, alarm bells rang.

What was wrong?

He wasn't imagining it: now he could feel eyes on him from among the isolated huts and lean-tos lining the dusty highway. His neck prickled. He listened to the cold flow of his instinct and tried to decode the messages.

Now there were faces: men and women dressed for working in the fields, but unquestionably following Robert's progress with their eyes.

As the road surface deteriorated, Robert slowed right down to twenty-five. He unglued his palms from the damp handlebars one at a time and wiped them on his thighs. He couldn't place a reason for all this unwanted attention. But he was damn sure this was as slow as he wanted to go. It was the same story – the watching – closer to town.

People stared as he passed, panning their heads as if following a tennis ball. Or like watching main street at *High Noon*, Robert thought. A last long look. I don't like it.

For the first time, the police road block ignored him completely. What could that mean? He crawled past their little cluster. He was even carrying an illegal weapon. Not a peep.

Those looks, though. What did these people know?

Robert revved away, taking several deep breaths, and told himself it might mean nothing, whatever the cold flow said. Maybe he'd always been watched and had just never noticed. After all, his might be the first vehicle on this road for an hour, or a day. And the police?

What a joke. Maybe the police were just sick of him and of not being able to extort from him. Yeah, chill out, Bobby boy.

No! There is something wrong. Something I don't feel in control of. Did you register that, Bobby boy? *I am not in control.*

In town it was worse.

The street below Bejteri's office was empty. The usual cluster of young men petitioning the lawyer to facilitate their escape to Greece was not there. Robert glanced up at the lawyer's first-floor door and green double shutters, and willed the right face to appear. He shouted. Nothing. He gave up, and wiped his forehead with his sleeve. The day was hot.

Killing the engine, he dismounted and tried to look calm as he took in every corner, every rooftop. Staying this alert was tiring.

When he squatted down to crack the road out of his knees, two flat-capped old men flinched and scrambled back into a doorway, sending pebbles skidding out from under their flat shoes. Then the shutters banged closed on a window across the street, and the sound echoed from three directions and made Robert jump. He swore, and sweated even more.

Straightening up, he looked in the direction of the first noise, then at the two men frozen with their eyes locked on him. I was right, he thought. This is like a fucking cowboy film.

Not quite.

This, it was dawning, was what he had read about, been warned about: The Day the Westerner Gets Too Cocky. A burst of shotgun or automatic fire, an implausible cover-up, a lost body, a sudden epidemic of *no spikky Inglese*, and a minor diplomatic incident. Then nothing: no credits, no house lights.

The day was very hot.

Robert started walking toward the dockside area, not wanting cowboy films clouding his mind. But nerves were winning over awareness, and Charles Bronson was stubbornly repeating the harmonica leitmotif from *Once Upon A time in the West*, again and again. Was that the one? Yeah, that was the one. He felt himself smile, and found he was whistling the tune at the men backed into the doorway. Why were they backing off him?

Three notes. *Once Upon A Time in the West.*

For a black second, a parallel second, he knew of death's hushed presence, and he felt the rifle with his fingertips; but then the knowledge was gone and he would never remember it until the day it came again in earnest, and then it would be different anyway.

In the doorway the men's eyes grew wide and then narrowed, grew wide and narrowed. *Today is a western. It's a fucking western today.*

Those three notes. The nearer he got to his destination the more clearly he heard them. Charles Bronson, guns. Calmly: oh, shit.

Seagulls shrieked. Fifty yards from the store Robert's legs stopped taking the right messages from his brain. It took a dizzying effort to lift them off the ground.

There was slow motion and then there was this. There was being alone and then there was this. His stomach twisted and he lurched and he tilted to his right. If I ever thought I knew what it meant to be alone, I was wrong. This is alone. At this moment I am hardly alive. No one is watching over me. *I do not count.*

Our man glanced up at the paneless windows in the Stalinist block which leaned out across the street and over the dock. People lived in that stone and steel wart. Robert felt a pull toward the building – toward any kind of life. He would be happy cowering inside with women and babies. This was too real. He blinked some stinging sweat from his eyes, and through the blur he saw open shutters and drying clothes, normal things. A small dog charged by, yelping, then two more.

And in front of him, in front of the cluttered dark store where he'd bought his rope and all his new tools, and the rank stuff to treat the veranda – where he'd come today to buy a pistol – four men were now assembled who had not been there when he'd turned onto the dock.

Now there were five, slouching in a half-star around the awning. The door banged shut from the inside and Robert swallowed, stopped, and stood still.

This was it.

It was almost a relief.

They wore combinations of baggy suits with kneed trousers, overalls, and off-white aprons. One had high boots turned down. One lacked an ear.

Reading their expressions wasn't easy when you didn't want to catch anyone's eye too long. Robert looked for the face of the young man who usually tended the shop, or for the armed sentry who knew him by sight now. Not there.

What about my *besa*? What about Bejteri? If Bejteri's not around – if he's cleared out – maybe I'm not protected. Shit. At the very least, Robert, at the very, very least, no one is going to sell you any more weapons.

He could hear men shouting down by the docks as they loafed and feigned the occasional stroke of work, and seagulls screaming, and a child somewhere laughing at another child who was singing, and above these the tide of his lungs filling and emptying and the dull pulse in his temples.

He slid a step backward and each of the men moved with him, one step: slip-slip. The group kept its shape. Robert knew that if he moved again in the wrong way they would surround him.

He could speak to them. He could speak in Greek or clear English and see what happened.

Then one of the men stepped forward and spat on the ground at Robert's feet, and Robert focused on him. Without thinking – *no, with thinking, definitely with thinking, and with new help from the cold flow* – Robert shucked the .22 from his shoulder and let it drop smartly into the waiting hook of his right hand.

The man who had taken a step forward – fortyish, scarred upper lip – looked surprised. He dropped his eyes to the weapon which was pointing at his groin. Then he flinched, and sneered, as if Robert stank.

But he kept his distance.

Robert felt a fresh cold sweat, and tried to keep his grip on the rifle.

A second man to Robert's left took a cautious step, and the rifle was at Robert's hip in both hands in a second.

Nobody moved now.

You're doing okay.

Robert couldn't see any guns – which didn't necessarily mean anything except that he couldn't see them. But two of the men who hadn't moved held lengths of grey pipe. For now they held them slack, pointed at the ground. Then the younger man to Robert's left spun the pipe over in his hand making a hissing noise. Robert and the rifle panned together, six elegant inches right to left.

In the corner of his vision – *and in the parallel reel of time where death had been* – Robert Maidens could see other people watching the confrontation from shop doors and from the windows of apartments. None of them were moving. Some of those people, he knew, would have guns, and could shoot him if they wanted to, if they could pick him out from among the shopkeepers and dockworkers. And he knew that that was probably how it would happen if it was going to, that someone from a window or a doorway or a corner in the middle distance, someone who wasn't right there in his face and seeing his anger and fear now, someone who would never think of him again except as the westerner he had bagged that day, that very hot day, would get one good shot at him and he would end up lying in the dust in this place for nothing. This knowledge settled on him like a feather falling, and Robert knew that he didn't mind any of it, that he might die and be kicked in the dirt by these shopkeepers. And at precisely the right moment he wasn't afraid.

And time flew by. Robert's head felt in reach of sky and clouds and in touch with courage that was a kind of bliss, a single, decisionless moment of living and dying.

They waited.

'You bastards,' he said quietly, and one of the shopkeepers shifted, and then someone else followed the shifting of the feet of the first to move, backwards this time. The young man with the length of pipe exhaled, and it was a signal for them all to slack off a fraction, and for Robert to edge his thoughts into the corners of the situation for a way out.

Not knowing what else to do he turned 180° and began to walk away. A long moment later he quickened discreetly. He couldn't hear anything bad behind him. And now, striding smartly to where his bike was propped out of the sun, Robert turned his head just enough to monitor the people still leaning in doors and out of windows, watching. It was the longest walk.

The bike was warm even in the shade. He was still being watched but he returned looks until they crumbled. He laid a hand on the bike and sent out other looks that said: this is mine, it had better be still here and still mine when I come back to it. The air was hot, and the street quiet.

Robert hoisted the .22 and slung it over his right shoulder and walked the short way he knew into the narrow alleys. For the first fifty yards he squinted into every shadow. Then he just gave it up, and walked.

If someone was going to put a bullet in him from a high window or a cellar door, his vigilance or otherwise wouldn't, he knew now, make a fart of difference. People could kill you. That was life: you could die anywhere. And, of course, you would.

Just before he reached the cafe Robert dared to ask himself: would I have fired that gun.

He was there with a cup of coffee. Neither man made a greeting.

The proprietor popped his head around the doorpost and Robert wondered if he was still welcome, or whether he'd stopped qualifying to buy beer in this town. Mostly he was just aware of shaking and of feeling betrayed, and worrying whether anything had happened to Bejteri and his *besa.* The proprietor appeared not to see the rifle. He vanished and reappeared in a moment with Robert's usual beer and the pissy undersized glass, then vanished again without a flicker of anything.

Robert poured a glass of mostly froth and drank it off. No one was at the other tables. The old man looked at Robert and Robert, had he been in a mood to muse, might have said that he looked sad. But he wasn't in the mood.

'I am sorry,' the old man began.

'It wasn't you.'

'But I am sorry. I knew it might happen.'

Robert grimaced and looked up.

'There are other foreigners here. It is happening to them all, in different ways.'

'Why?'

'They do not like that you have their land – oh, they liked it a few weeks ago, when they could think of your western money, but now you are just a foreigner and everyone who is not *fis* is to blame, and they are frightened. It is fear and panic, and knowing nothing else.'

Robert snorted. 'Yeah, tell me about fear. Fucking savages.'

The old man didn't seem to get it. He went on. 'It will not last – I hope. Most foreigners will probably leave soon anyway, before worse things happen. Robert, they are wise to leave.'

Robert poured the rest of the Amstel and wiped his forehead and then his chin and cheeks with his dusty sleeve. He wasn't shaking so much now, but he was drenched with sweat around his groin and under his arms, and down his back and in his boots. If it was possible for a man to smell his own adrenalin, that was what he could smell. It smelled like aluminium.

'Will I still be able to buy food? Shit, what am I fucking saying? Buy fucking food? How can I buy fucking food when everyone's trying to rip me off because they think my money fucks and reproduces in my pockets? How can I learn anything when no one will give me a straight answer?

'These, these *people*! Their lies and fucking tricks! No concept of honesty, or business. How the hell do they think the tourists will react to this? I'll tell you. They'll fuck off and tell their friends, that's how. Come to Albania and get lied to – oh, and maybe even beaten to fuck with iron bars in the market!'

The old man sat quietly as Robert ranted.

'I really want to believe what you said to me, about nothing being inevitable. But I fucking wonder. After today I fucking, *fucking* wonder!' He banged his palm on the table. 'Nothing will work here. Nothing has changed. How can I set up something even as simple as a guesthouse, in a country that hasn't progressed since the feudal system? It's like darkest bloody Africa. Blood feuds, bribes, *besa*, *fis*. It's like I've gone back in time. There is no reasoning with this!

'Maybe it's my fucking fault, I don't know.' He jabbed a finger at the old man, who sat still, saying nothing. 'It *is* the same as Bosnia. It *is* inevitable. And the reason we can't tear you away from each other's throats is that our notion of who the good and bad guys are is based on who happens to be winning or taking a hiding at a given moment. We make the winners out to be the villains of the piece because they're the ones with the opportunity to abuse someone. We don't open our eyes and see that if the positions were reversed it would just be a different bunch of savages being slaughtered. Macho bullshit! The middle fucking ages.'

Robert sighed. Some of the anger had gone. He went on.

'How could I have been so daft? People who think travelling to the next town constitutes an international incident, and grounds for a hundred years of bloody vendetta. People who haven't grasped the concept of the future beyond tomorrow or their next crummy meal. People who bandy around terms like Communist and Democrat, but to who it's just another extended *fis*. Fucking people.'

Robert's voice had tailed off with his last few words. He sat looking at the table, taking measured breaths.

After a few moments he said quietly: 'I'm sorry. I didn't mean it.'

'I know.'

'Not one word of it.'

The old man shrugged. 'I understand. I am sorry for what happened. And some of what you said is sometimes true. I am sorry.'

'No, I'm sorry.'

'It is enough. It has been a bad day.'

They sat in silence. At length the old man said: 'Come. What were you asking me before?'

'What? Oh, I was asking about food. It doesn't seem that important now. What the hell am I doing?'

'You have your gun with you.'

Robert had never sat at this table with the rifle before. He slid it from his shoulder and propped it against the next chair out of sight.

The old man went on, shaking his head for Yes: 'You have

your gun. Now you have started that, you will have to continue. You will have to take your gun everywhere.'

'Will I be in danger without it?'

'You are in danger every minute before you pack up and go home. But now that you have shown the gun you will have to carry it all the time.'

'Don't worry. I'll be keeping this toy with me.'

'And it will not matter.'

'How?'

'You know what I mean.'

Robert thought again of the men in the doorways and the windows, the ones not in his face, the ones who didn't care if he was angry or dangerous or not, or about his girl trouble and the pain in his sensitive wee soul. The old man was right.

'Will I be able to buy food?' he asked again.

'Yes, but bring your gun.' He leaned across the table conspiratorially. Robert leaned forward to meet him halfway. The old man whispered: 'You may have to haggle.'

They both chuckled. Robert ordered up. They drank, and Robert breathed deeply. He felt better.

'I'm impressed – you know "haggle".'

'Yes, I know "haggle".'

'What's all this about? All this today?'

The old man shaded his cracked yellow eyes and looked away down the alley, then back at Robert. 'It is about what I told you. Listen to the news. Then pack your things and go home to where there is no Kosovo.' He sighed. 'I did not think this would all happen so quickly. And I had hoped it would never become so bad, and that you would not have to go. But it is bad. I told you to listen to the news, because I knew you would be interested, because you are a man who thinks about things, and because I am – what is the word? – a *mischievous* old devil. But I did not know that all this would happen so soon. You must go home now. Home to England.'

Robert ignored most of this. 'Tell me about the history,' he said.

The old man nodded. 'There is no need. You are seeing it now, all of it. Our history of a man *who forgets* he is a man. After that he is only a Serb, or an Albanian, or a Gheg, or a Tosk, or a Communist or a Democrat. When a man does this, and he becomes a Serb or one or the other, then he becomes a soldier, he does not have to think about being a man, but only about being a Serb and a soldier – and that is no thinking at all, because someone else will tell him how to be those things, and he will believe what he is told. But no one can tell him how to be a man.'

'He probably thinks they're the same thing.'

'It is a man's favourite mistake. This being a Serb or an Albanian is a fantasy. I have travelled – there is no difference. We walk on two legs and drink *raki* and coffee, and chase women, and go hungry. And if we are lucky we think with our heads and that makes us men. Nothing else. Nothing else! A man is himself, he is not a nation, no matter what people like Milosevic want him to think.'

'You should go to Belgrade. They should listen to you. Milosevic should listen to you.'

'Milosevic is deaf. Milosevic is not a man.'

'And the future?'

'The same as the history.'

After a minute Robert said: 'I'm going to stay.'

'You have to think about it,' the old man said. But he shook his head. He sipped his coffee, which looked stone cold, although he didn't seem to notice.

'Yes, you have to think. Do you want to be a man with a gun here, in a country that may be going to war with Milosevic's army, or do you want to live? What are you doing here? It is not your fight.' He shrugged and sighed. 'Think about these things.'

Robert sat upright. 'Do you really think Albania will go to war with Yugoslavia?'

'It is possible.' The old man sighed and frowned – about the most emotion the old bugger had shown since Robert had sat down, possibly since he'd known him. 'But I am too old to have opinions on these things. I am too old to feel certain, or to want to – or even to believe that it matters what I feel.' He waved a hand at something only he could see. The creases on his forehead deepened. 'But it is possible. And even –' Leaning across, taking another small sip. '– if it does not happen, you are not safe here. You are a foreigner with Albanian land. A *foreigner*.'

Robert gathered that the word was supposed to carry weight. Foreigner: enemy. Was Robert someone's enemy? 'A war,' he said.

'I hope not. But think about the other things I have said. You can go home and be safe.'

'I want to stay here. I've done so much work. You should see the house.' Which sounded trivial, and Robert blushed.

'I know you have worked hard. And I would be happy to see your house. But if there is a war?'

'I don't have to get involved. I'm not Albanian. And my passport will protect me if it comes to anything.'

'No! Your passport is what will not protect you! Your passport is worth two thousand dollars on the black market! They will shoot you for it as soon as law breaks down and you become *invisible*. Did your passport protect you this morning?'

No, Robert thought. Not my passport. 'But I want to stay here. I've worked bloody hard to stay here. I've made something.'

The old man smiled. 'Yes, so far today you have made trouble.'

They both laughed.

'Tell me, Robert Maidens,' the old man said after a minute, Maidens sounding like 'May dance', 'what will you do if there is a war, and you stay here?'

'I don't want there to be a war. I don't think there'll be a war. Jesus, I have to keep thinking like that. I have to keep thinking that a lot of this is posturing and bullshit – do you understand posturing?'

'I understand bullshit.' Like 'Bollsheet'.

'Well, I have to believe that's what it is, and that it'll all die down and Albania won't get involved. And even if she does, we're in the south, here. Hundreds of miles from the border with Kosovo.' He shook his head. 'No, I just can't think there'll be a war.'

'You look like a man ready for war.'

'I'm a man ready for beer.'

'Why will you not go home, Robert Maidens? At least for a

while, until things are safe? Then you can come back to your hotel.'

'I can't leave again,' he said.

And then he stopped.

His hand reached for the bottle of Amstel. He wondered how to explain it. Only an ancient man and his own ears to hear the words. He tried saying them, but they weren't where they should have been. He couldn't think of what to say.

He'd been on the verge of giving the speech – the confessional one about saving face and not running away – but he froze. And he knew that something had changed. That his reasons for staying were no longer the same.

The drive back was miserable. It depressed Robert like a weight in the belly to have to return the looks of people who were mildly surprised to see you still alive. Okay, he could have just stared straight ahead and kept his eyes on the road, but he wanted to return the looks; if he didn't return the looks it would be like accepting his own death, even as if he were dead already, so that if and when the time really came, the impact of the event would be nothing, like a small gust, or dust blowing across worn stones.

What a shitty day. That's an understatement. Someone nearly killed me: a shitty day.

He wanted to hit something. He wanted to lie down and get drunk. Charlotte could fuck off until he felt better. Charlotte.

For a moment he wanted to hit Charlotte. How could she comprehend what the world did, what it had nearly done to him today? He was in no fucking mood, not for eating or cooking or curtains, or talking about the house or the mountains or the fucking starry stars.

He was nearly home. He didn't want to approach his home in this mood, but there it was. He turned into his driveway feeling no relief at being there.

And he was definitely in no mood to see four alien motorcycles parked in front of his veranda, and four rucksacks leaning in pairs next to them.

He steered to a stop, cut, and dismounted.

The bikes were smaller than his, but much smarter. He examined the backpacks. Three newish, one weathered.

He heard footsteps and Charlotte's silvery laugh, and five bodies turned the corner of the house, and stopped in front of him. Charlotte skipped out, smiling, from behind the four strangers, but stopped when she saw Robert aiming the .22 at them from his chest.

'Robert?' she asked.

Who did she fucking think it was?

The strangers stood stock still. One, the girl, began to cry.

'Robert?' It was a whisper.

He growled: 'Who the fuck are they?'

13

CHARLOTTE LISTENED CAREFULLY, then she kissed Robert and held him and said: 'It's serious now, isn't it?'

'It's that, my flower.'

'It means we'll have to go – you'll have to go.'

'No, flower. I'm not going anywhere.'

'Think about what you're saying.' Her voice was calm.

'I won't go yet, at least. It's not necessary. It could still blow over, and then we'd have given it all up for nothing. I mean, look on our porch. Backpackers are still coming from Corfu. It can't be that bad.'

'There's nothing I can say to you, is there?'

'What do you mean?'

She paused. 'You just think of yourself, don't you? There's one world. Robert's world. The little one you live in in your head. Everyone else can do what they like. Robert'll go Robert's way. But I don't really believe you want to live like that.'

'What do you mean?'

She shook her head. 'I know you like me. You can be what you are and be with me, too. Think about why I like you. Think about not having me. I'm not starting an argument. But don't get stuck inside there.' She tapped him on the forehead. 'And please don't shoot our new friends – and our first guests.'

She said *our*. Our guests. That had a good round sound to it. But at the mention of the visitors he reddened and hid his face in his hands. 'Do you think they'll speak to me yet?'

'I'll calm them down.' She stood up and walked toward the porch door, but stopped halfway and turned around. 'Coming here doesn't have to have been the final act of your life. Change isn't such a bad thing. And in case you were *wondering*, if you're staying, then I'll stay, because I think that once you start being honest with yourself, it'll be worth it, for both of us. If that's okay with you in there?'

Robert said: 'Wait. I've really had a day. Give me a chance to get straight.' He looked at her hard. 'But you're right, I don't want to think about being without you. But, boy, I've had a day.'

'I know. It's okay. We'll be okay.'

'I'll come out in a minute. I just need a minute or two.'

'I know. Don't worry.'

Robert was alone. He had the bottle by his chair but he didn't need to drink the day out of him anymore. Not so completely. He was still shaken but he was settling down. And he had guests. He had to shape up. In a minute, Bobby, in a minute.

He got up and hit play on the little ghetto blaster. Charlotte had the Jim Reeves in. *Distant Drums* played, then *Adios Amigo*. She said she loved it because she loved schmaltzy old rubbish, which was why she liked Robert. Schmaltzy? Robert just thought it was good. It was straightforward. He listened and hummed along for the two songs, then tapped a finger down on stop.

The four visitors and Charlotte were sitting around the veranda. A big blond snowboarder type was in the rocker. Or some kind of flash athlete. Charlotte sat on the deck near his feet. The girl Robert had made cry earlier was by her side. Two other boys in their early twenties sat leaning back against the two banisters by the steps down. The five of them were drinking beer from the bottle. There was a bucket of water filled with Amstels on the table. It was late afternoon now, and cooler.

Robert couldn't think what to say. It seemed bizarre to be making polite conversation just a few hours after thinking for his life.

And then he felt a little shock, and the scene around him flickered from monochrome into colour and he saw, not strangers and intrusions and distractions, but his girlfriend and his island(ish) paradise, and cold beer, and the wooden veranda being used for what it was meant for, and the circle of good-looking young people, and the cool orange late afternoon – all of this revealed in beautiful real colour. And the colour picture flickered brighter and he realised: God, he realised, this is why I came here. This is every single thing I came here for. Nothing could feel cleaner, or better.

The blond athlete stood up and smiled. He was closer to Robert's age than the others, and wearing paisley-patterned lightweight trousers in blue, and a red O'Neill fleece over an Australian outback design T-shirt. His friends were more brand-newly apparelled versions of himself. He offered his hand to Robert. 'Jeff,' he said. 'Look, I'm sorry we spooked you earlier.'

They shook hands and Robert smiled and shook his head. 'Don't apologise.'

Jeff said: 'I think I understand. Charlotte's explained about your bit of trouble. I believe you've had a bit of a hairy day.'

Robert nodded. 'I've had better – no, sit down, Jeff, I'm all right over here. Where are you from?'

Jeff sat down. 'Preston. We're all Preston. We were doing Greece and some of the islands. This is one of those places I've wanted to come for a couple of years now. No one would come with me on a proper trip, but I managed to drag this sorry shower over from Corfu, it being so close.' He sniggered. 'Although after hearing what you've just been through, I think they're regretting it.'

Jeff seemed polite. Maybe he wasn't flash.

'Preston,' Robert said. 'Used to be a team, about a thousand years ago, didn't they? Doesn't everyone watch Blackburn, now that they've bought a team?'

'And a ground and some fans. Walker thinks he can buy the league. But it's unsustainable. You can't just buy continued success and stability lock, stock and barrel like that.' He pointed to the table. 'We've brought beers.'

'Thanks, I will. What's your trip been like? Give us the whole story.'

'I think we're more intrigued by yours,' one of the boys by the stairs said. 'I'm Lee.' He stood up and they shook hands. 'You sound like you're having a bit of an adventure.'

'Oh, yeah,' Charlotte said. 'Laugh a minute, today.'

Robert nodded. 'Yeah. It's not what I'd planned.'

'But broadly, you're doing okay?' Lee asked. 'You look like you're doing okay. You can see there's work been done.'

'Broadly it's wonderful,' Charlotte said. 'We wouldn't leave here for the world.' She realised what she'd said, and looked a little sad, and worried.

Robert said: 'No, it's brilliant. It shows what you can do.'

Jeff said: 'We brought food as well. A few things from Corfu.'

'Delicacies to us,' Robert said.

'Luxuries,' Charlotte concurred. 'Thank you.'

'Pleasure's ours. Finding you was a bonus.'

Robert put his beer on the table, and frowned. 'Just how did you find us?'

'Little lad in the village, at the port. Directed us to the "American hotel by the lake".'

Charlotte laughed and clapped her hands.

'Jesus,' Robert said quietly. 'They can't decide whether to kill me or help make me rich. These fucking people.'

'So what did you do to piss them off?' the boy called Lee asked.

'What?'

'In the town.'

'Sarande.'

'Sarande. Why were they out in force with you today?'

Robert took a sip of beer, and said: 'What? Oh, I was trying to buy another gun.'

There was a silence, and the boy who hadn't spoken yet cleared his throat. Jeff whistled. The other girl tried to cover a cough.

Robert sipped his beer.

'So,' Charlotte said. 'Who feels like swimming?'

There was another short silence, before the girl said: 'We'll have to root out cozzies.'

'Ah, don't bother. We never bother. You're under our roof, now. When in Rome.'

Jeff shrugged. 'Sounds all right. Sounds good.'

Charlotte said: 'Who else is game?'

Robert picked up his Ray-Bans from the table, and slid them on. 'Moi.'

'What did you do for visas?'

'We didn't seem to need any. We just paid someone a few dollars – I knew we'd need dollars.'

Robert nodded, and penalty-kicked a stone, and whispered: '*Goooaal*! That sounds about right. How many other people have asked for a few dollars?' They were walking to the lake, carrying blankets.

Jeff blushed.

Jeff seemed to be the spokesman. Robert noticed that the others seemed to follow him, almost in a queue. It was sweet. Robert smiled to himself.

'Oh, a few,' Jeff said. 'They love their bribes, don't they?'

'Don't pay.'

'I paid the copper at the roadblock, but only ten. Much less than he asked for. I told him I didn't have any more cash. Pissed me off. I said to myself at the time: don't let it spoil your day, but thinking about it makes me really want to belt someone.'

'I know what you mean. Sometimes I could shoot some of these people.' Jeff looked startled. Robert continued. 'Just don't pay. Never look like you *might* pay – look like you'll fucking shoot them. They'll mess you around for twenty minutes, then give up.'

'Have you been ripped off much?'

'It's inevitable. But no, not as much as I might have been. I have a lawyer here, and he put the word about. And I'm taking that rifle everywhere I go now.'

'Guns and lawyers,' the other boy, Lee, said, and he laughed nervously. 'It's like Dodge City.'

Robert looked at him and didn't laugh. 'It's not so far off it just now.'

Lee cleared his throat and looked away.

'So, ah, so why do you need all these guns?' Jeff asked.

'I think I found that out today,' Robert said. 'Fucking savages. If you don't have any yourselves, and if you're planning to stay more than a few days, I'd suggest you look into it.'

'Jesus, no!' the other girl said. 'Don't let's get into that.'

Jeff said: 'I think we'll be okay. Give them a miss. We're a big group, after all. But we were planning on gadding about these parts a while.'

Robert looked at the girl. 'A girl, of all people, should be visibly armed.'

Charlotte sighed. 'I'm afraid it's true, for now.'

'But you came here alone,' Lee said.

'Alone, in a group, whatever – I wouldn't be without it. Plus it's fun.'

'*Fun*?' the other girl said.

Charlotte shrugged. 'Yes, fun. We shoot at targets. The forest's a good place. Robert's better with the pistol, and I like the rifle. We're getting quite good. Fun.'

Jeff said: 'It sounds okay when you put it like that. I'd love to try it. But I don't want to carry a gun.'

Robert nodded. 'But tomorrow – with the light.'

'Brilliant! You should give it a try, Mel.'

'Behave,' the girl said. 'I don't want you playing with guns.'

'Mel's my sister,' Jeff said. 'She doesn't approve of guns but she'll want me to protect her with mine.'

'You're not having a gun.'

Mel was going to say something else, but Robert interrupted. 'Look,' he said, quietly. 'Either go back to Corfu tomorrow, or get some help. They're just for show. But you need that show, or people will fuck with you.'

They'd reached the lake. Charlotte took over and laid out two blankets, and dropped her towel down on one.

'But you had a gun today, and they still bothered you,' Mel said.

'No!' Robert dropped his towel and, still wearing his sunglasses, pulled his T-shirt over his head. 'They weren't *bothering* me. They were going to beat me, possibly to death! But they stopped *bothering* me because I had the gun. Without it – well, you think about what would have happened to me without it. But I had it, and so I could have turned the tables.' He had raised his voice just too much, but he dropped it until he was speaking quietly again. 'I could have bothered them. I could have shot them if I'd had to.'

Everyone was quiet for a minute, then they began undressing. Jeff and the third boy, the one who hadn't said anything yet, undressed quickly on one blanket, horsing around and laughing.

Mel took off her baggy StoneWear jumper, and T-shirt, to reveal good tits under a plain sports-style bra. Charlotte noticed them, too, and threw Robert a mock scowl. He grinned back. Mel had good dark skin, and she was pretty enough.

Lee said: 'Would you? Would you have used the gun to defend yourself?'

'The point is I had it, so I didn't need to.'

'You're not armed now. Where's your gun now?' Mel said. She said it like a taunt.

Charlotte said: 'I have it.' Charlotte was naked from the waist up now, and not self-conscious at all. Good girl, Robert thought. She really is becoming confident. I'm proud of her. I'm proud for people to know we're together.

'What?' Mel said.

Charlotte bent down and unrolled her towel. The revolver fell out. Mel stared at it. The silent boy, who was naked now, ready for swimming, bent down and picked it up and held it carefully. He looked at Charlotte – a long look, Robert decided – and said: 'It's heavier than you'd think.' He passed it to Jeff, who weighed it in his hand and nodded, then returned it to Charlotte.

Charlotte offered it to Mel, who shook her head. Charlotte said: 'It's different rules here, Mel.' Mel shook her head again, and Charlotte put the gun on the blanket, and took off the rest of her clothes.

Mel took a long time to get from jeans and bra down to nothing, and Robert timed unlacing his boots so that they were the last two on the blankets. It excited him that Mel seemed a little scared of him, and also excited by her own fear.

He took a good last look at her before taking off his sunglasses.

As the girl was about to walk down to the water, Robert said: 'Look, don't worry about guns. I'm sure your brother can watch out for all of you.'

'Yeah, he can.' Then she added, coyly: 'When I want him to.' She took a few steps, then turned around. She looked good full on from the front. Short dark hair, full figure, tanned curves. 'Look,' she said. 'If Jeff and Lee and Simon had had guns today, when we came strolling round the front of your balcony, and seen you pointing that thing at us, what do you think could have happened? What happens when everyone's armed?'

Robert stroked his chin and smiled. 'Oh,' he said quietly. 'Any number of things.'

Mel looked confused for a moment, then smiled almost imperceptibly.

Robert sat and watched her run, shrieking, into the water. A self-conscious run, and a self-conscious, little-girl shriek.

Charlotte yelled at him and waved. He waved back, and took off his socks and trousers and stood up. The boys were throwing a plastic bottle, and swearing and laughing. The girls were trying to rob them of it but getting splashed and ducked. Simon, it seemed to Robert, was spending a lot of time splashing Charlotte.

But the two girls did look wonderful in the lake. Keep thinking like that, a part of Robert said to him. It peered in through the day's dark thoughts and said: keep thinking of girls in the lake, and a beautiful evening, and a long summer.

14

EARLY THE NEXT morning, Robert collected tools and rags and the shotgun, and carried it all out to the thinking rock.

The visitors' motorcycles were still parked out front. They were heading off to camp near the ruins at Butrint, but for now they were still sleeping in the second finished bedroom. They planned to call in on their way back to Sarande and Corfu.

The day was heavy and hazy. Even a light cotton shirt chafed Robert's neck, and the sluggish breeze was about as refreshing as a spray of warm glue. Sound wasn't travelling in the glutinous air, and Charlotte had to shout three times that they needed fresh water, only for Robert to promptly forget. He slapped his ears to try and knock out the plug, but it was the weather. What happened to the sun? Where did my paradise go?

He stripped to the waist and folded a rag into a pad and laid it on the thinking rock. He pressed the shotgun down on the rags and made a nick in the steel with the hacksaw. And then he stopped.

His conscience whispered to him that the thinking rock was the wrong place to work. But there wasn't another good rock. Robert wiped sweat from his chest.

He liked his new body. Charlotte said he looked good, too – although not that it mattered to her. Looks meant nothing, she said. Robert didn't believe her, and anyway it mattered to him.

He started again, and the noise cut through the peace and even through the gellid air. The heavy weather doubled the effort of the work, besides which Robert knew he was just guessing. How short do you leave it? He rested, and stood up straight breathing heavily, and wiped his left arm across his brow. How short?

He hacked up and spat, and thought: *Short enough so that when it hangs at my side it will look like the scariest weapon on the planet, and when those same people see it next time it will say to them: look, I don't even care who I hit with this thing but if you fuck with me again I'm going to use it and it will probably tear your liver out and pass it around among your good friends.*

There. About that short.

He found a rhythm and the sawing got easier. The weapon was an old style with the barrels side by side rather than over/under which, he reckoned, made it look more vicious and primitive. *Unreasonable.* That was the word. He threw the cut-away section over toward the trees, and started on the stock. When he'd finished it looked more like a pistol handle.

Without a proper bench with a vice, filing down the rough saw marks took even longer than the sawing. He wondered how he'd managed with the work on the house for so long without a vice. Pausing, he saw that he had new blisters on the newly-worked skin. Soon all of his skin would be thick. He stripped the weapon and wiped out the sawdust and metal filings.

Next it was the turn of the canvas shell bag. He used a knife to unstitch a hole in the front pocket just big enough for the two shortened barrels and the wooden stock down to the trigger guard to fall through. It would need stitching around again later. Slipping the gun through the new hole, he tried walking. It wasn't ideal, but he could think of some modifications. He'd fit the gun with a strap for his back, too, like on the rifle.

Robert wrapped the tools in a rag and laid the bundle beside the thinking rock. Then he shook out his shirt and slipped it on. It clung to his wet skin and he felt the warm-cold dampness spread down his spine and across his shoulders, until the shirt looked to have turned a darker shade. He walked toward the scrub forest with the gun hanging through the canvas bag. He stopped and looked around, then wandered a good way in.

The air was less heavy among the trees and he could hear the animals and birds. He could see light through the leaves and branches when he looked up, and on the ground dark browns and greens, and dead wood. He looked around for a target, then wondered if targets were even appropriate. How accurate was this thing? It occurred to him suddenly what a nasty, random weapon he'd made. Although it was just a frightener, surely – just a deterrent.

Deterrent. That was one of those words he'd always sneered at when he encountered it on the news or in the papers.

Anyway, he looked down at the gun and knew really that shooting this thing would just be a case of point and hope, that there was nothing of accurate intent about it. It was a catch-all weapon. He began to dislike what he'd done. This certainly wasn't a sportsman's gun anymore.

Sportsman's gun? Another lie, like deterrent. What am I thinking – *why* am I thinking?

The weapon snapping closed made a comforting sound, and Robert stopped thinking. He picked out a good-sized tree at thirty yards and aimed. Do you raise it to your shoulder and sight down it? No, he didn't want it anywhere near his face before he knew what it could do. Face? Never mind his face, it might take his fucking hand off. For all he knew about guns he might have just fashioned a suicide bomb.

Holding it at chest height was awkward, too; to get a good grip both hands had to be almost touching. And that barrel was going to get warm. Maybe duct tape – or gloves? What the fuck have I created? What an ugly thing. Robert spaced his feet and braced himself and, holding the weapon away from his body, squeezed the trigger its first notch.

The noise was horrible. It reminded him of something.

He surveyed the damage. He was right about the sloppy spread of the pellets. The tree he'd aimed at, a good foot across the trunk, was barely marked. So, thirty yards was too long.

He braced himself again and fired at the same tree from twelve yards and the result was much better, the trunk badly mauled. He was loading again when the shape of something – a bird – came into focus on one of the lower branches. Something big, like a pigeon.

A dove. Pink blood stained its grey-white head and chest, but it sat still and apparently stunned. Robert wondered that it hadn't fallen. It must be a hardy thing.

He snapped the gun shut and walked to within a few feet of the bird, which was shivering. But it didn't look too damaged; if he left it alone it might live. He raised the gun and looked into the scared eyes facing in two different directions and fired, then fired again, and the dove went up like a cherry bomb. Robert watched the heavier fragments fall and bounce off the forest floor, scattering blood and yellow fat and feathers.

Now he knew what this gun's noise reminded him of. It was the sensation of bad diarrhoea; the splatter and the messy shock and the rotten stinking. He felt ashamed, but only a little.

And at the same time he knew positively why he'd taken a saw to the gun, and that there'd be times when he'd be glad of this weapon. He toed the bits of beak and claw on the ground and blew a feather from his face, and nodded his head.

Charlotte wasn't anywhere around when he got back. The visitors' bikes were gone, too. They were okay, he thought. He stripped down to his boxer shorts and dumped his damp clothes in a pile. He started to clean the weapon but then got too tired and just sat and dozed. He didn't hear Charlotte until she was on the steps. He looked up and smiled at her.

She was naked, and holding a demijohn of water in each hand. Her straight hair was wet and flat to her head, but a few red strands had already dried off in the heat and were wisping over her head like baby snakes. At first she squinted and smiled, but when she saw what lay on the table she put down the water and stepped closer and the smile disappeared.

Robert sensed trouble, but he could feel himself getting hard, all the same.

She turned to face him. 'You've got blood,' she said quietly.

'What?'

'On your neck and your face. I've just noticed. You've got blood. How could I have missed that?' She seemed confused.

'Oh,' Robert said. 'The dove – a dove. Blood.' He touched his cheek and then his chin and sure enough blood had dried there. He even discovered some on his lips. He looked at Charlotte and wasn't sure if she was about to cry.

She bit her top lip and swallowed and then clenched her fists. She said: 'Show me.'

'What?' Robert's erection had shrunk away.

'Show me that thing, please? Show me what it does now?'

Robert stood up slowly and loaded the sawn-off, and stepped down off the veranda. His hands were shaking. He looked at her and she had folded her arms across her breasts and her whole body was shivering.

Turning away he spotted the broken plant pot at the corner of the veranda. The one Charlotte had been going to do something with rather than just let it sit.

He footed the pot away from the house and stepped back. Then he shot the pot to pieces. Charlotte winced and then jumped down off the porch and snatched the gun from him, and with the second shot blew what was left of the shards to dust, flinching again as the gun kicked back.

She handed him the gun and he followed her back up the steps.

'You're nice and clean,' was the first thing he managed to say.

'You smell of something,' was her reply.

'Bad?'

'Sweat and gun oil – and that blood. And just you.'

'I'll get a towel and go to the lake. Come with me?'

'You won't need a towel in this. But wait.'

He looked around at Charlotte and her expression had changed again. Her eyes were bright and her cheeks were flushed. Her nipples had stiffened. Taking a step backward he laid the gun on the rocker, but she stepped up and gently pushed him back so he had to sweep the gun onto the floor to avoid sitting on it. It made a lot of noise. Charlotte bent over him and breathed deeply.

She said: 'Take them off.'

He did as he was told and threw them somewhere and looked up at her body, at the honey brown and the goosepimples and tiny white hairs.

Desire gripped him, but in tandem with aggression. She made the first move, looking straight through him, kneeling down. Robert gripped her upper arms and tried pulling her up onto the chair but she pushed free and dropped her head and put him in her mouth. Robert could hear her breathing through her nose and something like humming and he closed his eyes as it got better – better than he remembered – and then he was gushing in a long flood and she was doing everything properly. When she raised her head, seeing her breathless blank expression and the knowledge of what she'd just done made him dizzy all over again.

They were standing waist deep in the water as the afternoon began to cool. 'Now you're doubly clean,' Robert said.

When she began to cry he wasn't surprised, but he didn't try to hold her because they were connected by the water anyway.

'I want to believe you're different from other people,' she said through sniffs. 'But it's not easy when I think about the guns and see you like you were today.' She talked slowly with pauses between each phrase and he didn't interrupt. 'I want to believe what I know about you, how you're funny and sweet to me, and full of ideas that make me think, and rubbish that makes me chuckle, or punch you.

'But I can see you changing, and I don't want you to go away from me into some weird place in your head.' She splashed a hand on the surface of the water and watched the ripples. 'I don't know how I'll react. I don't know who I was today. It was good but it was weird as well, and somehow not me. I don't know what's making me act like someone else just because you are. Those people noticed it yesterday. They like us but they think we're crazy with the guns. Are we crazy?'

'It's the place.'

'Don't blame it on the place. You don't have to become part of it.'

'Are you worried about what might happen here?'

'Yes. No. Not in the way you mean. I'm not worried about a war, because I can just leave – we can just leave. I'm not supposed to be tied to anything, I'm just travelling the world and this is just a tiny part of the world, and I wish I could make you think the same.'

She looked up at him and wiped her eyes, and went on: 'But I want to be tied to you now, and I think you want it, too, but you don't know how to put this other stuff out of your head and see it and *say* it. So maybe I can't travel the world the way I want, because I have to think about someone else, and I can accept that because I want it. And I'm not worried about a war because it doesn't mean anything to me. But I'm worried about what it's starting to mean to you. And I don't know if you're going to want to leave this place, whatever happens.'

'I can't answer that now.'

'I don't expect you to. That's not really what I'm getting at.' She'd stopped crying but was still sniffing and breathing hard. 'If you do it you do it. If you go you go. But think about me. Include me in your decisions the way you're part of mine now. Because I think that when your mind's clear, that's what you want. You talk to me, Robert, and you listen. Don't stop doing that.

'I'll leave with you or stay with you or whatever you want us to do. *If* you want me to. Don't say anything until your head is clear and you know what you want.'

All the time she was talking they were still just standing waist high in the cool water.

'I know you now, Robert. There's more of you in there than you're letting yourself think. Just remember one thing: this place is not the edge of the world just because that's the way it looks on Robert's map. You can steer away in any direction.'

Robert waited a minute, then said: 'What did you mean by different?'

'What, love?'

'You said I was different. How am I different?'

'Oh, God. You really don't know, do you? You really haven't a clue.' She sighed, and held his hands. 'I'd like to just say: think about it. But you think too much as it is. Just don't go strange on me. Don't think yourself into all kinds of trouble.' She tugged his fingers gently. 'You hear?'

'I hear.'

'You got me?'

'Gotcha.'

'Don't go weird on me.'

'I won't. Hey, I won't. And I haven't changed that much.' He smiled. 'I still have an eye for the ladies.'

'If you mean young Melanie, watch your step.'

'She's cute. But I meant you.'

'She's a flirt. And out of bounds.'

'Ditto Jeff. I saw you looking at him.'

'I suppose he's got a nice bod.'

'Watch it.'

'Just teasing. I'm happy with you, crazy man. Rub my back.'

She turned around and he splashed her with both arms coming from deep under the water.

'You bastard! I said rub it! You're a bloody bastard!'

And she was squealing and they were having a splashing war and then they were ducking and drowning each other in the cold water, and the diving birds were dive-bombing them and going mad at the sound of their laughter.

Tin cans he wasn't short of any more, and a rinse in the lake would get rid of the stench, and the runs of fishing line would be all but invisible. Of course he'd have to get used to distinguishing between the noises of the wind or small animals, and the clumsy clatter followed by the sudden silence that would herald the presence of something bigger, and more human, and less welcome.

It took him all that evening and the next day, working through all the daylight there was to fix the long lines. He told Charlotte he didn't expect her to help him do this, and she seemed happy not to argue. He said that when it was finished she would see that it would be good for their peace of mind.

She said that she had said her bit, and that he was supposed to be thinking about it. What's happened to you since yesterday? she said.

The weather was mercifully cool all the time he worked. The breeze came back and the forest lifted its leaves and the fresh wind helped in testing the wires.

Robert worked the tripwires in an almost unbroken D shape, eighty yards around the house in a semi-circle, and in the straight edge of the D as far as he could manage along the shore of the lake. He was pleased with the job, although eighty yards was still pretty near to the house. Anyone getting that close could draw a pretty good bead on them. But he wasn't sure he would hear anything further off. It was a compromise.

There were booby traps to think about as well, although he thought he'd let Charlotte get used to tripwires before he started sharpening stakes. Bloody hell.

As soon as the tripwires were finished he went with Charlotte to her farmhouse/squat and they collected her few last things. It was her idea, finally, but he said it was just as well, for her own safety, and that he was very happy.

For two days after setting the wires Robert circled the land around the farmhouse-turned-fortress – his home – clearing particular areas of debris, hacking out small bushes, creating flat, empty tracks several yards wide, radiating so they could be seen from specific windows in the house.

Charlotte had begun to help him now, and even to ask about the mechanics of what he was doing. Robert liked her more every day. But he didn't tell her much about what he was thinking.

He knew he was a competent shot with the .22 now and he knew he might only have to put one man down to make a gang think again.

You wouldn't kill anyone with the .22, but they'd get the message. The sawn-off was the best weapon in a close-up scrap. He thought about trying to make a bow, but he didn't know shit about bows and arrows. That was a stupid idea. Get a grip.

Charlotte laughed so much at that one, he had to chase her and pin her down and make her eat soil to show she was sorry. And she was still laughing. Robert felt happy. She hadn't laughed as much as usual these last few days, and the sound snapped him out of something for a few moments.

The fire lanes now spread out like the points of a paper star, five clear narrow paths at angles from the house to the edge of the forest, and one long panorama along the beach.

He tested his theory, and he was right – the ground around the house wasn't flat. Anyone wanting a succession of clear shots would have to break cover and be in one of the fire lanes. And as long as the night had at least half a moon, the chump in the open might as well be wearing a Davy lamp. Fish in a barrel. He was sure no one would attack along the open expanse of the beach. And who would attack him, anyway?

Who? Plenty of people. It could be Albanian vigilantes full of Amstel and testosterone, eager for the off; it could be someone assuming, as everyone seemed to, that he was foreign *ergo* he was rich *ergo* the house would be full of dollar bills and American passports; it could be someone who just didn't like foreigners and who wanted to get some use from their gun and a new stockpile of ammo.

Or it could be the JNA.

He thought about that a lot, because it seemed safe to think about something so unlikely.

Surviving something like that would make a hell of a story.

But if that kind of shit started in earnest he could just bug out and head for Corfu with his bike and his passport and his girlfriend and be out of there. That was an option. That's what the old man wanted him to do – and his girlfriend, too.

He remembered the old man.

He hadn't been back to Sarande since the day in the ammo shop, but he knew he'd have to go back soon. He missed the old man's company, and he needed to know the Bejteri situation. If the lawyer had skipped town, or the country, his *besa* might be compromised. Whatever happened, he knew he had to keep making appearances, show the locals he wasn't spooked. Oh, yes, and he had to let them admire his new toy.

Meanwhile, restoring furniture and scrubbing walls and ceilings and sanding and weatherproofing doors all but stopped, replaced by arranging crates and sacks to make firing nests under windows and by doors. Now Charlotte not only helped, but took the initiative.

She had begun wearing her gun in the house, pretending it was a game, but working as thoroughly as ever, making a good job of checking the positions of windows and blind corners in the approaches through the fire lanes, repairing shutters so they wouldn't let them down against things thrown. They both practised shooting down the fire lanes. When he asked, why the sudden interest in his 'schemes for their peace of mind', as he called them, she said it wasn't good for him to do things on his own.

Robert felt guilty, and said they'd start the real work again as soon as the house was ready and safe. He recited the list of his friends lined up to visit, and said she should invite someone. He said this, but there were no more tours through the rooms to plan layouts and requirements, or to test surfaces or swap thoughts, take mental inventory and plan the next job. Or to smile and kiss and make love on the dusty tables and floors, blowing out the ancient silence and waking old ghosts with their gasps and whispers. When they made love now it was in the bed in the one room with the shutters closed, and the guns close by.

July 25

Ray,

Situation mildly sticky. Best not come right now. Will keep you posted.

Later, ciao, R.

Then a PS

PS Don't worry about me. It's cool, I'm a long way from trouble. And I'm really happy. In fact I've never felt so happy or so at home. That's true. Home. So don't worry. I'm having a great time. I don't know how else to convey how great all this is. Later again.

He looked back over it, then took another sheet of airmail and started again. This one read:

July 25

Ray,

don't come.

Robert.

He sat for a long time at his desk thinking about what he had put into the two letters and what he had not put in. Later, he sat out on the thinking rock with a bottle of Cutty Sark, listening to the sounds. He hardly touched the drink.

He had decisions to make.

He could let his choices become practical, or he could admit they were still moral. Were they? Did he have to think like that any more? There was a war on, after all.

And there was a beautiful, wonderful girl.

But then, there's always a war on somewhere. And you don't have to go to it. This was not why he had come to live in this place. These choices were not ones he had expected to have to make or to want to. He screwed up his eyes and rubbed his temples.

If he stopped thinking about it, then it was all easy. Then the choices would be practical. But how long could you really stop thinking? It felt something like when things went wrong with a woman, and wanting her so much in the past tense pushed you close to madness, and you knew you had to stop thinking and be in some kind of waking coma until you could cope again. It was necessary, but the timing was important because if you left it too long you felt dead and scars formed over the important places in your heart and your understanding.

If he really thought, then the choices were hard. There were thrilling possibilities, things he might see. And there was the possibility that he was a hypocrite, and worse.

Fuck. All he could decide for now was that these were not easy choices. They were not like where to site a fire lane, or which bush to fix your tripwire to.

The tripwires were chinking gently now from time to time. A calm sound, like faraway cowbells.

Robert sat and faced the trees and traded thoughts with his conscience and his heart. It was a novel feeling, he realised.

There was a breeze. The trees swayed, and the wolves took up their impossible chorus in the real forest just across the lake. They're really not that far away, Robert thought. Just over the water. He tried to keep open those channels to conscience and heart, as the wolves sang up their hunger and their freedom, and the night came on.

Part Three

15

CHARLOTTE WATCHED HIS expression intently as they listened to the news together. Sometimes her features would betray emotion at the awful things she heard, but mainly she monitored Robert, her eyes flickering with any sign of change in his face. She watched him as if he were a retard, or a drunk who needed careful handling until you could get him to bed.

Get him away from here and on a boat to Corfu.

Then Robert would catch her eye and smile a blithe, half-fathomable smile that seemed to throw her off balance: a glimpse of sense, perhaps? A hint that she was getting through? Or a look that said he had gone beyond all reason? It seemed that she couldn't tell because, for the moment, she did nothing. And then his attention would return to the voices coming from the radio, and his thoughts sink far back from the surface of his face.

Albanian troops moved north toward the border with Kosovo, and fat men in Belgrade roared about provocation and acts of war.

Well – Robert yelled to Charlotte out on the veranda – they should know.

The Tirane government riposted that the few hundred soldiers headed north were destined for the UNHCR refugee hospital at Krume in the Accursed Mountains, a few miles inside Albania, carrying medical supplies, tents, and food.

Refugees were starting to turn up in numbers at Krume and the local police – who were little more than glorified *Çetas* or thieves, employed in plum jobs through *fis* connections – were overwhelmed and uncooperative. The Tirane government also revealed plans to send more men to help upgrade the emergency hut accommodation set up by German charities at Kukes and Bajram Curri, near to the border.

The American observers at their base in Tetovo in northern

Macedonia confirmed the initial Albanian troop movement but described it as 'negligible'.

Milosevic, however, referred to 'convoys of Muslim artillery'.

The Albanian military could not boast convoys of anything.

Next up, Belgrade claimed that Albanians had been smuggling heroin through Kosovo for decades, and that now they were going to bring 'tons' of the drugs north in 'hundreds of tanks'.

There were not even one hundred working tanks in Albania. And those not perishing from rust were only good as fixed artillery pieces as, when mobile, poisonous fumes from the ancient engines killed the crews.

And tons of heroin? Albania was certainly a known drug trafficking route, but its infrastructure could not support tons of anything, and Milosevic now sounded as paranoid as Enver Hoxha had at his most deluded.

But Enver Hoxha had stayed in power for forty-five years.

Words, words, words. It seemed to Robert that the more inevitable a conflict of some kind appeared to be, the more theatrical the bluster and sabre-rattling became – like the claims about drugs, which smacked of desperation – and the less likely it seemed that the fighting would spread beyond where it had begun. Robert knew he ought to be relieved: now his life could continue.

Yes, get real, he told himself. Who would possibly want to invade Albania? A bankrupt and starving country defended by a sugar-glass Maginot line; an agricultural and industrial wasteland foraged by goats and donkeys; its army engineless, its ghost-town airfields picked over by underfed children; its troops professional deserters who sold their Kalashnikovs in the markets and disappeared to Greece without ever looking back.

No, there was nothing worth invading or defending, and nobody who wanted to defend it. Robert joked to Charlotte that he was the only person in Albania who did not want to leave, then regretted saying it.

No, no one would invade Albania.

But Robert trailed a finger up to Krume and Bajram Curri on the map, anyway, just to see where they were. Bajram Curri, he remembered from the *Update*, was an outpost so primitive, a town so lawless that the authors had renamed it BC.

Yep, Milosevic was an interesting enough example of a sociopathic and psychopathic modern politician. But his sphere of influence was always going to be local.

Maybe I'm wrong, thought Robert, when the JNA poured into Kosovo.

It was hard to say which single event provoked the full-scale militarisation of the region. In the Belgrade press there were reports of KLA attacks on defenceless Serb families, which outraged Serbs in the rest of Yugoslavia, and put pressure on the politicians and the army to act.

Very clever, Robert remarked to Charlotte.

There was no mention in Belgrade, though, as there was on the World Service, of Milosevic's plainclothes thugs bussing in suitcase-loads of small arms to hand out to the Serb population.

One correspondent suggested as a probable last straw the 'human shield' incident, when hundreds of Kosovar school children were forced to march in front of JNA troops as they entered a shelled village in search of KLA snipers or, failing that, any adult males. The children were released by the army only when helicopter support arrived and the untouched houses could be rocketed from the air. The reporter couldn't say if all the children got away safely, as he was busy fleeing himself. This incident, he believed, so outraged the KLA and ordinary Kosovars that ambushes and rioting in the following days increased five-fold.

Whatever the reason, once the JNA invaded the situation exploded. The fighting spread west into the relatively flat Decane borderlands where the terrain was more suited to the Serbs and their helicopters, and where the KLA could find little cover.

Helicopters, rebels, cover. It all sounded to Robert like something out of Vietnam. Jesus, am I in Vietnam? *Hell no, I won't go.*

Still the KLA attacks continued. They seemed to have an inexhaustible supply of arms and ammunition, as well as of dogged determination. The JNA's leaders on the ground were forced to concede that they were no longer fighting terrorist cells, but an organised and trained army. They could capture the KLA's weapons but those weapons would be replaced. They could corner the rebels with tanks and machine guns and deliver ultimatums through loudspeakers: surrender or face the consequences. And the KLA would choose the latter always, and new recruits would step in to replace the martyred, or the wasted, depending on your outlook.

Correspondents reported the closing of all roads west of the axial Pec–Dacovica highway, after which it became difficult to monitor events and confirm details. Instead the journalists relied on gossip and what they could glean from Serb officials at the checkpoints, with many of whom they were now on first name terms.

Robert shook his head and laughed, dazed and delighted at the surreal nature of it all.

The constant complaint of the JNA officers against the western media, and the BBC in particular, was that the JNA was not being applauded for its heroic struggle against the forces of Islam.

Robert knew he shouldn't be shocked or surprised by this, but he couldn't help it. It was inconceivable. It was brainwashing.

Then he remembered what the old man had said about identity, and religion, Serbs and Muslims, shopkeepers and fishermen. No, it was not inconceivable at all.

It was merely evil.

16

THAT'S NOT AN *animal.*
That noise is not an animal.
They've come.

These were the dreams that hung on the tripwires. Dreams in which the rusty cans became fire alarms, and armies of men in aprons and overalls smashed through Robert's forest and into his house. The dreams jolted Robert from sleep, sobbing, or sometimes laughing.

Charlotte said, If you go back to Sarande, maybe the dreams will stop.

Robert found a town that, far from having returned to normal in the week he'd stayed away, had advanced another stage in its preparations for war, or the fallout from war. It was a phase in which people were preoccupied, which meant that it was safe to pass through and observe it, all but unnoticed.

Robert knew enough to know that that could change.

Bejteri had reappeared, thank God. Robert found his office once again besieged by the usual suspects. They yelled their petitions, as the lawyer whistled and waved to Robert from his high window. He must be making a fortune, Robert thought. Someone always does.

Still, Bejteri's return was a big relief: Robert felt it was his town again. This was what I needed, to come back here. Just like Charlotte said. Just like a driver getting back behind the wheel.

The harbour and streets crawled with armed men, but precious few in uniform. Predictable enough. Real danger? – *vamos* policemen. Probably for the best, Robert thought. He walked and observed.

Everyone was clearly trying to look necessary to the scene, but this pretence of action was too obviously a cover for strutting about armed to the teeth as an end in itself.

There were women of a certain type everywhere. It was unusual for them to be so visible. Do guns bring out the whores? Robert wondered. Clearly. Clearly guns change a lot of things. Jesus, is it me or is everyone – and I mean everyone – tooled up?

He wasn't imagining it. Boys of school age charged about with catapults loaded, not with stones, but a single bullet on an open groove. Accurate to, oh, four feet. Lethal, all the same. Put these boys in uniform, Robert mused, and you have hell on earth.

Yes, everyone felt it; the vibe of the place was all nervous action, all movement, and into it he melded.

Boats docked and embarked every few minutes. If anyone was supervising the unloading cum evacuation cum smuggling, you wouldn't know it. The Albanian way: the human chains slipped and knotted; instructions diffused into debates. Around it all, serious-faced messenger boys and girls raced in relay from shop to home to boat's gangplank to wherever, always at full tilt; and through it all, essentially nothing changed from one timeless moment to the next.

Robert scanned the bustle in the Russian-built harbour, remembering snippets of his research. The harbour: Hoxha had held it up as an example of *Albanian* engineering. But then, Hoxha had built concrete mushrooms; Hoxha had declared it a prison offence to grow a beard. He wondered. Information like that used to be strange and amusing to him: now it was just facts. Now he didn't give a fuck who built what.

He moved along the periphery of the mass of energy, of the town that couldn't sit still and wait.

They needed things: food, supplies. He bought everything without trouble. Only, after the first stop, for bread, he made sure he said something in each store he visited, a remark which required a response: as if the more people to whom he appeared as a talking, living being, the harder it would be for him to die.

Die. He had already nearly died here once.

He thought, this is hardly real.

Ray, if you could see me now.

Ray would scream: *Go home, you mad fucker. Get out! Come home; cut your losses and come home with a hell of a story to tell.*

And Robert Maidens would have replied, not yet: it's not enough of a hell of a story, not yet. Look at this place, this buzz: how could I ever think of leaving this?

The best place in the world is also the worst, and vice versa.

Yeah. Robert would have to be dragged out of this country.

'Woah, at ease, men! Welcome back, troops.'

Robert smiled and laid the shell bag on the milking stool by the table, and shook hands with Jeff and Lee, and finally with Simon. Simon had a weak handshake, he decided.

He kissed Mel on the cheek, then gave Charlotte a bigger kiss and a squeeze.

The four travellers looked tired and dusty and very pleased with themselves.

'So, what news from Butrint, lieutenant?' Robert asked. 'A bunch of ruins – or is that you lot? Ha ha.'

'Ha ha. I don't ever want to get on that bike again,' Mel said. 'I don't want piles. I don't think piles will help me get a husband.' She rubbed her bottom and pouted at Robert.

'So lady-like, sister,' Jeff said. 'That freak at Butrint was enough to give you mental piles, though.'

'Philistine,' Lee said. 'That was history re-enacted before us.' He gesticulated dramatically. 'That was a millennia of knowledge rendered through the ancient common language of interpretive dance.'

'That was gusset.' Jeff nodded to Robert. 'Some acid head actor prancing round the ruins in a toga. All very fucking authentic, I'm sure. Except it was all in Greek and we were the only audience.'

Robert laughed. 'Yeah, seen. This place has got some pretty basic catching up to do.'

'As long as you don't lose that innocence,' Jeff said. 'That untouched quality. That's why we're all here, right? Explore the untainted, return to innocence.'

'Right.'

Robert and Jeff clinked bottles.

'It really is a beautiful country,' Mel said. 'I never expected it to be like this. Not so wild. A lot of places you go to, you know what to expect. Not here.'

'Yeah, it's pretty much untouched,' Robert said. 'There are probably things here no one has seen.'

'Few more little guesthouses like yours and it'll be perfect,' Jeff said. 'Word gets around.' He reflected. 'Shame. You could have had a goldmine here.'

'How *could* have?' Robert said.

'Well, you'll be shipping out, with the war starting.'

'There's not going to be a war.'

Jeff looked amazed. 'We've been back across the border to Greece,' he said. 'From Butrint. They're gearing up for it. We're actually going back to Corfu tomorrow. Seriously, according to the Greek papers and telly, if you leave it much longer you'll be in the thick of it. The British government's recommending all its people get out.' He smiled uneasily. 'We feel a bit like cowboys. Last stage out of Dodge. We'll have a story to tell. I've taken sis and the boys on a real adventure.'

'You haven't got us out of it, yet,' Lee said.

'Get a grip,' Robert said irritably.

'Robert,' Charlotte said.

'I'm sorry. But look around. In the thick of it? We are in the thick of it, and nothing's happening. Hear any bombs falling? See any tanks?'

Jeff lifted his hands, palms outward. 'Hey, I'm sorry,' he said. 'I didn't mean to freak you out. These must be nervous times, considering your investment and all.'

'Yeah,' said Robert. 'They're nervous times. No offence.'

'I agree with Robert,' Charlotte said, and gave him a look. 'I think we should keep an open mind.'

For a second Robert felt snookered. Finally he gave her a look and said: 'Exactly. Open mind.'

Lee clapped his hands once, then rubbed his palms. 'My mind's open to a drag on that whisky you keep stashed, Robert.'

Robert went inside. He could hear them talking through the open door.

'I can't believe it's our last night,' Mel said, sighing. 'Then back to the fleshpots of Corfu. I tell you what, more than anything on this trip so far, I'm going to miss this balcony. It's such a simple thing, but it's perfect. You could transplant it to any warm country in the world and it would just fit right in.'

Robert felt a tug of pleasure in his chest. Then a pulse of sadness. He picked up an almost full bottle and went back out onto the veranda.

'Have you changed anything?' Jeff asked.

'In what way?'

'Well, the view looks different. You can see more. God, it's hot. No breeze.'

'Think yourself lucky there's no breeze,' Charlotte said. 'You want to hear the melodic tinkling of tin cans? Wish for a breeze.'

'What you talking about?'

'Tell them, sweetheart.'

Robert looked at Charlotte for a long moment. He took a pull at the Cutty Sark and passed it on. He was aware of the silliness in the sounds of the words he was about to say. 'I laid tripwires.'

Lee coughed on the whisky. 'Sorry! What?'

'Tripwires,' Robert repeated slowly. 'For our security and peace of mind.'

Silence.

Robert shrugged. 'Anyone tries to get near the house other than along the driveway, we'll know. And we can put a pin in them.'

'Put a what?' Mel asked.

'A pin. As in pinpoint. We'll know where they are.'

Looks passed between Lee and Simon, and Jeff and Mel.

Who were they kidding. Robert saw.

He also saw Simon look at Charlotte. The quiet one, Simon. He always seemed to find a perch next to Charlotte. Well, he had a pin in Simon. He'd heard him coming.

Lee cleared his throat. 'Robert, mate,' he said quietly. 'Okay, ah, after you know where they are?'

'Yeah?'

'What do you put in them next?'

'You f–'

'Whoa, whoa, whoa! Easy, boys.' Charlotte skipped over to Robert where he leaned against the table. She held his hands and began caressing his fingers, trying to calm him. 'Robert could be right. It doesn't hurt to take precautions. Like he said, these are tense times.'

Robert was still staring at Lee.

Lee shrugged and said: 'I didn't mean anything by it, man.'

'I think you meant something,' Robert said.

'Okay,' Lee said. 'Let's leave it. I'm sorry. But, it does seem a bit fucking extreme.'

'Lee,' Jeff said.

Lee went on. 'I mean, if you're so sure nothing's going down, why the fortifications?'

'Lee!' Jeff said again.

'I told you,' Robert said quietly. 'Precautions.'

'I'm, ah, I'm in agreement with Charlotte.' It was Simon. Robert didn't like the plum in Simon's mouth. 'Easy,' he droned, almost inaudibly. 'Let's all take it easy.' He put his hand under his T-shirt and into his money belt and brought out an Old Holborn tobacco pouch. 'Take it easy with some of these. Chill, children.'

Silent Simon, Robert thought. How fucking predictable. Another mystery solved. Another quiet sensitive type revealed as just another heavyweight fucking blowhead. About as deep as a pool of fucking piss. And 'children'? I've got his fucking number, and I fucking heard him coming. And I'll put a fucking pin in him.

'All right, man,' Lee said. 'No hard feelings?'

Robert shook off and buttoned his fly and staggered back toward the house. As he got nearer he began walking as quietly as he could. He didn't really know why.

He was stoned, and drunk as a monkey – they all were – but just about in control of his limbs. He tried thinking of anagrams of limbs. Blims, milbs. Jesus, get a grip, think about what you're doing; you're supposed to be listening. Am I? Yes, you're supposed to be listening. Sorry. Shh!

He tiptoed up the side of the house and leaned on the stone wall by the veranda.

'Don't roll another one,' Jeff was saying.

Robert could hear perfectly.

'Father, fucking forgive me! If you roll another one I'll puke. Someone stop him.'

'Or shoot him!' Lee said.

Simon chuckled. 'Don't say that when Rambo's here, man.'

Robert listened to the laughter which followed the crack, filtering it for sounds of Charlotte. No, she wasn't laughing. Most of it was Simon and Mel. Well.

'Seriously, don't roll another one, dude.'

'Don't have to partake, man.'

'Yeah but I'll puke just by knowing it's there. That it's alive in the universe. I'm an intuitive puker.'

'I'm sad we're leaving tomorrow,' Mel said.

'I'm not.'

'Simon!' Mel said. The exclamation had some consideration for Charlotte in it, Robert thought. He might not kill Mel.

'He's got a point.' Jeff, this time. Robert tried to control his breathing. 'No offence, Charlotte. You've both been great, and this is a brilliant place. I spend my life dreaming of places like this. Oases. I'm sure Robert's a great bloke.' He looked at his friends.

'But maybe we can see it and you can't. You've got to get out of this country, at least for now.' There was a pause, but no riposte from Charlotte. 'Robert's brilliant. I really admire him for what he's done,' Jeff continued. 'But – and please don't take this the wrong way – I think he's become a bit obsessed.'

After a moment Charlotte answered him quietly. 'If you all think he's so crazy, why did you come back to his house?'

'He's part of the trip, man,' Lee said. 'He's a feature. A story to tell. He's totally fucking trippy.'

'I don't think that's very kind, or very polite,' Charlotte said. 'You're misjudging him. I know him better than you.'

Jeff said: 'Charlotte's right. That wasn't polite. He's sorry, aren't you, Lee?'

Lee held up his hands. 'Yeah. Sorry.' There was another long pause. Then Lee said: 'Tripwires.'

Simon chuckled, then cleared his throat and said: 'Look,

Charlotte, if he's seriously not going to leave, then maybe you –'

That was enough. Robert coughed loudly and stepped away from his hiding place, and walked around to the steps. 'All right, troops?' he said. 'Blimey O'Reilly, why the big silence? Telling scary stories?' He smiled.

The five people on the veranda looked at Robert. They wouldn't know what he'd heard.

That's good.

Robert watched them examine his face for knowledge of what they'd said; he kept smiling, and shrugged, and saw their expressions relax.

Mel said: 'Travelling stories.'

'Travelling stories? I like travelling stories. Whose turn is it?'

Mel's mouth froze.

'We weren't really taking turns,' Jeff said. 'Just. You know.'

'Pass us that, Simon, old chap.' Robert took a long hit of the reefer. It burned his lips but he kept going. You could hear the grass and tobacco spitting as it burned, and see the veins in Robert's eyes fill with blood, but he still kept going.

Simon flinched.

'*Ouch!*' Lee said.

'*Travelling stories*,' Robert rasped as he exhaled. The smoke went on forever. 'I'll tell you a travelling story. Everyone sitting comfortably?' He looked around him. They looked more relaxed. They'd be thinking: perhaps he didn't hear; if he was walking he wouldn't have heard much. Robert smiled. 'Then I'll begin.

'Once upon a time I was in India.'

'Do I know this one?' Charlotte asked. Her voice was careful, testing.

'Not this one, dearest. Once upon a time I was in India.' He took another hit on the joint. 'Went to this place down by the Ganges. I forget what it's called. Where they burn the bodies.'

Lee swallowed: 'Bodies?'

'That's the one. Big pyres. Pyres for burning bodies in a sacred location. Indian crematorium thing.'

'Jesus,' Mel whispered. 'I don't think I want to hear this.'

Robert continued, a little louder. 'And they're burning bodies.

Loads of dead bodies. Oh, I forgot to mention, the food in India really chews cocks.' He looked at Simon. 'I mean, it really fucking chews big fat *cocks*! You with me? It sucks fucking *member*! All that freaking rice. Rice, rice, rice, *and a little cold rat meat.* Heh heh. And you can't eat the meat – the meat'll kill you.'

Mel whispered: 'He's out of it.'

'So I'm in this country without any meat, and I'm at the outdoor crematorium business. And this particular day, I am Hank fucking Marvin. Absolutely ravenous, and sick to the back teeth of fucking rice. And we're watching the sacred priest geezers burn these bodies, although it doesn't look much like a sacred operation, because they're just piled up and the shrouds on the stiffs keep slipping away and you can see them burning, and the flesh falling off their faces, you with me? Nasty stuff. Interesting stuff. But I swear – this is the funny bit – when I smelled those boys and girls burning? I just smelled food. I mean it. MEAT!'

Mel and Simon jumped.

He drew on the reefer again as if inhaling the aroma of cooked meat, then flicked the roach behind him into the dark. 'BARBECUE! And all I could think about, even with all the death and those burning bodies was, what wouldn't I give right now for a fucking great *burger*?' He drew the last word out, sumptuously.

After a few seconds Charlotte began to chuckle, then to laugh out loud.

No one joined in.

Robert said: 'What's the matter? Sense of humour haemorrhage? Fucking hell, try saying that sober. Charlotte thinks I'm funny, don't you, Charlotte?'

'That's not funny,' Mel said. 'It's sick. I think you're seriously sick.'

'Mel!'

'Don't defend him, Jeff! I've changed my mind. I'm glad we're going tomorrow. I think he's mad!' There were tears in her eyes. Tears of anger, and of the courage it had taken to release the anger.

And tears of unrequited flirting, Robert thought. A woman scorned. Well, I'll scorn the bitch. I can hardly see straight with this whisky and dope, but I'll scorn the fucking bitch.

'Mel, calm down, we're all mates,' Jeff said.

But Mel was on her feet. 'I'm going inside.'

'No time for another story?' Robert said. He looked at Mel and froze her where she stood. So, tears of fear as well? I'll scorn the bitch. 'No time for another story? Okay, I'll tell Jeff a story. Jeff, my old mucker. You asked me if I'd changed anything. You said you could see more from up here. And you can, even now when it's dark.'

'Robert, don't,' Charlotte pleaded. 'You're drunk. He's just drunk,' she said to the others and to herself.

'Even when it's dark,' he went on. 'Well, I have changed something. Watch this.' He staggered over to the table and reached underneath it, onto the milking stool, and took the thing out of the shell bag.

'What the fuck!' Lee pressed himself against the railings where he sat. Mel screamed and slid to her backside against the wall of the house. Simon took Charlotte's arm but she drew it away, quickly. Jeff hadn't moved.

'Come with me, Jeff,' Robert said. 'Bring a gun. Charlotte? Give Jeff your gun, dearest darling.'

'Jeff, don't go with him!' Mel shouted.

'Charlotte? Just for a minute. I need to show Jeff my improvements.'

Charlotte stood up slowly and handed Robert the pistol, then sat down again on the wooden deck.

'Loaded?'

She nodded.

'Okay. Jeff?' Robert offered him the weapon. He took it, eventually, and followed Robert down the steps.

'I doubt you'll like this story. It's not as funny as the other one.' Robert raised his free arm, palm down, and pointed out toward the forest in a gesture resembling a Nazi salute. 'Fire lanes, Jeff. Branching out from the house. It was hard work. But if anyone crosses them I've got a much clearer shot than I had before. I've got an advantage. I can put that pin in them first. There's that pin again, Lee. Did you get that? Try it, Jeff. Try shooting down the fire lane.'

Jeff stood holding the gun like it was a slab of raw liver.

'Go on, mate. Pick something at the end of the fire lane as a target. Have a go. Sight down the fire lane. Knock the safety off. *Have a go.*'

Jeff looked down at the gun and his expression changed slightly. He licked his lips, and closed his thumb around the grip. Then he looked up at his sister, hesitated, and handed the weapon back to Robert. 'No thanks, mate,' he said. 'Not tonight.'

There was a moment of waiting. Then Robert shrugged and walked back up the steps. He handed the pistol back to Charlotte, and there were several audible sighs of relief.

Then Simon stood up and began speaking quickly: 'He's lost it, Charlotte! He's crossed the fucking line! You should come with us tomorrow. You can – *ow, fuck*!'

Robert jabbed Simon lightly in the chest with the business end of the sawn-off. To Robert's surprise it sent the lad sprawling backwards onto the table. Bottles and plates went spinning and crashing.

'Fuck, *fuck*, *fuck!*' Simon was saying.

Robert whispered: 'Pathetic.' He walked toward Simon.

'No, Robert!' Charlotte cried.

'Your turn, Simon,' Robert whispered. 'Want to see the fire lanes? Silent Simon. I'm whispering. I'm silent, too.'

'No, Robert, please!' Charlotte crawled over to Robert and, still on her knees, hugged his thighs. She wasn't crying. 'Please, Robert, it's the dope. It's just the drugs, Robert. It's making you paranoid. Please stop, Robert.'

Robert laid the sawn-off on the table by Simon's right hand. Simon's face was grey and drenched with sweat. 'Silent Simon,' Robert whispered again. 'Roll a joint, silent Simon, why don't you? See if it calms me down? See if it makes you cool. See if it impresses the *ladies*?'

'Robert, please,' Charlotte said again. She was pleading but not hysterical. 'Look, I'm where you like me. I'm where you like me, Robert. I can stay down here. We can go upstairs and I'll be where you like me. Yes? Just calm down.'

Robert looked away from Simon to the other faces. Jeff's and Lee's were frozen in numb disbelief; Mel's was locked in a silent scream. He almost laughed – something else for them to take in. *Where you like me*. Digest that.

'Please, Robert? Stop it now? Please?'

Robert looked at Simon, and leaned into his nauseated face. 'Tomorrow,' he whispered. 'Vroom, vroom. You drive away.' He picked up the sawn-off and snapped it open. Simon jumped.

'Think you can waltz in here and take my girlfriend away? A limp-wristed fop bastard coward like you? Not even half a man? Charlotte knows you. Fucking blowhead.' Robert's eyes glazed over and he stood staring through Simon, as if unsure what came next.

Charlotte sprang suddenly off her knees and slapped Simon hard across the face, which at least ended the unpredictable stand-off. Simon fell back again, and his nose began to bleed.

He opened his mouth to object, but Charlotte said: 'He opened his home to you.' There were the sounds of the others clearing their throats, or swallowing. She went on: 'All of you.' Then she took Robert's hand, and led him inside.

That's not an animal.

And it's no dream.

What have I done.

Robert was out of bed in a volley of four-letter words, and hearing the sound clearly again as something stumbled and fell against one of his tripwires. It was no gust of wind, this time.

He made the tour of his windows, ducking, and levelling the .22 out of each, straining his eyes to cut through the black.

It was useless; to have a chance of hitting something you had to *see* the fucker. He hadn't put up any markers to mark off the distances between the trip points. How could he have missed that? Fuck! It was no good. Where are the fire lanes? He needed markers: loud, bright markers. And you can't hit anything with the .22 in the dark.

He headed for the porch, always ducking under the windows. The shells were waiting, but *Jesus* he'd forgotten the fucking sawn-off!

He had to run back through to the bedroom, under the windows again while all the time the enemy got closer. He'd *never* do this again, *never* make the same mistake.

He got the gun and ran back and out of the porch door and slid onto his belly on the wooden deck, winding himself and gritting his teeth. Load, level, watch. What can you see? What can you hear? He could see and hear nothing but the gun made him feel stronger and almost clear-headed. That's it, that's the fear receding now. Where are they? What could he see? What could he hear?

It was maybe sixty seconds since the first noise and now he heard a shout or something like a shout. It could have been a deer or a fox or he didn't know what. But he heard it as a shout.

And he heard its direction.

He fired twice.

Fucking. Eat. That.

He heard a shout, and now there were two more, and the tripwires going wild, and the noise of running through the trees. *There.* I heard it. I'm not paranoid.

He whispered *shit* and threw the sawn-off skidding across the deck, and dived for the .22, and was up in a kneeling position and getting off shots. One two three four five *reload!* The rifle felt charged with life in his hands now there was something to shoot at, but what was he shooting at, exactly? He reloaded and fired a second clip of five down the central fire lane, and waited nervous moments for the whistling to fade from his ears. It did, and he heard nothing else. And he knew they'd gone.

The next noise was Charlotte. He was surprised that she'd made time to put on jeans and the fleece. And then it hit him: a woman. A woman caught naked in the dark by men with guns.

He began to pour with sweat. He felt physically sick. What was he putting her through? He sat there in a pool of his metallic stinking sweat, watching her, seeing only a weak, vulnerable, potential – he didn't want to think it.

She doesn't deserve to be here. What am I doing?

She had her gun, and she had the hatchet from the living room table in her left hand, but she was shaking badly and didn't seem to know how she'd come to be holding these things. But worst of all she was standing in the open like target practice.

Robert ducked his way over to her and led her back inside, and gently took the weapons from her fingers.

She cried for a long time.

She managed a few words between sobs: 'I'm sorry. I was so scared. I didn't do anything right.'

'It's fine. It's just fine.'

'I'm sorry.'

'It's fine.'

What the hell was *she* apologising for? He held her and patted her like that and when he wanted to cry too he let it come and hoped that it might make her feel better to see him scared. And he was scared. As facts and possibilities became clear to him, oh, he was scared, and happy to be so.

Robert heard movement on the stairs, and a moment later saw Jeff, half-dressed, ducking in the living room doorway. His eyes were round and shining and he was shaking like a leaf.

'Jeff.'

'Robert.'

'Jeff, would you get the whisky?'

Jeff looked at Robert and at Charlotte, then back at Robert. 'Get it yourself.' He turned and began walking back up the stairs.

'Jeff,' Robert called after him. 'I was right.'

Without turning around, Jeff called out: 'We're leaving as soon as it's light.' You could tell he was crying.

Robert sat with Charlotte until she managed to fall asleep, then went back out on the veranda and stayed there the rest of the night. Not because he thought they'd come back, but just to be where it had happened, and to think.

What have I done, he asked himself. What have I misjudged?

Something like tonight just makes me think that the old man was wrong. I want to believe in everything he says, but this is just out there. Look at the way they act. Blood feuds, bribery, *fis*, *besa*. It's the civilised values of the twelfth century. It's like I told him: darkest bloody Africa. It's the law of the jungle.

I totally misread this place.

Here comes Bob Maidens wading in with his western twentieth-century ideas, hoping to make a free market killing in a place where the free market means literally killing the competition. Where ideas of right and wrong are based on what you can get away with, or on what tribe or *fis* they belong to. Your *fis* is right, everyone else's is wrong: kill them. How will I ever understand that? How can I possibly stay here and fit in?

Robert shuddered. Savages. Did he really believe that? Were the people creeping around his land really savages, or just thieves – which was understandable. Was it just high spirits, or kids? Savages? After all, it was him who'd started shooting, not them.

Robert thought about that.

But what if it wasn't kids, or high spirits? What if they'd got to him – to Charlotte? He shivered. What if he hadn't made the tripwires?

The night slipped by, chilly. 'Shit,' Robert whispered. 'Shit, shit!' It seemed the only eloquent comment.

He looked over at the sawn-off and cursed the damn thing again. It was useless like this, so was the .22. What he needed was another shotgun – not sawn-off – to give him some range in the dark. Because unless you were virtually shaking the other guy's hand you might as well throw pebbles as try and hit him with the sawn-off. And the .22 was for accuracy and you wouldn't get accuracy in the dark, maybe not even with markers. And the .22 wouldn't put a man down for good. All he'd done was scare whoever it had been.

So he needed another shotgun – which no one would sell him – and a handgun like Charlotte's, and actually he could use a pair of shotguns because they take time to load. And what about the Kalashnikovs? He wished now that he'd bought one, or a couple. One of those could rake across and up and down a fire lane in seconds. Thirty-two rounds in a clip.

What he also needed was to be rid of distractions like those people confusing him and making him lose his temper when he had other things to think about. They had insulted him, in his home. They had insulted him, and tried to take his girlfriend away. There had been no need. He hadn't wanted to start trouble, but they forced him. If someone doesn't give you a choice, well.

No, he didn't need that shit on top of everything else. He

needed more tripwires, and markers, and better fire lanes and to know where the fire lanes were in the dark, and all the guns he'd just listed blah blah blah.

Or he could just do what his girlfriend wanted and go home.

17

'IT IS GOOD to see you. But I am disappointed. I had hoped I would not see you again until all this was over.'

Robert nodded. 'I understand.'

'I hoped you would be in Corfu by now, or even England. But I had a feeling you were not. Still, at least you are safe.' The old man sounded tired. 'When did they come?'

Robert failed to hide his surprise. 'How did you know?'

'It was a guess. But I see it was a good guess. When did it happen?'

'Last night.'

The old man sighed. When the drinks arrived he looked up.

Now the summer was reaching its peak they were both drinking the cold Amstel, and a queue of empty bottles stood between them, glinting in the sun.

'Last night, you say.' The old man paused to take a drink. 'Yes, it has happened to other people. Most of the foreigners have left. Tell me exactly what happened.'

Robert opened his mouth to speak but stopped himself mid-syllable. He looked away down the alley to his right and began again. 'Your countrymen weren't very professional. They made enough bloody noise to wake the dead.' He paused again. 'They were lucky they missed the booby traps.'

'Booby traps?'

'Yes. Like snares, for animals.'

'And they missed them?'

'Yeah, lucky for them. I saw someone and fired over his head – I didn't get a great look at him. They didn't fire back.' Robert spat in the road, still facing away. 'Next time I might not fire over their heads.'

'They will probably not be back. You were lucky.'

Robert raised his eyebrows. 'I'd say our little friends were the ones who were lucky.'

'Oh, yes,' the old man said. 'The booby traps.' Then, quietly: 'But I think you were lucky.'

Robert turned back to face his friend. He looked at him for a long time, then sighed and said, quietly: 'I suppose so. Can you think who it might have been?'

'I think you were visited by bandits last night, my friend. Just bandits. From all the history lessons you have given me about my country – no, do not smile, I mean it, you have told me many things I did not know – from all your history lessons, I am sure you know there are many armed bandits.'

Robert nodded, trying not to look pleased with himself.

'But they are not stupid. Now that they know you will shoot, they will leave you alone. And the word will travel.'

'You think I'll be safe now?' Robert asked. He supposed he needed to hear – or at least to ask – the old man's opinion. But he didn't have to trust him. He felt a little sad thinking about that.

The old man shrugged. 'As safe as any of us. Come, let us drink together and talk about something else. I will help you to take your mind off fighting bandits in the night.'

Robert smiled. 'Okay. To not fighting bandits in the night.'

'Agreed: to not fighting bandits in the night, and to getting some sleep!'

'Perfect.'

As the afternoon waned the long shadows dressed the air around the two men in a cold-linen chill. Wafted awake, Robert felt suddenly, excessively, alive. He knew the feeling by now and knew not to trust it, but he let it take him a little way all the same.

It was a hard sensation to resist: the vibe of this place, with its serenity yet its brittle dangers; its loneliness yet its fickle, volatile crowds; its promise of freedom, yet its threat of instant dusty death.

Robert wanted to laugh out loud, and to walk the streets breathing it all in, living it. He was suddenly ashamed of the doubt he'd felt for the old man's integrity simply because, like the terrorisers of his home in the night, he was Albanian.

Gradually, the buzz subsided.

He looked across the white plastic table top. He saw the one native friend he had on this side of his small world, and on this side of a war zone – the lawyer was nowhere to be found once again – and conceded, once again, the instability of his judgement in this place he had chosen to make his home. He didn't want to think about that. Or maybe he did. If he wanted to talk about it there was only one man he could talk about it with.

I want to buy the old man dinner, Robert Maidens decided, and he was about to suggest it when another snap of cold linen, and the old man's voice, blew through the cotton-wool of his thoughts.

'Robert. Please tell me – and I ask you, not to try and persuade you, which I know is useless, but I ask because now I want to know – please tell me why you are here.'

Robert looked up into the old, old man's eyes. Something in the warmth of the voice speaking to him carried him back a lot of years.

What was happening in his brain? His heart? He was aware only of sitting in the cold, and feeling alive with a kind of life, but with no thoughts that would settle, and no urge to think.

The old man focused on Robert's face, as if reading, and shook his head. 'You don't want a damn hotel, Robert Maidens! The hotel is your excuse to stay here. There was one reason why you came here, but there is another reason why you will not go.' The old man broke off suddenly.

'The *Blue Guide* says the sunsets here are first class. I'd like to get us dinner.'

'The *Blue Guide*' – guide like 'geed' – 'whoever he his, is right. The sunset is in a few hours. We can talk until then. We can eat. I have no special place to be. And you have only your new fortress. I have plenty of time to listen.'

Robert wondered if he should be away from Charlotte for that long. But he couldn't really focus on the question. What the hell, she had the guns. And they wouldn't be coming back. He shook his head and tried to clear his mind.

'When I was a kid I dreamed of having a fort. I wanted to live in a fort in the garden. I'd have slept with my sword. I'll buy you dinner, you old swine.'

'Swine?'

'Pig.' For a moment Robert wasn't sure if he'd gone too far.

'For that terrible insult I will let you buy me dinner.'

'I'm here because I'm a coward.'

'I don't believe that.'

'It's true. That's the one reason I came. I'm scared.'

'We are all cowards sometimes.'

'In living? In pure bloody getting-on-with-it living?'

The old man looked confused. 'If you mean what I think you mean, many of us are cowards. But go on.'

Robert took a slow sip of his beer and wiped his mouth with the back of his forearm, and exhaled. 'I can't drive a car and I wouldn't know how to get a pension or a credit card and the thought of buying a house in my own country – one that costs more than Monopoly money – scares the life out of me. I haven't grown up. I wanted to come to a place where things are simple. Very, very simple, if possible. Where everything isn't ruled by change, all of the time. Where you don't have to keep fighting to stay ahead of the game. I wanted some time to, to just *be*.

'When I moved to London – Jesus, it was ten years ago – it was easy to get jobs. Good jobs. They didn't have the people to fill the good jobs. You could do well just by working hard and getting on with it.

'Now it's the opposite. Nobody needs people, and it seems so deliberate, so planned. I look ahead and I see a workforce of scared and unskilled people because no one wants anyone to have anything worth selling. There'll be a new job, a new field, every couple of years, then every six months, even. And I see directors and shareholders loving it, because everyone is replaceable. And everyone is replaced. My God, we're going backwards, it's Dickensian. Maybe it's even worse than that. The whole western capitalism thing is coming to an end. Hey, maybe you won't be plagued by tourists after all. It's true, though. The markets have failed. It can't go on. Am I losing you? Do you understand?'

'Not all the words, but something.'

'And I'm a coward because it was wearing me out.'

'I do not understand everything you are saying – there are many foreign words – but you do not sound like a coward, but like a man who thinks for himself. You must not stop thinking, my friend.'

'I think too bloody much. I worry about everything – I worried about everything, past tense. I was lucky. My job was okay – for now. I mean, when draughtsmen started losing their jobs in their hundreds I just adapted, learned CAD – that's computer design.'

The old man was shaking his head steadily, but it was hard to say how much he was taking in.

'I could still do my job and get a lot of money. A rational person, like my best mate Ray, can get on with it, keep up with the game – are you following me?'

The old man blinked his eyes Yes.

'But I couldn't be rational about it anymore. I saw friends doing desperate things to keep up with the way things are going – lots of change and all of it bad – humiliating themselves with paycuts; volunteering for pointless retraining; chasing carrots; crawling to jumped-up bosses younger than them and with half their knowledge and expertise. Expertise that would maybe be obsolete in two years, anyway. What was the point in learning a trade, or a skill, if you could just be screwed out of the market? When someone in the boardroom could fix it so your skill didn't mean shit, and you were one of the retraining classes again? No, sir. I didn't fancy sticking around to be a part of the "flexible labour market."'

Robert had been talking quickly, but now his speech became slower and less animated. 'Okay, I was all right. But for how long? I was scared. I adapted once. But it took a lot of energy. What happens when I'm too old to have the kind of energy needed to adapt a second or a third time? What happens? I don't think I want that kind of life with that kind of pressure. All that change.'

'You have nothing to punish yourself for, my friend.'

Robert didn't seem to hear. 'I'm not an entrepreneur. I don't enjoy adapting. I just want things simple, to see where I'm going. I'd be happy just with my little life, and to be a man.' He paused. 'All the rest can just happen in my head.' And then he stopped.

'All this is starting to sound trivial, do you see what I mean? Look at where we are. It's like you said, I came here for one reason, and I can't make sense of that anymore. So why do I want to stay?'

But it wasn't really a question.

There was another brief silence.

'All this – ' He motioned toward the harbour shaded in the dark pastels of the closing dusk. ' – all this isn't what I thought, is it? I wanted too much. Perhaps it serves me right. I was running away, do you see?'

'We have to run away from some things. It is how we survive.'

'That might be true.'

'And so now you can go back. You have a reason to go. No?'

Robert simply shook his head.

The old man said: 'I see.'

Robert noticed the other tables around them filling up. A boy by the door was tying on an apron over a grubby T-shirt. The logo on the T-shirt read: 'Baskin & Robbins.'

'We can have a good meal here, and it is cheap.'

'Good,' Robert said.

'Talking makes you hungry. Please go on.'

'That's about it. The rest you've heard before. When I heard about the prices of property over here and decided it would be nice to get away from lousy London and live an all-year round holiday in a country that had at least ten years left in it before it was ruined, there was only one thing I was going to do.'

The old man's eyes flickered. 'You think this country will be ruined? How?'

'Oh, yes. It'll be ruined. When the tourists start to come in numbers and the local businessmen get ideas into their heads about just what it is a foreign tourist wants, then it will all be ruined, you'll see. But you have ten years.'

'Oh. Then I hope I do not have ten years. This poor country. For years murdered by the communists and now by the tourists.'

'No – by the businessmen who try to control the tourists. Tourists don't ruin anything by themselves.'

'Oh.' But he didn't seem to understand.

So he doesn't understand everything, Robert thought. Of course not, why should he. Especially about his own country.

'But I was saying, now you have a reason to go back.'

'And I have a reason to stay. Or that's how it feels.'

'And what will you do if there is a war and the worst possible things happen? Will you die because you are afraid to look like a coward?'

'We have a saying in English: I'll cross that bridge when I come to it.'

'I have heard it. It's a good saying. You also have another where the bridges get burned.'

'And another, about old men who are too clever for their own good.'

On cue the old man laughed raucously. 'So, now I understand it all.'

'You do?'

'Of course. I understand enough of why you ran away to this place. I understand why you do not want to go home, and I think I understand the other reason which you have not told me, which I think is making you stay.'

'Yeah? And what might that be?'

'Call over that boy, I am getting hungry.'

Robert motioned to the little waiter.

'I will order for both of us,' the old man said loudly; he was a little drunk in a pleasant way. 'I know the food in this cafe.' He whispered a few words in the boy's ear and patted his backside, and the boy smiled and ran inside with the order in his head.

Robert said: 'So, go on. Tell me why I'm here. Tell me what's so wonderful about this place that I can't leave in the middle of a war.'

'Ah, my young friend, that is just it. It is not the wonderful country or your new hotel or your new simple life that keeps you here. You have said it yourself: we are in the middle of a war.'

Robert's eyes narrowed and he sat very still to hear the truth.

'Robert Maidens, my young typical friend. You have stepped around the sides of the truth. Maybe you wanted me to discover it, or maybe not; but I have, so that is that. There is going to be a war. And what young man, truly in his heart, could ever stay away from war?'

18

'But I'm a pacifist.'

'Oh. I am just an old man.'

'I mean it, I don't believe in war. There's never a good enough reason for killing people.'

'You had better tell the Serbs.'

'Wars are always in somebody's interest, but never in the interest of the poor suckers who have to fight them. The people who have to die.'

'You have thought much about this.'

'Absolutely. It always works out as kids being sent off to die for the sake of some old men in suits. I can't buy into that.'

'So why do you not go home? Refuse to witness this war. That will be your protest. Do not stay to see it.'

There was silence, and a stalemate, which was only broken by the arrival of the food.

The two men looked at each other as the boy laid out the dishes. The old man shrugged, and the young one rolled his eyes to heaven, and they both smiled.

There was *pilaf*, and a basket of dark crusty bread, and a salad of tomato, cucumber, and onion, and a plate of grilled peppers. Last came a dish of *fergese*, with its strong plain smells of liver and eggs and yoghurt. Charlotte deserved something like this, Robert thought. He should bring her, soon.

Soon? How long would the cafes stay open if there were shortages – and there would be shortages. He had a hunch that this might be his last good meal for a while.

The old man said: 'You have a good appetite, my young friend.'

'For food like this, always.'

'There is no better food in Sarande. You can eat pizza, but pizza is, I don't know.' He waved a hand.

Robert said: 'I know what you mean.'

'And I will always let you rich westerners spend your money on my dinner.'

'You old bastard.' Robert began to laugh.

'Robert Maidens,' the old man said suddenly, even aggressively. 'Will you sit here and drink and eat with me and still deny that you are waiting for this war?'

'You think all young men are fascinated by war?'

'All.'

Robert wiped his sleeve across his mouth, then drank. He cleared his throat. 'Then, yes, I must be as fascinated as the next man. Maybe more so because I'm actually here seeing it happen. So, does that make me a hypocrite because I want to see something that I've had such big opinions about for so long, at first hand?

'Maybe it makes me honest. Maybe it makes me not a coward. A witness, even. But no, I won't try and justify it that way. Maybe I am a hypocrite. Perhaps you're right – what man wouldn't be curious – curious? It's like fascinated.' Robert didn't seem to notice how loud he was talking. People were looking. 'Anyway, so, yes, I'm curious and fascinated. But that doesn't mean I want to jump on a tank and shout Tally-Ho! and head north with the cavalry. I'm curious, but I'm not a psycho! I'm not crazy!'

'I did not say you were,' the old man replied, quietly.

Robert lowered his voice and went on. 'Anyway, it's all hypothetical. There's no war here yet. But say I did want to see what it's like? Could I run away from that? Even if I just saw the start of it. I'm sure I'd always be asking myself what it would have been like.'

The old man shook his head. 'You are an honest man, at least: you make no excuses. You say nothing about right and wrong. And you are also a complicated man. Now, Albanians and Kosovars have little time to be complicated. Maybe people in your country have too much time to think about the wrong things. They should be hungry more.' The old man smiled.

Robert smiled back. 'You probably have a point.' He paused. 'In a way I'm doing what you suggest: I'm simplifying my life. All this trouble may come to nothing, or there may just be some more fighting in the north and that'll be the last of it. But to be here, to soak this up, to *carry a gun*.'

Robert drummed out a roll with his fingers on the stock of the sawn-off which took up the seat beside him. His face now lit into a smile.

'I carry a gun! I could never imagine that before I came here. I'm a different person here. I can do different things!'

'Things you do not believe in.'

'Yes. But I have to experience them.'

'Do you? Really?'

'Well, if I do it's my sin. And I'm not doing anything apart from witnessing – and right now I'm not doing anything but hypothesising about witnessing. None of it matters.'

'You are talking fast today. I do not understand all of your words, but I understand you: you are a man who thinks very much, and very carefully. Now think even more carefully – and quickly.'

The old man left a space between each sentence. 'Your thoughts now are not careful, they are simple.' Space. 'Think about what is brave.' Space, and so on. 'Will you hate yourself more for leaving this place and being a man of peace, or for staying and becoming –'

'Becoming what?'

'Becoming like the men who attacked your home last night! You have to think: if you stay here you will not see the war you think you will see – I can promise you that. You have to understand. You have to look inside and see where the true Robert Maidens wants to stand. Do you want to stand with your beliefs – what is the word?'

'Conscience.'

'Thank you. Or has your conscience changed? Think! Think, my friend! Think with the beer, and think without it! And think with your gun in your hand and then try thinking without that! Think while you sleep and when you wake! Oh, I know I can say these things to you, and you will not be angry. I can see you want to look angry, but you are not. You want to like me and you do like me. You have told too much of the truth to me today to stop and begin lying now.'

The old man leaned forward, gently pushing aside the last of the empty dishes. 'I admire you, Robert Maidens.' He dropped a restrained fist on the table every few words, for emphasis. 'I admire you and I wish you would listen to me and then to yourself and understand something. I am not a – a pacifist? No. I am just an old man and I have seen many fights and I will perhaps see others before I die – why not? – and I do not suffer like you when I think of these things. I do not suffer with the thoughts of the young. But I admire you, and I envy you your suffering because, with this suffering, you are a man, Robert Maidens. Do you hear me? *You are a man.*

'You have nothing left to prove. Your heart is pulling you different ways and you are fighting to find your conscience in all these difficult things –' His voice was shaky but still loud and strong. '– but you are losing your conscience. And if you want the opinion of an old man who has lived his life and now does nothing but eat and drink in good company whenever he can, I will tell you, there is nothing more, nothing more than this struggle, not anything in the mind or in the heart, to being a man. There!'

The two men sat looking into each other's eyes. The old man was in some discomfort as he got his breath back. It was the first time Robert had seen him really shaken. Robert raised his glass and waited. But the old man just continued looking into his eyes and breathing hard.

Robert said: 'I've listened, and I'll think.' And then the two men touched glasses and drank.

Robert surprised himself by sleeping soundly until well after it was light the next morning. The tripwires were silent all night, and for noise there was only the wolves and the cicadas.

The day promised to be hot and still, although, as always, startlingly alive under the painted Adriatic sky. My sky. No, though, it's everybody's sky. Whether you're a 'rich westerner' with too much time to think about what a fine sky it is, or a poor farmer trying not to be hungry, or a Serb, it's just a colour and it doesn't mean the same for everyone.

He wasted the morning lazing on his veranda, watching birds hop from the bushes in and out of his fire lanes. Every so often one, or a pair, would perch in the distance on one of the tripwires, making no sound.

He recalled his promise to the old man to think hard. But he was tired and hung over. Serious thoughts were not welcome. He needed life to be simple for a few hours.

And then it came to him.

Simple.

That was war. That was what he'd needed to say to the old man. That was what men thought they would like about it. In a war only the most simple decisions have to be made. Everything is a yes or no situation – that's what men think.

And much of the time it's just doing as you're told. A man could live with that. Take him away from the world and put him with comrades and give him simple things to think about, simple decisions to make. It might be a delusion – almost certainly was. But even the delusion was a simple one: easy to master.

Easy decisions: to march, to eat, sleep and shit, to say yessir, to kill, to hide, to make camp and move on, not to think, not to judge; to relax and laugh and wind down – and then to burn and wreck almost in the same breath; to be human and inhuman, to slip into terror, to cross the line and back again, to take, to rape, to go too far, to be another thing. And to be *allowed*. All these things were permissible, because a war was simple, and these things were excusable in a war; when you were a soldier all these things were someone else's responsibility.

Could he tell all that to the old man? Of course not. He didn't even need to.

He looked out at his paradise. The Garden of Eden with the fire lanes and the tripwires in the distance and the shotgun scars on the trees. What a time he'd have had as a child in this landscape.

What the fuck was he thinking of now?

He looked out across his land and felt the simple aching in his head, which would pass, and the simple misery in his body, which would slip away unnoticed, as always, at the very moment he thought he was never going to feel human again. He picked up a

12-bore cartridge from the box on the milking stool beside him.

He turned the plastic cylinder over in his fingers, like a big worry bead, or a rosary in a cup.

19

AN ESTIMATED 100,000 refugees hiked over the permanently snow-capped, ominous, ugly, magnificent natural border between Albania and Kosovo known as the Accursed Mountains. Another 50,000 made their way toward the American relief missions in Macedonia.

In northern Albania, German and Italian aid workers wrestled with the task of trying to produce something from nothing; to provide for refugees in a country without stores or resources. Without machinery, building materials, roads and vehicles.

Everything had to be imported, over disintegrating tracks which dipped and cowered through the bandit-ridden hills.

The task of bringing relief was close to impossible. Aid stations were robbed and ransacked by heavily armed mountain clans, who didn't understand any crisis beyond their own *fis* or village, didn't know these refugees or their plight, and saw in their presence only competition for food and space.

The relief workers on the ground described conditions as apocalyptic; the attitudes and level of comprehension among the mountain people as more primitive than anything they had encountered in the most under-developed areas of Africa or Asia. If you lived and breathed, they reported, you had better be armed to the teeth, or your life expectancy was measurable in hours. It was not what the liberal public back home needed to hear.

Robert imagined how hard it would be for people seeing the news and reading the papers to actually believe any of this: that the poorest, most desperate, and backward place on the planet was here in Europe.

Then he realised that none of it was going to make the news back home.

More self-deception. Help the refugees. But they're only refugees because the other bunch aren't. Because this lot lost. But you have to help. It's like fighting: it's what you do.

* * *

The aid workers doggedly persisted and people were, albeit haphazardly, fed and patched up. Their horror stories of life under the Serb crackdown were documented by the Red Cross, and Amnesty International. But the volunteers were fighting two battles: hunger and mass displacement with one hand, armed thugs with the other.

In the worst incident, an aid station was raided by a gang of over fifty, using jeeps ('Where the hell did they get jeeps?') mounted with heavy machine guns. Everything, from tents to shoes, was stolen, everyone – men and women – raped and beaten. The radio described it as like something out of a bad post-nuclear movie.

Inevitably, several charities threatened to pull out unless they were guaranteed increased protection. Tirane acted, and more soldiers were sent to guard the relief effort.

And Milosevic, the arch-opportunist, siezed his chance.

He would later justify his actions by describing the Albanian reinforcements as an expeditionary force sent to soften up JNA border patrols in preparation for a full-scale invasion.

Invasion using what, Robert wondered.

For the present, though, Milosevic didn't bother to explain anything. And on 5 August Yugoslavia invaded Albania.

The JNA did not attempt to cross the Accursed Mountains where, it knew, a few dozen fleet-footed shepherds with ancient .303s could make a good stab at stopping any army in its tracks. Instead it moved through the lowland corridor in the west of the country, down through Montenegro and along the passable Adriatic coast roads.

Robert spread out the map, followed the route with his finger, and nodded. Clever.

The UN, NATO, the EC, did nothing.

There were frantic street demonstrations not only in Tirane, but in Tetovo, Athens, Rome, Bonn, Bern, and Istanbul: anywhere where Albanians had established a community. But no one, it appeared, was moved to do anything more than make promises. The west had failed again. Albania was left to defend itself with an army which had spent the last decade rusting in a field, and a population barely recovered from the last upheaval and hardship, and the one before that, and the one before that.

Jesus, Robert thought: pity these damn people. What would they do? How would they fight?

He thought about Albania's ragged, scared soldiers. When he closed his eyes he could feel the sweat in the stiff boots of the young men, hear the flapping of the tarps on the rusting trucks as they drove to where, they did not know, to fight the Serbs.

He did not have to use his imagination for long.

The World Service told him how, from the very first confrontations, the extent of the decay which had accumulated around the nuts and bolts of the army was clear for all to see. Trucks broke down every few miles; boys and men had to get out and pick up their shabby packs and half-fit weapons, and walk.

Robert imagined them throwing away their army boots and belts and putting on their own which at least didn't chafe the skin and bloat and crack when wet. The officers would look away nervously and ignore these little infractions, and avoid eye contact with the men. The officers did not want to become objects of resentment: didn't want to add to the disproportionate number of officers in all wars in all armies unaccountably shot in the back. How long could they remain in control? How long before the cigarettes ran out and the men got tense? How long can I watch my back?

Communications systems failed and took hours to be rebooted. Officers could not talk with each other. The men talked too much.

Under Hoxha the paranoid, the making of maps had been a serious crime, and now the few maps that could be found were outdated and inaccurate. Not only that, but after half a century of unfamiliarity with the concept, hardly anyone could read them.

Deprived of basic data and expertise, rendezvous were missed, distances hopelessly misjudged, and supply convoys often ended up sitting in a field waiting for the sun and a sign from God.

Once in contact with the enemy, troops often found they had been issued the wrong kind of ammunition.

Try the dock in Sarande, Robert mused.

A few days into the invasion, and still the UN, NATO, and the EC had done nothing. Of course they're doing nothing, Robert told Charlotte. It had taken years for anyone to take even token action in Bosnia; why should things happen any quicker here. It was Bosnia all over again. Just substitute a few names.

Charlotte nodded and padded outside. Robert thought she seemed listless.

Robert stayed by the radio. He was always with the radio.

He listened as the JNA swept aside the defenders, but got bogged down on Albania's crumbling, pockmarked roads. He listened as Albania tried to cobble together some kind of defence of its towns, to fashion something, anything that would slow the Serbs' advance from Shkoder in the north, through Durres and Tirane, all the way down to the south, through Lushnje, and Fier, to Gjirokaster, and finally to within potshot distance of the Greek border, and Sarande.

And Robert Maidens sat waiting on his porch.

'You've got your bag packed.'

Robert stood staring at Charlotte's maroon Karrimor. It was in the middle of the living room floor, and it was indeed unempty.

'It's not packed.'

'You've got your bag packed.'

'It's not *packed*.' She looked at the floor and toed an invisible pattern on the floorboards. 'It's ready.'

'Explain the distinction. Please?'

Quietly: 'Oh, fuck off.'

'Were you going to tell me, or just leave?'

Charlotte shuffled out to the kitchen, made some noise, and wandered back in with a cup of coffee. She didn't have a coffee for him. Her shoulders were drawn in and she didn't lift her eyes.

Robert was still staring at the packed – or ready – bag. 'Of course, I don't own you. You can go anywhere you like, whenever you like. I just thought that – I don't know what I thought.'

'Robert, the question ought to be why aren't you getting ready?'

'Ready for what?'

She gave him an incredulous stare. 'Time's running out, chicky-pie. Haven't you noticed? This is it, decision time. That thinking

I asked you to do? You've had plenty of time to do it. Robert, this doesn't feel like a holiday to me anymore. With the way you're acting it doesn't even feel like much of a life.'

'What's that supposed to mean?'

He took a step forward and Charlotte flinched, spilling drops of coffee. 'God! Look at me, will you? You scare me more than the Serbs do!'

'Yugoslavs, technically.'

'Listen to yourself!' Her whole body was drawn in now and she was holding the cup with both hands. 'Look, that map you're moving pebbles around on and drawing lines on, it's not somewhere halfway round the world, it's up the bloody road, Robert! They're coming here, and I'm scared!'

'They won't go further than Tirane.'

'Oh! Oh, that's all right, then. You *know* that's bullshit!'

'Are you going today?'

'What?'

'You've got a bag packed. Are you going today?'

She paused and took a slow breath, and began again in a reasoning tone. 'Don't push me into something, and don't say anything we'll regret just because you're hurt. Yes, I've got a bag ready, but it can be unpacked, Robert. You know how? Very easily. What you have to do is tell me you want me to stay.' She left a gap, which he didn't fill. 'Do you love me, Robert?'

'I don't love people who bug out when things get a little uncertain.'

'Uncertain? Uncertain!' She was laughing now.

She sidestepped to the table and banged down the cup of coffee, spilling some more, and dropped her face into her hands. 'What have I done? Why do I always do it?' She wrapped her arms around herself and began pacing past the unempty bag as she talked.

'Uncertain. I'm on holiday. Let me get this straight in my head. I'm on fucking holiday! And I've fallen in love with this guy who is going insane and refuses to leave his house when there are tanks trundling down the road intent on doing a little extensive fucking gardening on his fucking doorstep! I'm ON HOLIDAY, Robert! And I don't want to DIE!'

There was a long pause.

'Just give me a couple of days will you? Get off my back!'

'I've given you plenty of time, Robert. Don't snap at me!'

'Are you going to unpack the bag?'

Pause.

'Are you going to ask me to?'

'Give me today. One day. I have to leave in my own time.'

'Just today? I need to know, Robert. This isn't like some Girl Pesters Boy For Commitment sketch here. I won't sink to that. I haven't done it all along and I won't do it now. A lot depends on this. Look around, it's getting serious.'

'All right. Just give me a day. A couple of days.'

'Serious?'

'Serious.'

'Robert?'

'I need to leave properly.'

'Well, how long do you need? I'm sorry, I didn't mean it to sound like that. Look, I don't want to leave here either.' She leaned back and ran her fingertips over his lips and cheeks and forehead. 'Of course I don't want to leave. It's heaven on earth. I'm a different person than when I got here. I feel capable of things now, you know? But all that's being clouded. We have to face facts. I'm relying on you.'

Robert looked deeply into Charlotte's eyes.

'If we leave here there will never be any way to come back. It will all be gone. It will, won't it?'

Charlotte nodded slowly.

'This house is the first thing I've ever owned. The first place I haven't let from some rack-renting vampire. The first place where the rent didn't depend on me chaining myself to whatever shitty, emasculating job I could find. It's mine. *Mine*! And to think I can't protect it is ripping my guts out. To just walk away with my tail between my legs and leave it to be ransacked by these, these fucking savage *cunts*!' He took a deep breath. 'But you're right. I've said it now, it's out, and it feels better. Let me leave properly. Then I'll be with you.'

She looked at him hard. 'That's fine, Robert,' she said. 'That's all fine. You've said what you needed to say, now do what you have to do. Yes? Robert? Don't fuck it up.'

One consequence of the invasion was that you couldn't buy petrol for love nor money. Robert was down to his last tank, and he hadn't told Charlotte, and it worried him.

But he had been making plans.

The night after the showdown over the unempty bag he waited until she was asleep, then he strapped on both guns, and pushed the bike to the end of the dirt driveway. Strapped to the bike was the pair of two-gallon fuel cans and a length of hose.

Once at the road he looked back toward the house, and started the engine.

20

He drove to a secluded property he'd been watching for a couple of days, and siphoned four gallons of fuel from a tractor hidden in the trees. It was ridiculously easy. Robert had been careful to check that the man owned no dogs, and there were no other hazards.

He half staggered, half swaggered back across country with the full cans to where the bike was hidden. Nothing bad happened. No one challenged him in the dark.

And, now he knew that he'd got away with it, Robert wasn't just swaggering, but laughing out loud. Suddenly he stopped and turned to face the house and the vehicles in the distance – but not so very far in the distance that he was out of danger – and strained his face into a snarl.

'Come on,' the words came out, not even whispered. 'Come out, you fuckers. Come out and see what I've done and fucking stop me! Come and do that and try and stop me. I'm ready!' He waited, and nothing happened, and he said again: 'I'm ready. Make me fight for it, motherfucking *fuckers!* Make me *fight!*' Flecks of foam spun off his lips as he spoke to the dark.

He stood a few more moments, then spat noisily, and turned and carried on walking.

It was a minute, no more, before he noticed a glare above his shoulder.

Headlights.

He felt sweat pour between his palms and the handlebars. He didn't know if the headlights belonged to the people he'd robbed coming after him, but he didn't know that they didn't. His stomach turned and his mouth filled with the aluminium taste.

He revved, forcing all the speed he could from the bike. Still the lights gained.

At the places where the road straightened out Robert tried to gauge the distance between him and his pursuers – if they were pursuing him, and he had to assume they were. But every time he turned to squint and measure distance in the black, the bike swerved so much he risked losing control.

Shit, the road was bending again.

He had to be nearly home.

And it dawned on him that he was leading them *straight to his home.*

Which fact was rendered irrelevant with the realisation that if they kept gaining on him at any kind of rate, he wasn't even going to make it that far. Fuck, which was worse? They would ride him down before he got home. They would catch the thief. And then?

Robert risked another glance over his shoulder. He had to make one last effort to get out of this, to cheat the shit he had brought down on himself – yes, he knew that now, that he had brought down on himself. Fucking *fuck.*

When the road straightened out at the next bend he could see that, okay, the light had gained on him a good deal, but that he still had a hundred, hundred and fifty yards' grace. He couldn't lead them back to Charlotte. There was only one thing he could think of to do.

Before he had time to scare himself to death with the idea, Robert flicked off his lights.

For another three hundred yards he continued to make all the speed he could, leaning forward over the handlebars, straining to see the road in the near blackness. If a pothole or a dead dog decided to show its cards about now it would be thank you and goodnight Robert Maidens. Strangely, this realisation helped him relax. At that moment, knowing that you couldn't be held responsible for, and couldn't control absolutely everything, seemed like an important insight. Then, as sudden as one of his rushes of adrenalin, the insight was gone.

When he recognised the shadow of the flat clearing he was looking for, Robert let go an involuntary rebel yell. Rolling off the dirt road to the right, into the grass and scrub which bordered it, he slowed to a stop. He vaulted two-footed from the saddle and ran fifteen yards before skidding onto his belly.

The sawn-off was out of the canvas bag and aimed at the road before he even knew about it.

He'd chosen this side of the road so that the arc of the turning headlights wouldn't pick out the silhouette of the bike on its near side. For a second it seemed to Robert that he had thought of everything. And now he was grinning and talking to himself, saying things like he'd been saying back at the farmhouse, grinding his hips and elbows into the dry ground, waiting for the headlights of his pursuer to catch him up.

The car was long and wide and low, like an American cop show car, and it passed in and out of his vision in a few seconds. It never slowed down. He was safe.

For a few moments, as its dust trail settled, Robert felt almost disappointed. He pursed his lips and blew a thin whistle. Then he shook himself and replayed what he had just seen in the car.

Two men up front and at least two in the back and, even at the speed it passed him, the unmistakable silhouettes of Kalashnikovs.

Robert picked himself up, and slid the sawn-off back in its cloth sack. He swiped half-heartedly at his dusty torso a few times, but all his strength and will to move were suddenly gone. He knew now that the car hadn't – at least initially – been following him. But that hardly mattered: it was a car full of armed men prowling around in the dark. It was not a good sign. He dragged himself back to the bike, mounted, and keyed the ignition. He drove slowly with the lights on, watching the road, prepared to repeat what he'd just done. But all the good adrenalin was gone. His jaw was slack and his arms shaking.

Fifty yards along his dirt drive he stopped the bike and scrambled out of the saddle and vomited.

He locked the bike in the outhouse. He'd find a place to bury the fuel in the morning. Four gallons wasn't much but if it was enough for Robert to steal it was enough for somebody else. But only four gallons a time. There had to be a better way. He'd have to think.

He'd have to think about a lot of things.

He walked a circuit of the house, looking at the ground, and then followed his feet all the way down to the lake. Death was here, he thought. Drowning was one way to die.

Tonight. It had been something. A night like no other. He experienced another flash of what he thought was insight, and this one told him: *this is what my whole life is here.*

I am visited by death and danger and the highs and lows that people in some countries have lost over the centuries, and that I never, ever knew back in my old life. I'm powered by the electric beauty and the exhilaration of the presence of death, the sweetness, the *tangible sweetness of the taste of death in every waking moment.* Death at the edge of life. And cheating it, cheating it was what gave you life, real life, not just existing. Life and power.

In the second that Robert registered the presence of the moment of insight and tried to catch it in his mind, it was gone, and it was forgotten. But something stayed, perhaps like the scar on a burn.

Then, as well as the insight, all the fear was gone. And then Robert was thinking how good everything felt in the aftermath of the fear. And that made him think of other things, and suddenly of Tina. Tina, who'd wanted him the night they'd gone out to see him off, in the restaurant. He tried to picture that night. How long ago was it, three months? Lifetimes.

Remembering the details took effort, so he just tried to picture Tina. In the restaurant, in her good clothes, good-smelling, and then there beside him, naked, delicate, uninitiated into any of this. Innocent as Eve.

He'd show her who had faced death, and who deserved admiration, and she would have to give it to him. He'd show her who was a coil of muscle and nerve, and she'd like it. Of course she'd like it, it was what she'd liked back in the restaurant, the thought of danger. He'd force her or he wouldn't, but she'd get it. He took himself in his hand there by the lake and gritted his teeth. If she was here now she'd get it so fucking hard.

The bedroom smelled of whisky and of vomit. There was an empty bottle by the bed. She must have been terrified waking in the night and finding him gone. Who wouldn't drink?

And now, drunk and nauseous, she didn't need to sleep next to someone who reeked of petrol. She'll understand in the morning, though. We need fuel.

Robert took the pillow from his side of the bed, and his sleeping bag, and left the room, and then the house, and made his bed on the veranda.

He jumped awake. When he saw it was only Charlotte he sighed and laid back down.

She didn't look good. She was leaning in the doorway, dressed in jeans and a T-shirt. She held her revolver limply in her right hand.

Robert said: 'You scared me.'

'I smelled something.'

He sat up. 'That would be the petrol. I managed to spill some.'

'You stink.'

'I know.'

'No. I mean it. You really stink.'

Robert looked up at her face, and down at the gun, and started to say something. But Charlotte turned around and slammed the door behind her, and he closed his eyes and listened to the thumps of her feet mounting the stairs.

He followed her into the house.

She leaned over the banister. 'I see it now,' she said. 'I see it. You see yourself in your combat gear, creeping around, with a two-week beard and a thousand-yard stare. And lots and lots of guns! In your trenches with your toys. But I don't know why. That's as much as I understand. I don't know any more than that.'

She turned away, and Robert made a move to mount the stairs, but she was back, leaning over again.

'Don't come up! Don't come up, soldier boy. I do know. I do understand more. I thought it was the house you wanted to stay with. But you're a liar. It's the bloody war. Don't come up, because you stink!'

Robert didn't move or speak.

'Shit. I'm leaving in the morning. That's all there is to it.'

* * *

It was almost morning, the morning of 14 August. The lake was blanketed under a silky mist and in the forest the trees would soon be limp with dew and midsummer fatigue. By the afternoon it would be so hot that the birds wouldn't stir from the branches and the cicadas would meditate in silence.

'It's going to be a plum day for shooting,' Robert murmured.

'Robert?'

'I heard you.'

'Well?'

'I think I'll make some coffee.' He turned to her where she stood in the doorway, and smiled.

Charlotte looked at him for a long moment, and then said: 'I'll make it. I think I need some too. I won't sleep any more.' She went into the kitchen and returned a few minutes later and handed him a cup at arm's length.

He said: 'Thanks,' and walked out onto the veranda.

Charlotte followed him. She cleared her throat. 'I'm going to Corfu. I'll get a room at the Prasinos. If I can't get one I'll leave a message there for you. I'll stay there a week, until the twenty-first. I'll wait that long, and then I'm going. I don't know where. I'm just going to go. I figure if you haven't come to your senses by then, it's not going to happen. This is messing with my head too much. Robert? Say something, please? This is not just another discussion.' Her voice had that quiet in it. She left a space, then began again. 'I have stopped waiting, Robert. This time when I pack my bag I really am going.' She paused and, when the sky didn't fall in, continued again. 'I'm not going to repeat myself, because it's not a threat, I'm just telling you what's going to happen.

'I want you to put some petrol in my bike – I know you've got some, and I don't want to know where and how you got it – and I'm going to Sarande and then to Corfu, whether you come with me or not. Think about it, Robert.' She put a carrot in her voice. 'Corfu. Corfu is safe, and beautiful. We can do what we like.'

Robert sipped his coffee and stared out across his land. It looked magnificent in the half light.

She said: 'You think about it. I'm going to swim and get clean for the trip, and then I'm leaving. Robert?'

'This isn't what I expected.'

Charlotte's brow creased. 'I warned you. I've given you time. Jesus, you must think a lot of yourself. Just how long did you expect me to sit here waiting for the worst to happen, or for you to make up your twisted mind?'

'I don't mean that.'

'Tell me what you do mean, then.'

Robert sighed. 'I mean the war. I didn't think it would happen this way. I mean, I've *studied* that map.' He shrugged. 'Still.'

Charlotte sighed. She was talking to a child. 'Well, it's happened now. And we have to accept it. And if we stay here even another two days we could be stuck. Please.'

'I thought it would be different,' Robert said. His voice was thin, so that he sounded like someone else. He shook his head and blinked in mild surprise. 'A lot different. But then everything that happens is like that. You think things will be a lot different. You think things are one way, and then they happen another way that just doesn't seem fair. I don't suppose you ever know anything until after it's happened.' He nodded his head at the apparent wisdom of his own words.

Charlotte looked angry, then nervous. 'But it's happened. I don't know what to say to you.' She walked up behind Robert and touched his shoulder, and then moved closer and slowly wrapped her arms around his chest. She kissed the back of his head, then closed her eyes and nuzzled her nose and mouth under his long hair, and kissed his neck. Robert stood still.

'This must be a terrible thing for you to have to accept,' Charlotte whispered. 'But it's time to go. Please think of what we have to do now. This is all gone. Let's go somewhere else and find it again, or something even better. But we have to start by getting to Corfu.'

Robert stepped away from Charlotte as if she were not there and turned and looked into her eyes, and said: 'I don't have to go anywhere.' He spoke the words flatly, like it was a tiny, average discovery. I've found a fiver I didn't know I had; I don't have to go anywhere.

Charlotte took a step back and returned his stare. Then punched him in the gut.

Robert slumped, wheezing, to his knees, just managing to fend off Charlotte's ankle as she aimed a follow-up kick with her right trainer. He hoisted her foot high and she landed on her backside on the wooden deck. Picking herself up she ran sobbing into the house, slamming the porch door behind her.

Robert scooped the plastic cup off the deck and walked, bent double, to the table. He put the cup down next to the sawn-off and thought about making another, but decided he'd better stay out of the house.

The coffee had made an awful mess, though. Look at it, sprayed everywhere. And for what? The cleaning rags were all inside, though, and Robert remembered that he shouldn't go in the house. Why was that again? He grabbed his head and shut his eyes tight.

Then she was back, slamming through the porch door once more, her eyes red with rage and tears. Robert noticed some tresses of hair had slipped from the red towelling tie. That's untidy, he thought. He watched as she marched past him, dragging his empty Berghaus Alp by one of its loose straps. When she reached the veranda rail Charlotte launched the rucksack over it. They watched it land in the dust, twenty feet away.

'Fetch it and fucking FILL it, Robert! We. Are. Fucking. LEAVING!!'

'I don't have to go anywhere,' he said. 'And don't hit me again. You spilt the coffee. Look.'

She actually staggered. It took her a few moments to compose herself, and when she spoke again her voice was hoarse and incredulous.

'Jesus Christ, they'll be spilling your fucking insides a couple of days from now! What is the *matter* with you?' She waved her arms at her sides, trying to give flight to the words. 'You are sick, Robert. *Sick!* You need some kind of medical attention. You're not thinking straight!'

She paused, breathing heavily, scratching her head and pacing. Turning to him again: 'Just let me take you, Robert. Leave everything up to me. You won't have to think. Yes?'

Robert's expression hardly altered.

Charlotte stepped toward him and took his right hand in both of hers, which were trembling. 'I know you love me, Robert.'

Nothing.

'Come *on!* Come out of there! I'm trying to save your bloody life!'

Somewhere in Robert's consciousness it registered that this was a strong girl, and that that was both admirable and sexy. Nothing much else got through, though. And her voice was starting to sound like a gnat.

Charlotte went on: 'I promise you wherever we go it will be just like it was here at the start, because we've changed forever now. Inside ourselves we will always be in the best place in the world! But we have to get out of this place now. And it's just a place. It's nothing more than that. It's not the world, Robert. It's not the world we can make for ourselves. Robert, we have to go to Corfu now!'

Still nothing.

'You told me your sodding self' – loud again, pulling at his fingers now, as if she could drag him out of himself – 'you told me you'd never spent as much as two meaningful bloody weeks with a woman in your life. Well, you've done it now, or are you going to tell me this meant nothing? Well, are you going to tell me that? Are you?'

'No.'

'Right. I know you don't want me to go without you. I know it, Robert! You're just *sick*, that's all! Please let me *help* you?'

Charlotte fell against Robert and tried to hold him. When he failed to respond she pulled away and the tears stopped at once.

Robert's expression hadn't changed in five minutes.

Charlotte wiped her eyes, then slowly shook her head. She said: 'You've really gone, haven't you?'

'What's that, chuck?'

She was almost whispering. 'You've gone far away. It's not my fault, now. I can't do anything else.' She sighed with fatigue, and even relief, and glanced around her as if looking for something. 'I've got to go,' she whispered. 'I've got to go.'

'You're right,' Robert said.

'What?' Her face froze with hope.

'I said you're right. I have got some petrol. And you can have some.'

Charlotte screamed suddenly, a long scream that didn't show any sign of stopping soon, and Robert suddenly screamed back and slapped her face hard, knocking her sideways and to her knees. He turned and started to march toward the steps but she grabbed him from behind, and he spun around, trying to shake her off.

Grabbing his T-shirt, she cried: 'For God's sake! Wake up! Wake fucking up!'

He grabbed her wrists and pushed, slipping in the pool of spilt coffee, and landing painfully against the table. Wheeling around he grabbed the sawn-off and slammed the barrel against Charlotte's face.

She collapsed without a sound on the wooden deck.

Robert leaned over her where she lay on her front. 'Charlotte?'

As soon as he lowered the sawn-off, she rolled fast to her left, whipping the pistol from the rear waistband of her jeans. A second later she was lying face up and pointing the weapon at Robert's groin.

Robert hissed, 'Jesus!' and swung the sawn-off back up until it was level with the girl's head. His eyes widened, just a little, and he took a step back from where she lay.

She cocked the hammer on the revolver and got slowly to her feet, still aiming between his legs.

They stood there like that, a tableau, for a good thirty seconds: Charlotte panting and bleeding hard, Robert staring and saying: 'Jesus!' over and over. Eventually he said, quietly: 'Please stop pointing that pistol at my balls.'

She raised her aim to his head.

'Thank you.'

Another thirty seconds passed. Occasionally Charlotte made a sound somewhere between a groan and a sob.

Thirty seconds more and she said: 'I'm going. I can't wait till it's light. I'm going to walk to the porch door and inside, and finish packing a couple of things. When I come out again I expect the bike to be filled up with petrol. I want my Nike baseball cap back, because without it the sun will get in my eyes.' She paused and spat out blood. 'Shit! And then I want you to walk down by the lake and out of the way. And I want you to leave that gun here on the table where I can see it. I want you to stay by the lake until you hear me drive away.'

'Uncock the pistol.'

'When you agree to do what I said.'

'No problem. The pistol now? It's not safe. It's damn near a hair trigger.'

She reset the hammer, but kept the gun pointing at Robert's head. 'Now put down the shotgun.'

'That's a little unfair, don't you think?'

'Put down the shotgun.'

'Not first. Not when you're acting crazy.'

Charlotte laughed long and loud. 'I'm not the crazy one here, Robert!' She raised her left hand to her swollen cheek and touched the skin and looked at the blood on her fingertips. 'Shit. You've deformed me, you fuckwit!'

'It's just swelling and a small cut. You'll still look lovely.'

'And my mouth.'

'Yeah, that'll hurt for a while. Avoid eating salty things or it'll sting. And take Ibuprofen rather than Paracetamol. That'll help the swelling. Some ice would help, but that's a non-starter, obviously. I'm going to put the shotgun down now.'

'Good.' She laughed again. Everything seemed funny.

'There.' He raised his hands, like in a western.

'You can put your hands down. But apart from that, don't move. Don't you dare move until I say you can. Shit! This isn't happening! Turn around.'

Robert descended the steps, apparently unpanicked. At the

bottom he stopped and looked up. His brow was furrowed with the effort of some great thought.

Then he turned away again and, true to his word, walked all the way to the lake.

21

THEY MOVED FIRST in small groups, which soon joined together to create a massive moving thing: a flow of blood. Or what international agencies would call, from a safe distance, a Significant Problem. And day by day The Problem grew more Significant. And perhaps when it graduated from Significant to Desperate, something more than a few prefab huts and soup lines might be done for the people. Don't hold your breath, says Robert, out loud, to no one.

Don't hold your breath.

The refugees were not only the Kosovars now, but Albanians fleeing towns and villages taken by the advancing JNA. The World Service was there for all of it. The refugees listed for the reporters the names of relatives they had seen robbed, beaten, or summarily executed, or who had simply disappeared in the chaos of the fighting. The newspaper men and women got great pictures. Radio journalists reported it all. From their mouths to the ears of Robert Maidens.

You could get tired of hearing about the refugees.

When he drove out on his bike to the edge of his land, as he did several times a day now, he could see them, bands of women and children and the old, huddled on horse-drawn carts, or simply walking, south toward the Greek border. And he could see groups of armed men moving north from the villages south of Sarande.

Near to Sarande he drove out to where two buses from Shkoder had skidded off the coast road and down a steep cliff face to the rocks below. The buses had contained children orphaned by the fighting.

The World Service said accidents like this were happening all the time on Albania's notorious rocky roads and tracks, even to JNA tanks and APCs. It was, said the chief war correspondent, the main reason the JNA's push south was taking so long. Roads so bad you couldn't tell which had been shelled by mortars and which just always looked that way.

The real flood of refugees hadn't arrived this far south yet. Although, Robert guessed, it would come soon enough. But he couldn't really picture it. What would a human flood look like? Not something you wanted on your doorstep, anyway.

He wondered if people might take the better road east through Delvine: the Xarre-Cuke road wasn't much better than a wide dirt track which would become broken up and impassable with every snake of people trampling over it.

If the few military vehicles left were pushed back this far they would ruin the surface completely, and Robert Maidens would be stranded. And the last straw would be rain. Rain would turn the road into a river.

The Greek embassy in Tirane was besieged by Greek nationals, and Albanians with ex-patriot relatives, all seeking visas, although how they thought they would get to Greece was another matter. Maybe they just thought that papers might protect them, either now or when it was all over, and the UN was in control. The UN will come, they told the reporters.

The embassy which the British shared with the French in the capital had become a virtual bunker for any EC nationals who could find their way to it: you didn't have to be French or British. The British consulates in Gjirokaster and Kosca, as the World Service pointed out, had closed down a few months previously, as had the one in Sarande.

Robert hadn't known this.

22

'AH, ROBERT MAIDENS. How is the hotel business?'

Robert laid the sawn-off on the table, then thought again, and moved it to a chair. He sat down. 'Business is quiet,' he said. 'But it could boom at any time. Boom. Geddit?'

'Please?'

Robert shook his head. 'Never mind.'

So, among all the chaos in the town the cafe was still managing to function, for the moment. Robert scraped his chair along the ground until he was comfortable, and looked around for Safet. He wondered if there was any more beer. It seemed unlikely. Petrol and booze, the first things to run out or become gangsterised.

Then Safet appeared with two open labelless bottles and a glass for Robert. He said something Robert didn't catch, and poured the drinks himself. 'Thank you,' Robert said in English, and for the first time saw the proprietor's face register the beginnings of a smile.

'Safet says this is the last crate of beer. There will be no more.'

'Please thank him for all his hospitality. He's made me feel very welcome.'

'I have thanked him. But there are more important things than beer for you to think about now.'

'Name six.'

The old man ignored him. 'There is plenty of beer in Corfu. And plenty in England. Go there. Go there before you cannot.' There was a silence. 'There. I have said it once and it will be the last time. Now, let us drink and be friends.'

Robert smiled. 'Thank you.'

They drank.

'You have seen the people on the road?'

Robert nodded and swallowed. 'Yeah. Will you go to Greece?'

The old man waved away the suggestion.

Robert nodded again, and there was another silence. He was

glad the old man would not be leaving. He didn't want to think about him on the road with the refugees.

'I have heard people will kill for a tank of petrol. Soon they will kill for food. A foreigner they will kill for fun, believe me.'

Robert cleared his throat and shifted in his seat. 'I can defend my home.'

'Do you know what that means?'

'I'm starting to. I don't mean to run out of food and fuel.'

The old man's eyes narrowed and then opened wide. He shook his head. 'Yes, you are learning. Perhaps you will not die here.'

'You don't think what I've done is wrong?'

'The only thing you are doing wrong is to stay in this place.' He shrugged and sighed. 'But you are determined to stay here, and when I was a young man I did many stupid things, things I was determined to do, and I have lived to be an old fool who knows nothing.' He chuckled. 'So maybe you will do okay.'

They touched glasses and drank. Robert nodded to one of the boys, who then slipped inside the cafe.

'I will miss your company, Robert Maidens,' the old man began again. 'I have enjoyed talking with you more than anything I have done in a long time – it is not often anyone has time to talk to an old man. Yes, it is good to talk with people from other places. To imagine the world outside the place where you live.'

'Hey, hey, don't start saying goodbye just yet.'

'But it is goodbye. I do not know how the roadblocks let you by today. A foreigner came through two days ago and left for Corfu. We thought all the foreigners had gone. She was a young woman. The police were so amazed to see her here, they did not even try to take her money.'

Robert clenched his fists and leaned across the table. 'She got away?'

'Yes. On the boat.'

'She was okay?'

'Yes, Robert.' The old man smiled. 'She was quite well. You have too many secrets, Robert Maidens. And I will not ask about them. But I can promise you that a young foreign woman left here safely on the boat for Corfu. She came on a motorcycle, from the direction of Butrint, the police said.' He paused again, and watched Robert relax, then said: 'I hope it is true what you said about having plenty of food and fuel.'

'Enough for a siege.'

'And I hope the roadblocks let you go home. Things will change in the next few days. The police and the soldiers will become the most dangerous people here – if they do not run away and hide. Either is possible.'

'I can handle them all right.'

The old man looked at the table. 'I see.'

'The Serbs will never come this far south.'

'You are the only one who is so sure.'

'The Americans will come in, or NATO. They'll have to protect people like me.'

'Now I know you are being stupid.'

The boy brought two bottles and Robert signalled to him not to pour them.

'Okay, so screw the Americans. But this war won't last forever and when it's over I want to be here holding on to my land and my house and start running my hotel. I want to be here, sitting in this cafe with you.' Robert blushed and began pouring the drinks.

'And tell me,' the old man said. 'Will you carry a gun after the war is over?'

Robert put down the bottle he was holding and didn't move or speak for a while. When he moved it was to draw patterns in the sweat on the side of his glass. He sighed. 'I see what you mean.'

The old man spoke quietly. 'This war will not last – you are right. But neither will this country as you know it, not now. But the rest of the world will be here when it is over. The same world that was here before it started. The same world you say you ran away from in England, and that you say you want to stay here to defend. Do you think you have stopped running away from things now? Is that it? Do you think that to stubbornly shove your face before a gun, or a gun in someone's face, is to stop running? Or are you saying something else? Or have you just turned stupid?'

'You're right. You can't find what you're looking for in a place.

You're the second person who's said that to me recently. But about the other stuff, I don't know yet.'

'And it is for you to think about and to decide. And you do not have to tell me.'

A thought occurred to Robert. 'What's your name?'

'What?'

'Your name? You've never told me, and I thought it would be rude to ask. You may be right, we may not meet again – for a long time. I'd like to know your name.'

The old man smiled. 'There was a story from the Bible I remember from when I was a child, when the Bible was still allowed, before Hoxha. A story about how the people did not give their names out to just anybody, because they believed that when someone knew your name it gave them power over you. That story always stayed with me. My name is Harry.'

Robert smiled. 'Harry. It's good to know you, Harry.'

'And it is very good to know you, Robert.'

'Cheers.'

'Chin chin.'

Robert laughed again. 'But what's your Albanian name?'

'Oh. You would not be able to say it.'

'I could learn.'

Harry closed his eyes. 'No.'

'I see. You're probably right.'

23

THE ROADBLOCK WAS across the mouth of the Cuke road.

It was at this same roadblock – possibly even by the same soldiers – that he'd been waved through into Sarande that morning, once he'd promised he was on his way to board a boat for Corfu. Robert wondered what story he could give for going in the opposite direction now.

He took a good look around.

No police, just plenty of regular army. That was good: a police presence could mean an extortion attempt, and a delay. And a delay at a checkpoint, and in this atmosphere, could lead in all kinds of bad directions.

He knew the procedure with the soldiers by now: a couple of nervous boys would glance at his passport, ogle his bike and the sawn-off, then whistle over Corporal Hassled, who was just as young as them, but who could at least get by in English.

His speech would translate along the lines of: *get your arse back to Corfu while you can, you dumb foreign bastard – like I care this much. But it's my job to tell you what's what. Now fuck off.* And Robert would nod his head and thank the corporal, sir, and say that was exactly what he intended to do, sir. And he'd salute the corporal as he drove off, thinking: Jesus, those kids should be playing basketball or blagging Radiohead bootlegs.

Forget it, you're looking out for yourself now. Yourself, and your home.

Am I still sticking to that story? Oh, Bobby boy, you pick your times to question your existence, you really do.

At first glance the scene at the roadblock hadn't changed since the morning. There were the same two shabby Nissen huts: one for communications, the other a whistlestop medical centre where refugees could be patched up on the hop. There were long queues outside both prefabs. But Robert noticed one difference.

Since morning a large patch of mud had appeared around the two huts. It hadn't rained more than a pint in weeks, and there was no piped supply anywhere that Robert could see. The medical hut would only have a small tank.

He didn't care where a patch of mud came from but seeing it made him uneasy. It felt like a warning. Robert decided to trust his instincts, and he slowed behind a huddle of families clutching their papers for inspection, and killed the engine.

Taking stock, there were maybe two dozen soldiers clustered in threes and fours, scattered around the checkpoint. To a man they looked worn out, and sick to their guts of the whole cabaret. A group at the mouth of the road – there was no physical barrier at the checkpoint – appeared to be picking on anyone not sufficiently visibly traumatised, or not coated head to foot in ubiquitous death-grey road dust. Away to Robert's left two uniformed boys were half-dragging, half-carrying a weeping heavy-set woman in a stiff headscarf toward the queue for the medical hut. She walked spastically, her head lolling and jerking as she attempted to marshal some rhythm into her legs. Robert watched the soldiers deposit her at the back of the line and walk away. Almost as soon as they had gone the woman scuttled off at surprising speed to rejoin the snake of people following the road south. The two soldiers turned and shook their heads. Some of their comrades laughed.

Robert strained to see among the crowd, but couldn't make out if there was anyone waiting for the old woman. Family? Shit, she couldn't be on the road alone? He swallowed a lump, and looked down at the ground. This was not what he had stayed to see.

Robert didn't know who to pity more: the refugees, or the troops. The soldiers looked as lost and hopeless as the lines of people they were herding – at least the refugees had an objective – and in a few days they would all be prisoners, or worse.

Robert felt the warning twinge again. He knew now that he wasn't imagining anything. It was something about the gait of the soldiers. They seemed more jumpy than they had that morning.

Shit, that could be it. Had he happened along here at the wrong time, just as the boys with dangerous toys were overdue to let off some steam? It was as likely as anything else. It was late in the afternoon and getting chilly, and they all wanted to get back to camp and let the night shift take over and good fucking luck to them.

Which was when three of the soldiers saw our Robert.

He felt the stares and keyed the ignition but didn't go anywhere for the moment. He was waiting to see what they did. He was forty yards from the circle of mud which marked the boundary of the military presence. His engine drummed over, ready.

The three uniforms conferred, and one waved him toward them as a second – here it was – raised his rifle to cover the bike as he rode in.

A weapon had been raised. Instantly something in Robert's gut said: no, it's one more bad sign. And if I let these boys stop me it will end somewhere bad, and I will not ride away from here.

The boy waved again, more impatiently, and the one pointing the gun shouted something. Robert spat, and revved the engine hard, and moved off to his left. Nothing happened, no warning shots or shouts. He carried on circling around to the soldiers' right and, just as all three raised their weapons together, he held up a hand, palm outward, and made a U-turn toward them at a steady, unthreatening ten. Two of the boys lowered their rifles and stepped forward.

Then at twenty-five yards off, Robert gunned his engine, spreading a peacock fan of grey mud behind him. At fifteen yards he was standing out of the saddle spraying up a mud shower and aiming the sawn-off in the soldiers' faces.

Robert heard a scream and saw three rifles clatter to the ground as the soldiers ducked to their knees, covering their faces. But then the bike was struggling in the mud, the tyres threatening to slip in the wet.

He held it steady.

Five seconds more, no shots fired, and Robert was approaching the refugees who had passed through the roadblock and been okayed to move on.

Six seconds. Robert swerved straight into the line of people. Arms grabbed children, and feet scrambled out of his way and into the roadside scrub. By the time his temporary human shield had scattered, Robert was out of range of anyone but a marksman, and the shots he heard behind him swung high and wide into the trees.

Ten seconds, twelve. Robert slowed to about twenty-eight, laughing hysterically into the rush of air and dust. Let them follow him. He was invincible. He'd beaten the army now. Nothing was going to touch him. He laughed again and let go a rebel yell. It was the best he'd felt in days. *No, that's just the way you live here: it's the best I've felt in my life. Forget everything else: all there is is every desperate second. I've won again.*

There would be another, smaller, roadblock coming into Cuke, but fuck them, too. He wouldn't even stop. They'd get the sawn-off in their faces and see how they liked it. Whatever. Fuck them.

Robert Maidens rode toward home feeling fine fine fine.

He lay on his back in the hollow he'd cleared among the stones and scrub, hands behind his head, chewing a stalk of fresh grass. The sky was dim with the first signals of dark, and you could look straight up without squinting. Robert lay watching the changing shapes above him, enjoying the hypnotic growl of distant shelling.

One more hour, he said to himself. One more hour. Nobody heard. Robert closed his eyes.

The bike was hidden under a green tarp and covered in weeds, two hundred yards away. Two hundred yards in the other direction was a white and red house with two working Chinese tractors. The vehicles were well concealed amongst the trees, or the army would have taken them, but Robert was learning about where things were hidden.

He'd started early and stashed the bike while it was still light, because driving after dark wasn't clever any more. He still had to get back, of course. And he was a good way south here, past Ksamil and almost into Xarre. He'd searched in vain for vehicles to hijack nearer his house.

He wasn't happy. The road at night would be clear of refugees, but it was still a long way. He remembered the last time.

No point in worrying.

Robert's eyes locked shut and he drifted into a good sleep, the far-away booming of the shells wrapping his dreams in a lullaby of flapping bedsheets. He drifted with the music of high explosives, and the hour passed, and then another.

When the cold eventually shivered him awake it took him a moment to recognise the explosions for what they were. Had they moved closer?

He sucked a deep breath in through his nose, and roused himself. It was a while after he'd planned to start, but what the hell. He stretched and yawned, and the dark spreading out around him did not feel threatening or dangerous. Not when you were invincible. He stamped his feet and shook his head and tried to connect with the danger in what he was about to do: he needed an edge in his thoughts, not this complacency. Think sense.

Think.

Suddenly he clutched his head and groaned, and screwed up his face. It was just a stray thought, but it clubbed like a migraine: the thought being the sudden urge to leave and to be with Charlotte in Corfu. But the idea and the picture couldn't get a footing and all it did was stab at his temple and Robert was back alone in a field in the middle of the night in a country at war and without a friend. He tried picturing Charlotte again, but the image of all that good feeling was just an ache. He couldn't see her in the future any more.

Robert rubbed his face and took several deep breaths and looked away toward the house and the tractors.

Now he was into the doubt phase, the low, when your fingers shook and wouldn't hold anything, and you fretted about what could go wrong. When you felt anything but invincible. The real adrenalin high only came afterwards. He didn't know how long expeditions like this would remain practical. They played bad games with your head, on top of which, the return for all that stress was lousy. He needed to get two full cans every trip or, what with the fuel he used getting there and back, it would hardly be worthwhile.

Robert walked in the near black until he saw the shadow of the house.

He didn't see a light.

That could be good or bad, but he'd rather have seen a light and been able to place the people in the house. But of course they wouldn't be putting lights on. Even with the area a no-fly zone, there would be a blackout or at least a blackout mentality. Or maybe it was yet another power cut – if they had power, that is.

This didn't feel good. There were too many uncertainties. He could always give up and go home – and have made a wasted trip, and used up precious fuel for nothing.

He picked the tractor furthest from the shell of the house, then felt prickly about it. Maybe the other tractor. But that was more visible from the house. It was only then that Robert noticed there wasn't a simple escape route from either: no trees or bushes for cover once you were ten yards from the vehicle. In fact, all the cover was near the house.

What an idiot. He thought he'd planned this properly.

In the end he went with his first choice. He laid out the gear and went to work. The fuel cap was too tight and wouldn't give. Shit, in this country of amateur mechanical wizards, he had to stiff the one bunch of gyppos who hadn't heard of rust.

He tugged harder. Nothing. He took a real vice grip and twisted hard, then lost hold when it came off too easily and the metal disc cymballed to the pebbly ground. Making a grab to pick it up, Robert collided with the fuel cans, banging them against the tractor backboard.

'*Shit shit shit!*'

He looked up at the house and listened intently over the sound of his breathing.

He gave it a minute.

Everything seemed the same. He went to work again and, once the petrol started flowing, managed to calm down. He was holding back an acid sickness in his stomach now. The first can was half full when he thought he heard a sound.

A growl.

Robert wheeled around and fell on his backside, skidding up stones. There were sounds in the trees to the left of the house and, disappearing back into the cover, two pairs of eyes near ground level.

How could he see the eyes? Where was the light coming from that had illuminated the eyes of the dogs?

When the can overflowed onto his knee Robert whipped away the tube. Then he dropped everything and grabbed the sawn-off. How far away were the eyes? Maybe fifty yards. Out of sawn-off range. He scrambled to his knees.

But what about those eyes?

A flash of realisation spun him 180°.

He stared into the dip in the ground behind him – the one he'd used to shield his approach. It stretched away for several dozen yards and, dark as the night sky was, he would still be showing a silhouette. That was all they needed, and that was how he could see their eyes: he was – albeit only by the moon – backlit.

Robert moved a few feet from the tractor and raised the shotgun in front of him, which seemed to be the signal for more dog sounds, and for the unmistakable sounds of the voices of men.

He could only be calm. There was nothing else. Thinking that way seemed to slow time down to a controllable speed, and Robert could almost imagine he heard music. Then time was back and it wasn't music it was dogs and he could hear them perfectly, and distinct from each other. One was much bigger, covering several yards in single leaps. The second was smaller, panting, growling, scuffling at stones.

The bigger dog barked. Thank you, you dumb fucking animal. One undisciplined sound and Robert could see its approach in his mind: twenty-five yards, twenty. You big bastard. You beauty.

He saw an outline then, and his imagination filled in the gaps to create something like a Doberman. And at fifteen yards Robert aimed, blinked, and fired at the lean black shape.

Straight away he knew he'd shot a fraction too soon and to the right, and he braced himself to have to fire again. But there was a howl and the scraping of the animal changing direction in the dirt – it was running away! Its next yelp came from thirty yards off, and Robert hissed: *Yes!*

Then the second dog betrayed its position by barking at the first, and Robert could see the smaller animal.

Something in his stomach jerked and twisted.

He'd pictured it about right, as something near to a pit bull. This dog wouldn't turn tail if he stung it at fifteen yards. This dog would kill him.

Robert joined his eyes with the beast's. He heard the rhythm of its growling breath and the clawing up of pebbles, but then his fear lifted off him and hung just above him in the air. The dog was barely running, just trotting, absolutely confident. But Robert was confident, too. He watched the green darts roll closer – watched them, smiling – and lowered the weapon. At twenty yards he could almost hold its gaze, and feel the rage that provoked in the animal.

At ten yards he felt the rush of his fear lifting again, and they were the same animal. There was no gulf of strength or of will between them. At six, Robert levelled his eye along the short barrels and strung it to the green beads, and fired.

This time he didn't blink, so that the flash blinded him. He waited, expecting teeth on his throat. But there was only a skidding sound and then silence.

When Robert could see again, the dog's eyes had blinked off. Squinting, he made out the animal's body jerking in the dust and weeds, but no head.

Robert heard sharp laughter coming from his own throat, laughter that sounded like someone else's. He snapped the barrel and reloaded with shells from his pocket, his hands shaking, his voice still cackling outside of himself, and ran stooping to where the thing lay, and blew its hind legs to jam.

Two shotgun blasts ripped the skin off the ground where Robert had crouched to shoot the first dog. Dirt and pebbles and sparks jumped up around the petrol tank, and Robert ran crouching in what he hoped was the right direction.

Then another shot, and a stray spark too many, and Robert felt himself lifted on warm air, and then laid down, almost gently, ten feet from where he'd been running. Something landed smoking beside him and then he was rolling but not gently any more, and he turned to see the wide puddle of fire on the ground around the burning tractor. His eyes lit up with the flames and for a tenth of a second he had six senses, and he could see in infra-red and hear everything as if through headphones. He could hear the staccato yelps of the wounded dog and the footsteps of the men and the rumble of the fire like a high wind. He got to his feet.

His right sleeve was on fire, and he dropped down and rubbed it in the dust. He wasn't panicking. It wasn't a long way to the bike, he'd be okay.

He turned and ran fifty yards, head down, somehow managing to keep his feet as pebbles rolled themselves under his boots and small rocks moved to block his way. Then suddenly he stopped. He was almost away.

The fire was far behind him. But Robert trotted back toward it, and crouched behind the remains of an old stone trough. He could be away and safe in three minutes if he kept moving. But he sat behind the stones and waited, and pretty soon he heard the two men.

He fired and two shapes dived to the ground. A few seconds later two shotguns boomed and grapeshot rattled off Robert's hiding place. Robert laughed out loud and was off running again, this time toward the bike.

Another fifty yards and he skidded into a hollow in the ground the size and shape of a shallow grave. He threw himself flat and waited until his pursuers were thirty yards off.

Robert fired twice and the men dived in the dirt and one cried out as if stung. Robert was up and off again before the bushes around the hollow where he'd lain were massacred by four shells exploding in the dirt.

He gave them one more shot at him before he hit out to find the bike. It was closer than the others, and it scared him and stopped him laughing. The one he'd hit had managed to circle around to his left side. One more round of the game and they'd win.

Now Robert just ran. For a second he saw Charlotte in his mind again, clearly this time and without the jabbing pain.

The men would have been well over a hundred yards off, stalking his shadow in the dark, when they heard his engine start.

24

ON THE MORNING of 19 August Robert Maidens opened his eyes and came to his senses. It didn't take him long to realise just how narrow his escape had been, and to be seized by a degree of shock that he couldn't wash away with whisky. But more worrying than that had been his willingness – no, his determination – once the shooting started, to put himself in as much danger as possible. Charlotte was right. He wasn't thinking straight.

Well, all he could do was seize the opportunity now that he was acting rationally – because there was no guarantee it would last – to get his unstable backside out of here before he flipped again.

It hadn't been him out there in that field.

No, it had: that was the problem. It was a version of him. And it could come back.

It was enough. He knew he had to get out. He had to leave the country today.

During the night the World Service had announced the fall of Fier.

Fier was barely seventy miles from Sarande as the crow flies, maybe a hundred by road. It was the last substantially garrisoned town. Nothing else was left after Fier. The World Service spoke of this as the end.

As he listened Robert experienced a sensation like floating above his body, watching the changes in himself as they happened, as the calm and the reason resumed control. He saw his two selves merge, and he was happy with that. He would need both of them, working together, to get out of here.

The sombre reports painted curious, moving pictures. Images of Albanian soldiers watching impotently, weeping as the JNA tanks rolled through the old town. Fier had fallen, said the anchor, in his best tone of frustration and irony, not because the defenders had surrendered or been defeated, but because they had simply run out of ammunition.

But that's good, thought Robert. That's good, because they didn't have to fight.

There were poignant descriptions of bewildered JNA troops openly acknowledging that the Albanians' ill fortune, rather than their own military prowess, was the source of their victory. In some parts of the town the invaders seemed almost ashamed of how they had come to be there, and unsure as to whether to bother disarming the defenders. There appeared to be a strange bond between the victors and the vanquished, an understanding peculiar to soldiers. The Albanians were numb, the Serbs awed and subdued. Perhaps, said the correspondent, perhaps someone is at last beginning to wonder what we are all doing here.

Robert sat upright on the grey blanket and rubbed his eyes. He had slept on his porch – as he had every night since Charlotte left – absorbing the news as it broke, blacking into sleep when he could no longer focus his conclusions, convulsing awake just before the headless thing leapt at his throat. Now he was very awake.

The World Service recapped it all: the siege of Tirane; the outflanking movement by the JNA; the isolation of the capital; the final push south to consolidate the gains in the rest of the country.

Sarande would be next. Gjirokaster, although protected by the mountains, would only take a little longer.

The radio news was assessing the implications for Yugoslavia, for Albania, for the region, for the UN and NATO, for Uncle Tom Cobleigh.

Robert switched it off.

Enough.

It wasn't the dreams, and it wasn't even the invasion. It wasn't gun battles with strangers and being attacked by dogs.

Enough.

He had allowed something to take over from his reasoning self.

Charlotte had been dead right.

Charlotte.

But Charlotte was still within reach: she'd said she would stay at the Prasinos until the 21st. He had treated her badly – God, that's an understatement. He remembered exactly how badly, now. He dropped his head in his hands and cringed and rubbed his eyes. But she had offered him a chance. He had two days.

He could conceivably be there by this evening. The radio had mentioned a flotilla of small craft making the crossing between Sarande and Corfu, called it a miniature Dunkirk.

Yes, he would get on a boat if he had to jump off the dock and swim to it. It would be a tricky journey to Sarande, but even if he had to surrender to the soldiers at the roadblock at Cuke – if they hadn't abandoned it by now – that would be enough. They would have to deport him as a matter of urgency by the quickest possible route, and that would mean across the water to Corfu.

Thinking straight felt wonderful. Complicated thoughts did not hurt his temples. The opposite: thinking soothed; thinking flowed. The dead dog in his dreams was just a dead dog, and there was no need now for anyone to be shooting at him. He was no longer a man with a gun, but just a stranded tourist. This was no longer his house or his land and it did not matter. It was anyone's to take and he wasn't going to try and stop them. He didn't want to fight anyone.

I have said things about war, and believed things, and I have acted a different way. I must put that behind me. I'm not a savage. I am part-savage but then we all are and we have to know it but then control it. It's such a simple thing. I should have thought that way all along.

Robert closed his eyes and pictured the reunion with Charlotte, the initial anger and distrust in her face replaced by relief and joy as she pulled him to her and held him. Then he could feel her pushing him away and her fists pummelling him as she told him how part of her had spent the last week loathing the memory of him. But now he was here and they could survive anything because they had already been through the worst things people like them should have to imagine.

I'll carry the smell of burned skin and hair, and gunpowder, with me forever. And I have earned that: earned the good and the bad of it. And, Ray, will I have some stories to tell?

Suddenly the stories themselves seemed to justify everything, and to be enough to get him home. The stories would be his scars and his medals. The stories would wipe away his shame at leaving his paradise.

He got up from the porch, still wearing the petrol-stained gear, and drank water. He stepped down from the veranda and checked the bike which, although it had taken some punishment, seemed as good – or as bad – as ever. At worst it only had to get him to the Cuke roadblock.

He swigged down some more water, then jogged down to the shore of the lake, stripped, and waded in for the last time. As the rainbows filmed the brown water, he wondered what he'd think of from now on whenever he smelled petrol.

Then one last submersion in the dark water, one last chill deafness, surfacing back into the air and spitting a cold fountain from his mouth, and shaking his whips of hair.

He left the petrol-ruined Levi's jeans and jacket on the shore and walked naked, CAT boots in hand, back toward his house. Halfway there he dropped the boots as well.

Then, at the foot of the veranda, he froze.

It was distant, but clear. Artillery. But not like yesterday.

Everything heard it: him and the house and the trees, and for a moment his world fell silent. No birds, no cicadas. No wind in the treetops. Silence – *baboom!* – then silence. Then again. *Baboom!*

They were coming.

How the hell could they be this close?

Does it change anything?

No!

Yesterday the guns had been so far away as to sound almost comforting, a pillow of sound. Now the sounds were more distinct, and harsh, and terrifying. Was the radio news lagging behind? Were the Serbs closer than it had said? Jesus, there wasn't much margin for error. Robert ran up the steps to his house.

He dressed quickly in the clothes he'd arrived in: lightweight trousers, long-sleeve Timberland T-shirt, purple-blue Berghaus fleece, Gore-tex AKUs. There would be no mistaking him for anything but a tourist. He looked in the mirror, glanced around the room, patted his pockets. Passport, visa, wallet, cash – Greek,

American, Albanian, Sterling – fished out from his floorboard stash. Swiss Army knife. Bottle of water in the daysack.

He'd leave everything else. It wasn't that he didn't imagine luggage would be allowed on the boat, or that he wanted to travel light, or even that the more stuff he carried the more time it would take should the kids with popguns decide to search him. It wasn't any of those things. He just didn't want this stuff any more. He had what he had in his head, and everything else was replaceable. He felt calm.

All he needed now, he thought, was a good Al Capone scar – a wound sustained in battle. Well, he hadn't been far off. He laughed out loud at his own bullshit. A scar, for Christ's sake.

He tried but failed to drag himself from the house without a final tour. Just one last look at his half-finished dream of escape. But he felt no bitterness or renewed fear. The only small, whispering terror was the knowledge of the thing he'd been close to becoming. Robert shuddered.

Yes, he'd come to his senses. He was Robert Maidens, Londoner, standard issue backpacker. Dressed like a geek and going home. He walked, past the new paint job on the walls, the chairs and tables and drawers he'd sanded and stained, the mirror he'd hung, the beds he'd planned to prepare for guests. Down the stairs he'd partly rebuilt, past the two guns on the porch. He didn't see himself in any of it.

He turned away from the unlocked house, no longer his, and walked to the bike. He was carrying just the daysack and a bottle of Cutty Sark. He opened the whisky and took a long swig, which became a deep, rhythmic draught. When he took the bottle from his lips he was gasping, and he smiled to see he'd drained almost a third of its contents. It felt good, and he half-moaned, half-sighed. He stood looking into the gold liquid in the bottle for a moment before tipping it, all that was left, into the dust at his feet.

25

THE BIKE FELT strangely light and manoeuvrable. It took a minute to sink in that it was because he wasn't carrying the guns. It gave him a feeling of freedom, as though shackles had been removed. Robert opened up the ancient engine.

The retreating hills and trees and houses pushed him on his way toward the port. His body felt as light and mobile as the machine. Robert recalled watching the eagles, all those months ago, and, for a second, felt capable of flight. Cuke was less than three miles away, ten minutes at the most, even on this cut-up road.

There'd be some talking to do at the checkpoint, but what could they do? He might even get an escort – every other weird thing imaginable had happened to him in this country.

And, once in Corfu, a couple of phone calls home – calls he should have made long ago – then a taxi to the Prasinos, and Charlotte.

A mile from Cuke Robert saw the first refugees.

He didn't care. This wasn't his home, and this wasn't his war any more. He wove the bike through the clusters of shellshocked human beings as if they were so many footsore shoppers.

More and more refugees, now. People were beginning to crowd the road from the sides inward, and he had to dodge and swerve his way through. They weren't making it easy. Small children were the worst, just accidents waiting to happen. Robert attracted grimaces and a few shouted insults – he guessed they were insults.

He'd noticed before how particular clusters of people on the roads shared a group vibe; well, today's vibe was anger. This group was not passive and resigned, nor listlessly weary. Robert didn't like that. He felt their energy, and it made him wary. A worrying possibility occurred to him: could they be from Fier? Surely not so soon. Think straight, Bobby boy.

A youngish man with a bandaged head stepped out of file and spat at the bike, then gestured and shouted. Now Robert felt the absence of his weapon.

There was the roadblock. Robert exhaled, relieved.

He revved the engine to signal his intent to approach, and the grey tide grudgingly parted, closing in again behind him. There were more comments; he began to recognise the same words.

Up ahead there was virtually clear space for nearly a hundred yards – God knows how or why – and soldiers slouching under the overhang from two scrim-draped tents. But Robert couldn't see an actual manned stopping point. Whatever. This is it, he thought. The start of the journey home.

And then a familiar bad feeling: the spasm in the neck that signalled trouble.

Ignore it. Keep driving.

Then, without warning, the unmistakable report and echo of a shot.

The front end of the bike wobbled in Robert's grip, and the refugees collapsed to the ground in one motion, like a human blanket.

Robert, now a conspicuous upright target, tried placing the source of the shot. He cut the engine and squinted, and made out three crouching figures in green, all aiming Kalashnikovs in his direction. He raised his arms and opened his mouth to shout, but didn't manage to get the words out. Three shots broke the air. Then three more. On the ground some people began to cry out.

Robert could make out other soldiers now, appearing from cover and dropping to crouching positions, and aiming their AK47s at him.

What the fuck was going on? For one second he allowed himself to think that he had misunderstood, that there was someone else directly behind him that the soldiers were popping off at. He glanced around for who it could be.

But no. Now they were running in his direction and one was shouting orders. There must be eight or ten of them now. And then, *crack-rack*! A volley of four shots and he felt the bullets wrecking the air as they ripped past his face. He grabbed his head as the vibrations rattled through his upper body. The soldiers were sixty, maybe seventy yards away and they were lousy shots, but not lousy enough to keep missing him if he just sat here.

He revved and turned a one-eighty as a volley of four or maybe six shots snapped around his ears. Tiny pops in the distance, then hideous fizzing cracks. A bullet passing that close hurt like a glove-less hook.

God help me, *what is going on?*

Robert executed the turn and pulled away, while the firing intensified. What had got into these people? Did they think he was the enemy? Even so, there were people everywhere. They couldn't keep shooting like this. Could they?

Robert could hear the curses of the men and the shrieks of the women and children as the gunfire came closer and grew painfully loud. Just drive, just keep going, he told himself. Just DRIVE!

And then it all went bad.

Twenty yards ahead to Robert's right a scream cut through the other sounds. He saw a thin woman leaning on a bedroll clutch an arm to her breast. And then he watched as the arm went limp. A tiny girl kneeling at the woman's side closed her eyes and locked her features in a silent yell as blood sprayed across her face and chest. In seconds the child was drenched as the woman's chest pumped out.

A bulky man who'd climbed to his feet next to the shot woman fell backward like a dropped sack, pink blood geysering from his neck.

There were so many shots now that you couldn't even make out which was the one that hit someone.

Oh my Lord, what have I done?

Robert drove straight for the bodies. He couldn't help himself. This was his doing. He had to see. *What have I done?* He had to see it. They'd arrest him now. Surely they'd just arrest him and realise their mistake and send him to the port and he'd be away and be done with it. He slowed the bike and looked at his mess.

Almost immediately a grey-brown arm whipped across his line of vision and he fell backwards and the bike spun away from him, the engine still grinding and now throwing out fumes. Robert staggered to his feet and dived for the machine. Just as it registered in his consciousness that the shooting had stopped, another blow caught him on his mouth and he felt his lip split. He made it to his feet a second time and two more blows caught him simultaneously, one in the ribs on his right side, another on the back of his head. He didn't see any of the blows coming. But he saw his mother and sisters, and Ray, and faint images of his father and grandfather.

That was the last he knew about anything for an unspecific spell, but which he knew when sensible once more couldn't have been more than five seconds.

When he came round he was in pain, but at least no one was hitting him. A space had opened up between him and the bike, and people were running back toward the checkpoint and shouting. Then there were more shots and the people were running at the soldiers. The people's anger had shifted from him to them. Robert tried to move but the pain in his side held him down. But he had to move.

The bike's engine was still rasping in the dirt, dying, and if he didn't get to it soon he knew it would all be finished. It seemed to him that the soldiers were being driven back and then he saw why.

More refugees were on their feet and picking up stones and running back toward the checkpoint. He couldn't see the soldiers, but they would be retreating fast. Maybe they'd have to abandon the checkpoint, or maybe they'd start shooting again. Now the refugees were stoning the soldiers, and the soldiers were shooting into the air.

Get up. Get up and move.

Robert gagged, and spat out a wad of blood and phlegm. He managed to crouch. The bike was only a few feet away, but each step was agony. Tears blurred his vision. Lifting the bike from the ground almost sent him down again, but he got up and onto it, blood spotting the seat and frame. He forced his arms to stretch and grip the handlebars, and the pain in his ribs settled into something he could recognise and carry. Then he was off.

He passed the two people who had been shot, the thin woman motionless and white against the bedroll and the little girl shaking in shock beside her; the woman's eyes closed, the girl's wide enough to see for two. And the round man lying in an attitude of sleep on his pillow of red dust. Robert skidded off and left them behind.

Then there were stones landing around him. Up ahead the road was chaos but he wasn't stopping for anyone. These people had tried to shoot him, and to beat him to death, and finally to stone him.

Get. Out. Of. My. Fucking. Way!

Suddenly there wasn't any way.

The refugees were zigzagging across the road in groups, their heads jerking left and right. Each volley of shots prompted a chorus of screams. Robert could stand the shots, but not the screaming.

Somehow he had to drive through this. He revved high and made all the speed and noise he could, and God help them and him if they didn't move. It seemed to work; a path cleared before him, each diving body a split second away from a collision.

And then around a turn there was absolutely no way through. People were crossing the road in a huge clump and they couldn't have moved out of his way if they'd wanted to. Why were they crossing the fucking road? There was nothing on either side to cross to.

He went straight for them. They'd have to move.

They'd have to move.

At the last moment, as the crash loomed, the cluster of children now in his way screamed and fell backward like skittles. Lifting the front wheel Robert went for the lowest part of the dusty mass and just rode straight over it. He felt the softness and the slipping under the tyres but didn't look down. He was doing nearly forty, God knows how, and he didn't come off the hump of bodies well. The bike went through a clumsy three-sixty as it landed, and Robert was forced to stop to regain control of the machine.

And to see, in turning, the faces and the bodies he'd run over.

Whatever. What *fucking* ever.

He balanced through the three-sixty and was away again, and soon into the empty place on the road south of Cuke.

26

WHAT NOW? HE still had only one objective: Sarande.

But he couldn't get to Sarande: barring a five mile trek across country hugging the coast – which the bike would never handle – the Cuke road was the only way he knew. Jesus, this wasn't happening. This just was not happening.

Come on, Bobby, you don't have time to think like that.

But was the Cuke road the only way? Robert scanned the maps in his memory: maps in the *Blue Guide*, the *Bradt Guide*, the Vickers & Pettifer book. Was it the only way?

Maybe not. It took him a minute to picture it, but he seemed to recall something.

What he had recalled was this.

A donkey track just south of Cuke snaked north, through what he knew was decaying forest and abandoned arable land, to a biggish village called Gjashte. And west out of Gjashte – *think* – there was something west of Gjashte. Yes! West out of Gjashte hooked the last branch of the north-south throughway into Sarande – the Bartholomew map's Big Red Road. Of course. Gjashte was the settlement marking the broken crossroads for routes west, north, and east. Robert had never really acknowledged Gjashte before because he had never needed to – all his business had been in the port. But it could be done if he could get to Gjashte.

He felt a momentary rush of elation. Although, would the donkey track take the bike? Robert doubted it. He'd have to try, though. It was either that or give up and – and what?

Approaching an empty stretch of the road, he stopped to take stock. The simple fact of not being able to see any refugees either in front of or behind him, just for five minutes, was a relief. Besides that, he could hear neither small arms fire, nor the grind of engines behind him. Also good.

Now, the track to Gjashte was back in the direction of the roadblock. Not good. He'd have to go across country. And being only a battered backpacker on a resuscitated Honda, and not Steve McQueen on a vintage BMW, he'd also have to get off and push.

He dismounted and peeled off the fleece, which made him wince. But everything that should move or bend did, and he could breathe pretty well. His fingers found pain when he walked them over his ribs, but only dull pain. A break, he decided, would feel sharper. And anyway the task at hand was the same, broken ribs or not.

What a fuck-up. What a flying fuck-up! I'd laugh if it didn't hurt so much.

Feeling suddenly hot Robert knotted the fleece's arms around his waist, and let the warm air dry some of the sweat. Now thirsty as well, he drained half the bottle of water from his daysack in a few gulps, then used the rest to clean the dust and blood from his hands and face. He felt calmer now. He reckoned the track was less than a mile away. And the sooner he started the sooner he'd get there.

Humping the bike over rocks and grass in the hot sun and in his state was no fun, but Robert began to feel better, and to recognise something like composure returning to his muscles and bones. There was a calming rhythm in the boredom of the job at hand. If he could just carry on facing his situation in the same way he faced this trudging: one careful step at a time.

He couldn't afford any more lapses, though – like stopping to gawp at the people who'd got themselves shot. Fuck them if they got themselves shot. It was terrible and awful but he had his own problems.

His mind suddenly flashed him an image of the pile of children back there on the road, and he was silent.

When did that happen? Did he do that?

It struck him that he'd almost managed to forget the episode – no, not to forget it, but to have never even registered it, a negative which had faded before there was time to print it to paper. But he saw the picture distinctly now.

There'd been three children. Ages, oh, anywhere between six and ten. Yes, one boy and one girl both lying face up. Then another smaller shape face down, hands over its head, one side of its mouth visible in a howl.

He remembered two pairs of wide white eyes.

Or was he imagining the eyes?

Robert shook his head, No, and spat some pink foam.

The kids would be okay; they'd be more shocked than hurt, and shock was something these people and their children had better get used to for a while. They'd survived and he'd survived and it had happened and he couldn't help them now.

He remembered the girl's eyes. Big, pretty.

Get out! Get out of my head!

Why did he have to remember that? He stumbled on a loose rock and dropped to his knees. The eyes.

Get out!

He got to his feet and pushed on.

When I am away from here all this will leave me. It will be different when I am away from here. I will not think of these things.

Robert stopped and let the bike lean against his hip. He grabbed his hair in both hands and pulled and growled and gradually the sound grew into a scream, as he recognised the horror and the stupid falseness of the lie he had just told himself.

In a couple of minutes he seemed fine again, and he took a deep breath and spat once more, and pushed harder against the bike.

If he kept it down to fifteenish and didn't get cocky the track was manageable. Guided by the mental map of where he thought he was, he followed the worn trail north-west, skirting in a crescent around Cuke, toward the village and the junction. Gjashte was about three miles from Cuke, Sarande maybe another mile. In places the trail seemed to disappear for as much as fifty yards, and Robert was having to hunt among the weeds for where it restarted – and this thing qualified for inclusion on a major map.

North of Cuke trees closed in on both sides of the path and Robert could see less and less up ahead. Finally, after what felt like an hour, but was only about fifteen minutes, the trees thinned out and he could see the first low houses, with the outsize red roofs, and the wood and stone barns and outbuildings.

And, there in the distance, the cloud of grey dust, and the tangible rumbling and scraping of activity that could only be from the road junction. And, between it and Robert, maybe five hundred yards of scattered huts and blind corners, of high barn windows and unpredictable strangers. Of ominous silence. Robert frowned and clenched his teeth, and gripped the handlebars. What did his instinct tell him now?

He cut the engine and surveyed the scene in front of him. Well, there simply wasn't a choice.

With no detour around the wide scattering of buildings he would simply have to drive straight through Gjashte. End of story. Robert nodded to himself, and keyed the ignition, and gave it some gas.

But something made him hesitate, and he cut the engine again.

It was the middle of the day and there was not a living soul in sight. Had the village been abandoned? He clocked a couple of dogs warily eyeing him, and other wandering bits of untethered livestock which had – so far – escaped a soldier's pot. Goats, a donkey. But no two-legged animals.

He keyed the ignition once more and revved the bike.

Let it mean what it wants. Let's get this over with.

He never heard the shot.

The bullet caught Robert under the right eye, snapping his head and shoulders backward, and bounced back off his cheekbone. Blood erupted in front of his face.

A second shot exploded the bike's headlight and sang away off the mudguard into the high grass. Robert didn't hang around for the third.

Skidding the bike off the track, he gunned and ground hell-for-leather toward the cover of a tent of orange trees fifty yards to his left. No shots followed him into the cover. He stopped and cut and listened.

He scanned what he could see of the village, which wasn't much. But at least here under the trees it was harder for them to see him. He felt his face. There was numbness, and plenty of thin runny blood dripping from a rip an inch or so across. His fingers were shaking, and his breathing staccato. Jesus, would people leave his fucking face alone?

Robert couldn't believe either that he'd actually been shot, or that, now it had happened, he was still alive. It must have been a small round. That was lucky. What? This was luck? Well, at least he had his Al Capone scar now.

Get a grip!

God, he'd hardly felt the bullet, and it still didn't really hurt, not like he'd always imagined it should. And he hadn't heard it – so that was true, that you never hear the one that hits you.

This was too much, it was too much to do. All he wanted was his girlfriend, all he wanted was the girl. They could let him have that much, they could give him that, couldn't they?

Listen to your voice: now, you can turn around and head back to the farm. From there you can check your fuel, and gauge how near it will get you to the Greek border. It might even get you all the way there. Yes, this is fucked up: you tried but it's fucked up, and the Greek border is the only way left now. Accept that.

But damn it Sarande was only a mile away. If he could just somehow get through this village and to the port he'd be almost home. But Robert didn't believe that anymore: they'd pick him off before he got fifty yards. Blood dripped onto his chest and thighs. Why was all this happening?

Perhaps the JNA was closer than either he or the World Service had realised. Whatever, Robert realised now that even if he made it through Gjashte – not a chance – Sarande would be one big practice range through which he'd never make it. There would be no organisation; passports and visas and citizenship wouldn't mean a thing. Between here and safety were a thousand men with guns. Robert had to concede that he couldn't compete with a thousand men with guns.

He had been hiding among the orange trees for maybe a minute when he heard a shout not fifty yards away, and another in reply. Fifty yards was close, damn it. Automatically he reached back over his shoulder for the .22. What .22?

Figures in civilian clothes made a crouching dash between two outhouses in the middle distance. Robert saw their rifles. Two behind the outhouse, at least two in the trees. He longed for his guns.

Hearing the same sequence of shouts again convinced Robert that they were trying to surround him.

He was being hunted.

He spun a one-eighty on the back wheel and, ignoring the rocks and dips, hurtled, jolting and bouncing, back toward the donkey track. If he was followed out of there – back the way he'd come – by shots or shouts he wouldn't have heard them through the fatigue and despair smoking out the last spare space in his head.

Risking twenty-five he growled, then screamed and raged as the village receded into the trees and Sarande shrunk far away and the image of it became dim, and the knowledge that he had to prepare himself all over again dragged him low, low.

After a while, the walk across country between the track and the Cuke road seemed, once again, to help Robert to some degree of calm. This was the plan now: he would return to the farm, maybe try and eat something, clean his cuts. Attempt some kind of butterfly stitch repair job on his face. One more thing: he wasn't going anywhere without the guns this time. Jesus, they'd have to fight him for them at Heathrow after today. He chuckled in his throat at that. Him in his ragged shot-to-pieces state toting two cannons through passport control. Yes, laugh, Robert. Laughing makes you stronger.

Fifty yards from the road Robert put the bike on its stand and wandered away toward the trees. He returned with a straight stick about three feet long, and an inch and a half thick. He untied the fleece from around his waist and put it on, then slipped the stick down the neck across his back. With the fleece zipped up tight the stick wouldn't slip out. He would not be without a weapon of some kind, even just a stick, again.

And then it rained.

He cursed himself for not having noticed the dark clouds thickening in from the north until it started to pour. Shit. If you wanted to survive you stayed alert. He couldn't have done anything about the rain: but to just not notice?

It rained like the end of the world.

Robert slowed down and concentrated on the disintegrating road five yards ahead, no further. Visibility was so poor that it was as much as you could do to stay upright. Watching the periphery for danger was out of the question. Damn it, he'd known, he'd *known* this would happen to the road if it rained. But then why not rain? Everything else was going to hell, why shouldn't the fucking ground he walked on?

The turn off through the trees to his house was clear of refugees, but the driveway was a royal mess. Robert had never seen a storm like it. The broken road surface expanded like sponge, then crumbled into porridge. The deluging water transformed small ruts and dips into bogs and small whirlpools. Avoiding them required absolute concentration.

Suddenly, something away to his right caught his eye, and he flinched in the saddle. Then, turning his head again in an awkward double-take, he seemed to lose control of his arms.

The bike's front tyre slipped, and wedged in a rut, and Robert was hurled forward over the handlebars. As he flew and fell, he registered the dying of the engine, and a splintering sound, and then he was face down in the mud and hearing himself gasp.

He clawed his way to his knees. It was a colour that had caught his eye and frozen his muscles: the same dirty dead grey he'd been seeing on the road for weeks.

The only sound in Robert's ears was the relentless drumming of the rain filling every hollow in the ground, every corner of his skull. And the only thing before his eyes were those patches of grey. He knew he had to get to the bike. But first he had to know about the grey.

Walk away, he told himself. *You know what it is*. You know and you can do nothing about it so just keep doing what you have to.

Robert rolled onto his back. He couldn't move his right leg. He saw where a sharp branch half an inch in diameter had pierced his thigh, and he felt the blood drain from his face. He reached down and pulled out the stick. Why couldn't he feel anything? Prodding the area a few times with his finger encouraged some small sensation. Okay.

He began crawling away toward the bushes.

He felt something across his back – the stick he'd secured under his fleece. He slid it out over his shoulder and, using it as a crutch, staggered through the puddles toward two small prickly pear bushes, beyond which lay the bodies.

There were three.

Two men and a woman. One man was probably a few years younger than Robert, the other was maybe fifty. He couldn't see the woman's face. He hobbled closer. There was no bad smell. How long, then? Minutes? Were their killers still nearby? Robert looked around.

The two men lay face-up, side by side. Robert couldn't see any wounds. They must have been shot in the back, and then turned over. The woman lay face down, partly underneath them, which seemed wrong. Robert felt ashamed and ill-mannered that this woman should be lying face down in the mud on his land. Her hips were narrow like Charlotte's.

It occurred to Robert that she would be more comfortable on her back. Yes, he'd wake the men and they'd make her comfortable. Rest was what they all needed, and to get out of this rain. He could light a fire. Then he thought to wonder why he could see the woman's hips, not covered by anything, and he knew what had happened to her and that these men were her family and that they had died with her for being her family. And then the wrong of it all, the sheer damn wrongness took hold of him.

He closed his eyes and collapsed to his knees by the pile of bodies, and began scooping handfuls of mud over their soaked forms. But the mud was quickly washed away again by the steady rain. Robert dug harder and shovelled more mud onto the corpses. But they wouldn't stay covered. The rain kept coming, and kept washing away all his work.

Robert stopped digging, and slouched forward on his knees, and wrapped his arms around himself, and wept and moaned, rocking back and forth in the mud.

27

'YOU SHOULD HAVE a wife at your hotel.'

'Huh? What?'

'A wife. You should have a wife at your hotel.'

'Jesus. What's going on?'

'A hotel without a woman? It will be strange.'

Robert jerked and twitched on the wooden deck as Harry's voice crackled in his head.

'A hotel without a woman will be a strange hotel. Your guests will feel that it is not right.'

'What woman? What . . .'

He drifted back into deep sleep, then moaned and muttered as the voice, and now an image of Harry sitting outside the cafe, materialised in his dream. Robert could see Harry was not alone. There was a stranger standing at his shoulder. A stranger? No, Robert recognised this man, but he could not remember from where.

'Well?' Harry asked.

'Well what?' Robert groaned.

'Where is your wife?'

'Wife?'

'You must have a wife. You want to know why? Ask him.' Harry pointed over his shoulder with his thumb.

'Ask who?' Robert creased his brow as he tried to see deeper into the dream, into the face of the stranger.

Harry pointed with his thumb again at the man standing behind him. A man with long wet hair and a round belly, and a bloody stump where one of his arms should have been. The one-armed man's eyes were a dark, expressionless blur, as if he were wearing sunglasses. Robert knew he had seen this man before, but he still couldn't place where and when.

'Ask him,' Harry said, smiling. 'He knows.'

'He knows what?'

But Harry was gone, and the one-armed man was holding a sawn-off shotgun and pointing it off to the side, indicating that Robert should look there. Robert turned to see the three grey and white, milk-white bodies dumped there in a pile. Robert thrashed and struggled to reach the one-armed man – he sensed that he had answers for him, things he needed to know. But he had stepped back into a blur of the fading dream, and was gone, like Harry.

28

HIS HEAD SWAM, his joints clicked, and pain and stiffness locked across his shoulders and hips where they'd pressed on the bare wood. A sour odour reached his nose and he realised he'd pissed himself. How long had he been asleep or, more likely, unconscious? He worked it out. He'd have crawled up here about mid-afternoon. So, eighteen, twenty hours ago? Was that possible? Feeling this stiff, yes, it was possible.

Everything hurt, he stank, and he could taste his own rotten breath, like something was dead in his stomach. He rubbed his eyes and glanced around the porch: a bloody towel, a whisky bottle, a foil of Ibuprofen.

The two guns.

He sighed and attempted to take in enough to get him started. The storm had given way to a brazen white light which spared you nothing of its empty sameness. This is it: this is what's left, it seemed to say.

Robert could hear the birds going crazy, and the dripping water that was probably making them that way. It was dripping off the roof and the veranda rail onto damp wood and drying brown grass and stones. It made a pleasant flavour in his nostrils, like wet plaster. He closed his eyes again.

He knew he was never going to see Charlotte again. Tomorrow she would leave the Prasinos and Corfu and go where, he did not know.

The day was warming up. The hole in his leg was itching and his cheek was throbbing, but that was less of a worry than the leg. He peeled off his trousers.

The front of his right thigh around the hole was a big leaf-shaped bruise. Robert wondered about infection. He remembered something he'd seen in a film, and poured whisky into the wound. Bad idea.

When the pain died down and his head stopped reeling, he tried lifting the limb, gave up. He remembered the bike: where he'd come off it, the splintering sound, the bodies.

Those bodies.

The bike was gone, dead as them.

Robert dragged his dead limb down to the veranda steps and sat and looked out across his land. His land: that statement didn't mean anything now. This land belonged to anyone he couldn't stop from taking it.

That sounded like something Harry would say.

The mist was just about gone. It had looked pleasant while it lasted. He found himself wondering how he might describe it to Ray in a letter.

Robert Maidens leaned back against the top step, and stretched out his bad leg. What would he do? What should he gather around him? Tins and the opener, and a couple of spoons. A bottle of water if he had one, purification tablets, and the last of the whisky. If there wasn't water anywhere in the house he'd simply have to cripple down to the well for it. He could wash while he was there, clean off this smell. Then back here he'd get coffee going, and strips of plaster.

Get the guns ready.

His wounds made him think of Charlotte. He allowed the pain of the memories to suffuse. What hurt most was what she might think about why he had never shown up at the Prasinos. He knew it would give her pain for a long time, and he was sorry for that. But it was just another thing that had happened now that he couldn't change. He could love her in his memory, though. And he did love her, he knew that now. To have the memory of love, he decided, was something. Loss was not just a void. Charlotte was a good thing even when you had lost her. It was a shame. It was all a shame.

Just then all around him, sounds began stopping.

It happened in a wave, spreading toward the house bird by bird, scuffling thing by scuffling thing; even, it seemed to him, drip by drip: stilled.

And then, in the distance, he began to hear the other sounds.

Yells and long whistles, and other whistles in reply, and the tap-tapping of small arms fire. Worst of all, engines. Good, big engines, not Albanian tractors or antique Chinese APCs. Robert sat up, dragging the dead leg straight, and hissing curses through his swollen lips. He hoisted himself to his feet and hobbled to the table, and swept the .22 and the sawn-off toward him. He sat in front of the table on one of the two wooden chairs and positioned the other so it would support his leg.

The shouts were clearer now, and the engines louder, and not just from the road, but coming through the trees on his land. In a few minutes he would hear the tripwires.

Suddenly he froze.

Who was the one-armed man in the dream? He could see him in the dream, but couldn't picture him anywhere in his memory. Why was he thinking about him now? Just another example of losing his concentration. Not that it mattered. *But he was so vivid.*

Tripwires. Booby traps. My land. *There is no safety, ever.* There is simply the world in which you find yourself. There is the world you can try and make for yourself to live in alone but someone always finds a way into your safety. It can be a woman, or it can be an army.

But that was all right, now. For the first time Robert thought he understood what had brought him here, and what kept him here when he should have gone. Maybe he even understood a bit about what should have made him stay home in the first place. He couldn't say he felt anything like peace or completeness, because this was not the time or the place. But then, there would probably never be a time. So maybe this was all okay.

What I do feel is that little understanding. Much less seems certain to me now, and that is always a good thing to know. That you are certain about less, and you can just see things happen and know they are not happening to you or because of you but just happening.

I love you, Charlotte.

Robert laughed.

I love you, Charlotte. Did you hear that?

Mum. Charlotte. Ray. I can hear them on my land. I can hear their vehicles breaking down the low branches, and I can hear the shouting of men. Why my land, I wonder. Does it have some significance? There's the lake, I suppose. And the archaeological stuff over the way. These are the Serbs. This is the JNA. The World Service said they were coming, and I stayed to see them do it. And now they are here, all of us waiting for what comes next.

Robert Maidens sat at the table on his porch and loaded his guns and listened to the sounds that would soon become visible things. He sat and looked out across the land he had bought, and waited for whatever was going to happen to him to happen.

Part Four

29

Iraklia, Greek Islands, 1990

ROBERT MAIDENS HATES watching the octopus hunter, but he watches him all the same, every day. He stops reading – today it's A Farewell To Arms – and uses the book to shade his eyes so he can follow the big man's descent into the sea. He's a big man across the chest and shoulders, and he knows it. He loves himself. But he's big around the belly as well. How can he love that, thinks Robert. How can he love his ugly belly.

He watches him wade out about thirty yards from the shore to where the flat reef begins and the water is waist deep on a man. The man turns around to face the beach, and to pose for a few seconds. Then he bends at the waist and dips his good arm into the water. His thick silky hair falls forward. You can see his shoulders and his head and the stump of the missing arm. The sea hides everything else.

It only takes a couple of minutes. The octopus hunter's body swings up and back – Robert always waits for him to fall comically and for his catch to drop – splat! – onto the surface of the blue, and then sink, but it never happens.

He holds up the octopus. Its wet form turns on his fingers, reflecting drips of light, like a melting mirror-ball. The octopus hunter's wet arrogant belly heaves in and out. He stands there so you can see. No, he stands there so long that you have to look.

Robert has heard the story of how he lost the limb – a German girl who carried a sleeping bag to the beach so that she and Robert could do it 'really under the stars' told him how she heard it was dynamite fishing, back when that was allowed. Robert reckons this is a macho bullshit myth, and says so, and that the explanation is probably very dull. 'Maybe an octopus bit it off,' he suggests to the girl, whose name is Ilona. 'You are so fucking romantic,' she replies, lighting a cigarette.

The sea monster's wife now walks down to meet her husband as he struts up the beach looking cocky. She falls in behind him, her head bowed, and follows him to the rocks at the far end of the beach by the cliffs. She is smaller than him and sometimes has to trot to keep up.

He goes to work on the fish (is it a fish?) and she sits in the sun and watches. He picks out a good rock and slaps the dead thing against stone again and again.

Robert recalls the rubber feel of octopus flesh in his mouth, and wonders if the one he had that one time was softened up enough. It didn't feel soft. He watches the impact of the fish against the rock and a second later hears the sound of each blow like an echo.

Robert gets up to go snorkelling. He keeps his T-shirt on because he's not great with the sun. The fish in the reef are quite something to see, but they are not an octopus. Their colours are like the colours of tropical fish he remembers from pet shops and aquaria.

Evenings, the octopus hunter always brings his catch to the same small taverna, the one Robert and his friends use. The wife is dressed up, but the octopus hunter hasn't made an effort. He slouches at a table in the courtyard while she looks around nervously for a chair. When he has rested he carries the octopus past the outdoor grill into the gloom of the kitchen. Again, so everyone can see. He reappears followed by the proprietor, who is carrying a dish of legs. The proprietor lays them on the grill and it spits back. Cats hover, and a small boy carries drinks.

The legs still look exactly like what they are. For a minute, when the plate walks past, their smell is everywhere. The proprietor presents the plate in front of the wife, who picks up a pink and black leg in two fingers, and bites and swallows, then smiles. Then the husband begins eating. Robert has to clear his throat and swallow saliva.

Robert goes back to his tricky fish and concentrates on the needly bones. He is not watching the couple any more, and he doesn't see how scrupulous the husband is that despite being twice the size and with, presumably, twice the appetite of the wife, he doesn't take a morsel more than his share.

ACKNOWLEDGEMENTS

Of the many books which helped in my research I would like to pick out three for special praise – not just from the point of view of research, but as a reader for pleasure. They are: Robert Carver's *The Accursed Mountains*, Michael Ignatieff's *The Warrior's Honor*, and Laura Silber and Allan Little's *The Death of Yugoslavia*.

Grant Stewart

Kenny Rogers Sings the Gambler

'A page-turning thriller that delivers' *The Times*

'In this racy first novel, three young graduates – clever enough to know better but too desperate to care – turn to black magic and crime as a "temporary" solution to the inescapable bleakness of their poverty. The harrowing tale is alleviated by the author's wit and the compassion he inspires for his characters. The informal, engaging narrative voice is sequinned by astute, offhand observations ("gatecrashers are not pretty – pretty people get invited to parties") and sardonic asides . . . Stewart never becomes sensationalist or tacky – he examines violence and mysticism with a chilling intelligence. Exceptionally good.' *Literary Review*

'Natasha, Rob and Rich are apparently destined to make do with menial jobs or the dole queue. During a party the mysterious Madeleine introduces them to the rituals of the Ouija board. They find that the spirit who has been assigned to them is soon obliging the three with betting tips and urging them to "risk everything", which they proceed to do . . . An open-air heist is convincingly drawn, and the moral and spiritual deterioration of the three friends is disturbingly rendered.' *Observer*

flamingo

Robert Carver

The Accursed Mountains

Journeys in Albania

'One of the most exciting travel books for a generation'
Spectator

In the spring and summer of 1996, Robert Carver managed to make a series of remarkable journeys through Albania in the brief interregnum between Communism and anarchy. High adventure, danger and comedy exist side by side in this sharp and spirited travel narrative, set in a mysterious mountain land now once more closed to the Western traveller.

'A memorable debut. Robert Carver has fulfilled the dream of every travel writer to find somewhere strange, remote and unvisited, and to pin it to the printed page. *The Accursed Mountains* is a tale at once endlessly diverting and profoundly tragic.'
WILLIAM DALRYMPLE

'A dazzling account of a journey – always bizarre, often comic, and increasingly nightmarish – through one of the most dangerous backwaters currently to be found anywhere.'
PETER HOPKIRK

0 00 655174 2

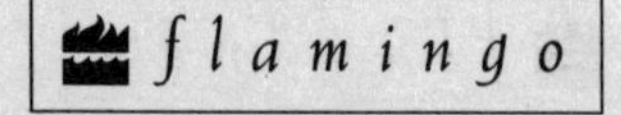

Peter Landesman

Blood Acre

'For readers who like their thrillers in pure noir.'
Literary Review

Nathan Stein has just run out of time. He is the son, and partner, of one of New York's more shadowy, pugilistic and successful lawyers. He is the maybe-half-brother of a *barrio* cop who was once his best friend. He was the fiancé of a public defender who now picks up the cases he drops. And he is very, very ill.

Nathan has also inherited his father's appetite for philandering and for moral slipperiness. *Blood Acre* opens with the corpse of a beautiful young woman, Nathan's secretary and secret mistress, washing ashore on a Coney Island beach. Stein is the prime suspect, but when the woman's true identity floats into sight, he becomes a man wanted by more than just the police.

'A genuine tour de force . . . *Blood Acre* deals with financial and sexual corruption and its corrosive effects on the human psyche with all the moral seriousness of a classical tragedy. Not only that, but it demands to be read in a single sitting.'
Literary Review

'Peter Landesman brings to radiant life a dark, disorienting, and violent vision, rendered in gorgeous prose.'
ANDREA BARRETT, author of *The Voyage of the Narwhal*

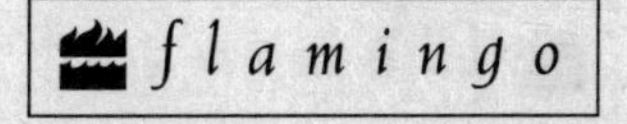

Jim Lewis

Why the Tree Loves the Axe

'A clever, weird, utterly absorbing story told by a rare talent.'
The Times

'Caroline is a compulsive liar. She ends up in Sugartown, Texas, after fleeing a broken marriage and suffering a car crash, and makes up an identity for herself to get a job. She lives a shadowy fictionalised life as an orderly in a geriatric ward, getting involved with a sinister old man, who confers on her a strange box to deliver, and a soul-mate girlfriend whom she strangely resembles. Sugartown descends into hellish street riots during which Caroline kills a policeman, and learns that her girlfriend has died . . .

Jim Lewis deserves a wider audience . . . The narrative here is modern American Gothic, with a Pinteresque menace, and a nice twist in the tale . . . Lewis covers a wonderful range of American experiences. Midwest pieties and dreams of a new city on the plain are transformed into a nightmare of social unrest, sinister geriatric decay and necessary lawlessness . . . wise, lyrical and refreshingly astonishing.'
ADAM PIETTE, *Evening Standard*

'A literary suspense novel that actually delivers – a page turner that will keep readers guessing until the end, their curiosity fuelled as much by the book's gorgeously inventive imagery as by its seductive plot.'
SARAH FERGUSON, *New York Times*

'By releasing the tallest of stories in a rush of rich language, Jim Lewis dazzles you into credulity. An unmissable novel.'
She

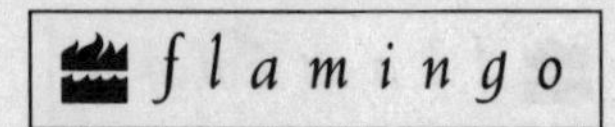

Richard Beard

Damascus

'It's the last day of the holidays and Spencer Kelly (12) wants to hold Hazel Burns (12) by the hand. This is the meaning of life. He wants to sit beside her on a sand dune and hold her hand and then kiss her. Just kissing, in a nice way, on her cheek perhaps and then a little bit at the top of her arms . . . If he can kiss her this once then he'll always have kissed her, and everything which follows will be different. It's to be the one moment which instantly changes everything.'

'Richard Beard's second novel is something of an event, given the widespread plaudits for his first. In that book, *X 20*, he arranged an ingenious and unconventional structure around tobacco smoking. In his new novel Beard uses similar techniques, but this time in a romance . . . Beard is a talented writer, crafting many scenes with luminous precision.'

PETER CARTY, *Time Out*

'The climactic showdown is not only an apt marriage of the novel's form and content . . . but also gently comic, the characteristic tone of this undertaking. Ludic in a peculiarly British manner . . . an assured achievement.'

STEPHEN KNIGHT, *TLS*

'Lovely, funny, touching, and exciting.'

HARRY MATHEWS, author of *The Journalist*

'A book with a real difference.' *Irish News*

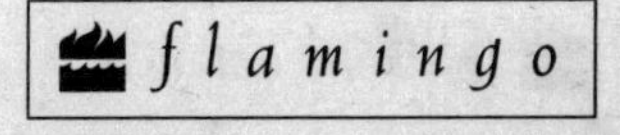

J.G. Ballard

Cocaine Nights

Five people die in an unexplained housefire in the Spanish resort of Estrella de Mar, an exclusive enclave for the rich, retired British, centred around the thriving Club Nautico. The manager of the club, Frank Prentice, intends to plead guilty to charges of murder – yet not even the police believe him. When his brother Charles arrives to unravel the mystery, he gradually discovers that behind the resort's civilised facade there is a secret world of crime, drugs and illicit sex . . . At once an engrossing mystery and an unnerving vision of a society coming to terms with unlimited leisure, *Cocaine Nights* is a stunningly original work of the imagination from one of this country's most acclaimed writers.

'The arrival of a new Ballard novel has become a literary event. He is one of the few genuine surrealists this country has produced, the possessor of a terrifying and exhilarating imagination – and a national treasure.' NICHOLAS ROYLE, *Guardian*

'Utterly compulsive. One is constantly being brought up short by the sheer strangeness of Ballard's imagination.'
JOHN PRESTON, *Sunday Telegraph*

'As *Cocaine Nights* progresses, it becomes that familiar Ballardian object, a vision of apocalypse. There are those (I am among them) who would back Ballard as Britain's number one living novelist. This adds a glinting new facet to his achievement – Ballard, detective-novelist extraordinary.'
JOHN SUTHERLAND, *Sunday Times*

'Dazzlingly original.' *Independent*

ISBN 0 00 655064 9

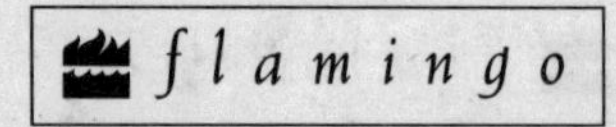